WHO'S DRIVING THE BUS?

My Year as a Kindergarten Mom

Tracy Egan

ISBN: 1453620931
ISBN-13: 9781453620939

Acknowledgements

Much gratitude to *Mothers Who Know*: Elisabeth Bald, Jean Fies, Patty Fitzgibbons, Pia Griffith, Amanda Hanley, Heidi Lott, Lydia Morrisey, Betsy Neumann, and Eileen O'Halloran. And to Francine Allen, Robert Egan, Kate Glass, Carla Deaton Lev, Teri McEvoy, Annice Moses, Susan Schulman, Joanne Sekulic and Amy Teschner. Gold-star-stickers to Kindergarten Teachers; Adrienne Drucker, Wendy Harris, Lisa Nielson and Kelly Post who generously allowed me to be an oversized student of their amazing classrooms. Littlest but not least: to the children, especially my own, who endure us as advocates, lobbyists and mothers.

Moving was Ted's idea. Cornwell Indiana, where we live now, has been our home since before our daughter, Emma, was born. It's a charming town, where relatively little money will buy you a decent ranch house on a good-sized chunk of land; a rolling, grassy lot large enough to justify a riding mower, sport a basketball court or lay in a crop. My husband Ted was only ever loosely attached to the town and, apparently, to his job. He was let go six weeks ago along with half his team. After a week careening between disbelief and outrage, he stood up from his recliner and announced that the firing was the opportunity we'd been waiting for. We will move to a recession re- sistant community just north of Chicago where he can start his own Identity Theft consulting firm and have plenty of small businesses to draw upon for clients. I was unsure if he could call himself a "firm" being a solo guy in the enterprise. Otherwise, I was on board quickly because the school system is supposed to be stellar in Lake Park. And the selection of the school district that will hold and mold our only child from age five through eighteen will be made in tandem with finding a place to live.

I thought choosing a stroller system was difficult. The prospect of committing my child to a specific grade school comes wrapped in a coating of thick, hard responsibility that makes me feel like tiny Alice toppled into a world far beyond her ken. At each Lake Park house we tour I raise a finger to inquire about the neighborhood school on the listing sheet. "It's great!" our realtor says with the same identical lilt she used at the house previous. This is my first indication that she doesn't have children. I wander the bedrooms of strangers, envying their plump, coordinated bedding and looking for a sign, other than well-placed electrical outlets, that this is *the one.* The only time I can relax is on the drive from one house to the other, sunk into the creamy vanilla back seat of our realtor's Lexus sharing a snack-sized bag of goldfish with Emma. I suppose, if all else fails we could live in the woman's luxury car. Of course then I'd have to car-school using only the Jump-Ahead-Shape-Finder workbook in my bag and some shrunken, travel-sized board games with minute, trachea-sized pieces.

Still high from the exhilaration of making broad life decisions, I bring a Chinet plate loaded with Toll House cookies to my Cornwell Lamaze/book group, formed when Emma was still no bigger than a doorknob. Ten minutes later I blurt our news, then I cast around the room as bits of chocolate chips along with reactions of shock and dismay settle on the faces of my friends. For the first time I think through what it means for me to leave them; these other mothers I can count on seeing three days a week at Miss Suzette's Happy Child Preschool and regularly at the Piggly Wiggly on Broad Street. These are the women who provided me rescue, guidance and commiseration through the first four years of motherhood. Together we figured out where to get the cheap cotton onsies, which irreverent parenting books to read, and what to do when Harold-the-biter sunk his teeth into our child's shoulder. At the conclusion of my breathless announcement I burst into tears.

On the third day of touring Lake Park houses, our realtor says, teasing, to Emma, "I've a surprise for you!"

A lollipop, no doubt. The surprise for children under the age of ten is always a lollipop.

"Do you know where you are?" Our realtor asks this question quietly, smugly, after we'd driven twelve more blocks. Her crescent brows arch in the rear view. Her question is a trick one, clearly. The kind you're not expected to answer. Before we can take a stab at it, she sallies forth as if we'd spoken.

"Yes. We *are* still in Lake Park, but the city isn't what I had in mind. *This* is a special house," she says, maneuvering us into the one available spot in front of the tiny brick bungalow with the *For Sale* sign sunk into the front yard. Old green paint curls off a long, empty window box that tips out from a dark picture window. An empty, ill-defined border of bare earth abuts the house. The only life in the yard is a sole, leaning crab apple planted too close to the front walk and a straggly stand of yews bowing out over a narrow strip of side yard.

"*This* house is in District 47." Her voice is tremulous. She glances at Emma.

Ted and I give her the look of polite amazement she clearly expects.

"You can tell you're passing over into District 47 when you spot the *Creative Learning Toys* store on the corner. Did you see it? An adorable little place. I know the family who owns it. Waldorfians."

A polite silence. "The hotel people?" Ted asks.

Our realtor exhales once in an impersonation of mirth. "That's right," she says, ignoring Ted. "Very little plastic, mostly wood. Melissa Doug, Spiel & Holz, Chelona. That's all my niece gets from me. Yes, that little girl has been BPA free since her inception. But, and you're gonna love this. *This* house has Jefferson as its neighborhood school."

Both of us, husband and wife; Ted and Jen in concert, say, "Oh!" Though we don't learn the full significance of her announcement until the next moment. After our realtor licks her finger and pages rapidly through a blue plastic file sleeve next to her.

"Mm hmm!" she hums, as if answering a question; confirming a suspicion we'd pressed her about. Ted and I exchange a glance, and a copy of a Chicago Tribune newspaper article lands in our hands. The headline reads, *Jefferson Grade School Rated One of State's Top Ten*. After giving us a second to take it in – to absorb the importance of the location of this particular listing, she says, "Two blocks down, then a hop skip and a jump around the corner. Yep!"

Here she takes a moment to be pleased with herself, then she twists full around, slings her elbow over her seat and juts her head towards our little girl who sleeps deeply in her booster next to me, her cheek compressed against the window. We all watch as gravity pulls Emma's glistening thumb from her mouth. Then without any discernable effort, it floats up again and her sweet lips part for it.

"Awwww. Look at her," moans our realtor, her hand pressed to her chest in a theatrical pantomime of emotion.

"Need I say more?"

May 22nd

The school ranking sells us. Ted counts outlets and paces out the master bedroom while I devour the article about Jefferson School. The following Monday I spend the morning casing the new neighborhood. When I first round the corner, my heart does cartwheels against my chest. The neighborhood school is an iconic place; a two-story red brick building with stacked, uniform rows of tall windows and a protrusion of cement cornice rimming the top. It's a picture-book school. You half expect a furry round Berenstain Bear (with his own cartooned image on his lunch box) to pop out the door and bound down the front stairs on his squat legs. A recent addition in brick a couple of shades lighter than the original structure, corners off one end. And the L-shaped building safeguards the playground and adjacent field like a looming crossing guard with his arms spread.

After circling the school six, or maybe twelve times, I drive on and find in the entrance to the *Creative Learning Toys* store a flyer in a pile next to last month's issue of Organic Baby. The next night, the very next night, Jefferson School is hosting a Kindergarten Information Event. Holding the flyer in both hands, I present the sacred paper to Ted as if I'd engineered this fantastic coincidence of timing, and come Tuesday we are there at the main entrance to Jefferson School when the doors open at 6:30.

Inside the school, one whiff of the construction paper, graham cracker, and spilled-milk bouquet fills me to the brim with a promising brew of nostalgia and optimism. I clutch Ted's hand and tow him towards the stairs at the end of the wide hall. On either side of the expanse the walls are filled with colorful bulletin boards and, below them, slender metal lockers painted midnight blue. From the top of each, the name of a child written in friendly bubble-letters dangles in a cartoon cloud. Closed classroom doors interrupt the flow of lockers at twenty feet intervals. Other early parents jiggle the knobs, and finding the doors locked, gaze through the dark rectangular window sunk into each door. Arms splayed, they stand there waiting for their special powers of night vision to kick in.

Quickly the hallway fills. Some parents bring their noses close to the bulletin board displays, duck into the pint-sized restrooms and casually flip open a locker belonging to *Sarah* or *Emily*. We are detectives at the scene of the crime that has yet to occur. Quiet and reverent in the land that will shape and guide our children. Outside the auditorium a table offers papers on hot lunch, aftercare, busing, disciplinary procedures, tuition requirements for those outside the district, and information on the necessary immunizations and registration materials. I wait while a woman wrapped artfully in a voluminous chocolate Pashmina pauses in front of me, pen in hand, frowning at the sign-in sheet.

"It's okay," says the teacher from behind the table. "Just write the name of the child who's starting Kindergarten here next year on the line." It sounds simple, but the shawl wrapped woman straightens defensively and regally. She looks down her Roman nose at the desk woman as a pouf of red hair dives from the clip atop her head.

"Just the name of the child, and then your name and your phone number below. Right here," repeats the teacher with droopy eyes and a weary smile. She unpeels a banana as she speaks, but waits to take a bite. It will come as a reward, no doubt, for resolving the sign-in situation.

"What if I'm undecided? What if I don't want to commit yet?" Pashmina looks down over her craggy nose. "And I don't want any solicitations from you Jefferson people. I might go with Sirius Academy or Jumpstart Montessori." Determined to be anonymous, she plants her knuckles on her hip. Eventually she is waved in without having to supply any information at all. As the teacher sinks her teeth into her banana, I sign in and drag Ted through the auditorium doors and down to the front row of the auditorium. Two free chairs beckon. On one side of them, a pant-suited woman frantically pushes numbers into her Blackberry. The small boy beside her is equally engaged in a hand-held gamer that leaks tinny explosions as he tilts and shakes it unmercifully. A daydreaming, freckle-faced woman who nibbles the ends of her hair then brings them from her mouth to examine them is slumped in the chair on the other side of the two empties. The blank page of an open spiral notebook waits on her lap.

"Are these seats taken?" I ask the latter, who seems infinitely more approachable.

She snaps out of her dream "No. My husband wouldn't come with me tonight." Here she bristles with resentment. "Apparently, he doesn't care very much about our son's education." With pleading eyes the woman pushes the seat down and tugs on my sleeve.

"Sit, please," she implores. I do. Introductions are made. Ted sinks down into the creaking seat next to me. The freckled woman, whose name is Peggy, continues defiantly, "Of course our son is only eighteen-months old, but you can never start too early with the preparation. You know what I mean?" Her eyes are huge and frightened.

I have no idea.

"I do," the pant suited woman sings loudly. She is suddenly looming, towering over me, Blackberry at her hip. Her suit is tailored to fit like skin. The coordinated belt cinches in her waist. "That's why my son . . ." she shoots a pointed glance at the woman next to me, "who *is* starting here in the fall, does the Sylvan Pre-K prep class, a Kumon pre-reading program and of course Montessori preschool."

Her voice rises and falls over the heads of those seated in the front three rows. At the conclusion of her contribution, she pulls the gamer from her son's face and holding him by his shoulders, she pushes the scowling boy forward. Presenting him with the bravado and pride that an artist would a portrait that took many years to complete, she says, "This . . . is Duncan." As she speaks, the little boy's hand slips down the front of his pants. As he gropes there, the focus drains from his eyes.

When I told Miss Suzette we were moving, she threw her arm around my shoulders and squeezed. Miss Suzette was Emma's pre-school teacher. The only "teacher" Emma has ever had. On Monday, Wednesday and Friday afternoons, kids ranging in age from two-and-a-half to four gathered in the basement of Cornwell Christ Church to sing rhyming songs, play house with a set of grimy plastic plates and dress up in a slew of raggedy costumes donated by families with older children. Miss Suzette gives Creative Memories scrap-booking classes in her home, and all the mothers already knew her as being infinitely patient. The reason for choosing her went something like: if she could stand supportively by you during the two hours it took to fashion a Lake-Michigan-Vacation-page-border out of vellum, then she'd likewise stick by your mangy toddler as he worked his way out of Pull-Ups for pooping and that horrific spitting stage.

The preschool year ended with a little celebration last Tuesday. There was a sheet cake, a skit based on a Curious George book, and a performance of a single song by the fidgety kids. After the song Miss Suzette tearfully exclaimed that all of the kids had learned, over the last weeks, to clap together at the exactly right moment of, "If You're Happy and You Know It." Color bloomed in her cheeks, as if this single accomplishment exceeded even her lofty expectations. In the ensuing parental applause, a sticky sentimental affection arose in me, and alongside it, a certain kind of terror.

I feel exactly the same way now.

When the Principal enters from a stage door and takes her place at the podium, I relax into my seat because she wears a pale blue pantsuit and is perfectly pear shaped. How could you not warm to someone attired in such a fair-weather, blue-sky kind of outfit? Atop her head a uniform protrusion of short, jet-black hair points admirably skyward, perhaps with the aid of some Herculean mouse or gel. She looks stunned, as if she expected the room to be empty. The already subdued audience sinks into a deadly expectant hush, and the Principal shuffles her notes here and squints at us. It is a closed mouth expression and as she casts around the room I realize she's taking us, next year's Kindergarten class, in with the same scrutiny we're giving her. She takes a long time to work over the room. Someone coughs.

Ted's elbow lands in my side. His hand covers his mouth. "What's she waiting for?" he whispers, and Peggy scribbles furiously on her pad. Then she leans over me to address Ted in a loud whisper. "Class size. There were two last year, but one of the teachers is retiring. This year they'll have to hire if there's gonna be more than twenty-six kids. Which, F.Y.I., there will be."

"Okay. There're quite a lot of you." These are Principal Otis's first words. She is clearly daunted by our mass. For the next ten minutes, she speaks at length about her prior experience as a second grade teacher and the Doctorate in Education she's finishing at the University. Higher education, it seems to me, is the last thing the gathered people want to hear about. Ted yawns into his fist but a peek around the room reveals a rapt audience. An engaged crowd of smiles and bobbing heads. An audience of family and friends. A dream of an audience. I used to be a stage actress and this group is definitely a Saturday night sort of crowd. The ones who'd lubricated their good will and found their chuckle over two or three dirty martinis before the show. Casting about the appreciative house from the front row, so close to the lip of the stage, takes me back to the eight shows a week our theater company performed at a tiny storefront theater on the western fringe of the city. Our plucky troop was comprised of seven of us who left Baylor after sophomore year to pour our hearts out in works by Shaw and Simon on our ten-by-five stage. In winters, audacious mice competed with us for backstage space and inadequate radiators clanked and hissed over our lines.

The audience assembled tonight is the kind of crowd that rewards the actors, despite some dropped lines and a blown entrance, with a confounding and undeserved ovation. Now Principal Otis steps backwards to look offstage before introducing two Kindergarten teachers who each pop out on cue from behind the stage curtain. The first one, grandmotherly, doddering and demurring, shuffles self-consciously towards the onstage chair reserved for her. Her entrance gets a swell of applause from the gathered audience. As she bats away the adoration with a swipe of her hand, she is reverently introduced as the one retiring at the end of the current school year. While delivering this news, the Principal wears a childish pout, and a sorrowful moan travels the room in response. The teacher is round and jolly, with a face like a shriveled apple-doll, and from the expressions on the faces of the parents whose older children have been blessed by her tutelage, beloved. Embarrassed by the applause, she can't take her seat fast enough. The second teacher, introduced as Miss Barbey, 10 could be the first's granddaughter. She looks to be fourteen or so, and is lovely. She has a cascade of wavy dark hair and wears a denim pencil-skirt paired with tall black boots with spiky heels. She winks with an open mouth at parents she recognizes in the audience and I can't help wondering if she baby-sits. Her arm shoots straight up into the air and she waves like she's squeezing a lemon with that hand.

The program shifts now and Principal Otis stands off to one side of the stage while the teachers run us through a Kindergarten day. Much of the subject matter is in code. There's the "DEAR" time in the morning and then again in the afternoon. I've missed what the letters stand for until my eyes fall on Peggy's page of copious notes.

She's written out the words, "DROP EVERYTHING AND READ" in caps at the top.

The house lights dim. On stage the Principal wrestles with a long pole in an attempt to catch a hook on the overhead roll of movie screen. We watch through several goes at it and applaud when she latches on. Suddenly we're smack in the thick of a PowerPoint presentation with assessment goals for Kindergarteners during which my antiperspirant fails. The Principal spends a good deal of time on Diagnostic Reading Assessment numbers and Illinois State Achievement Test scores. Leaning over the lectern when the lights are raised, she says into the microphone conspiratorially. "Across the district, the DRA benchmark is a two to a four by the end of the Kindergarten year. But what say we set the bar high for your children and make our goal for this incoming class a six? Shall we? A six for the whole class?"

She shields her eyes from the light trained on her to better view our response. A smattering of applause is led by a mother in a sari at the end of our row who calls out, loud enough for the Principal to hear, "My son, Ahmed, is already a six."

Now how does she even know that, I wonder. At her feet is a precocious boy with an enviable mop of black hair and a peeling Spiderman tattoo on his check. He's one of the few children here, and he has my attention now because he performs every gesture with the Principal. With exaggerated flourish he waves his spindly arms in augmented imitation. When she pokes the air with one finger to announce her testing goal, so does he. And rather than still him, his mother watches proudly, her fingers entwined over a knee, blinking lazily at him as if some latent disability of hers requires her son to interpret for her. I am distracted and enchanted. The boy is a fantastic bother and in another arena I'd pay to see his show. But here in this auditorium I want to sit on his hands and run his so-called DRA through our noisy paper shredder.

Finally Principal Otis leans a shoulder into the podium to coyly announce that the time has arrived for us to tour the classrooms! It's like she's unveiling a tray of free samples at the end of the chocolate factory tour. Instantly the cavernous room bustles with paper shuffling, as parents stuff the notes they've taken into three ring binders and hard shell briefcases with snapping clasps. The parents of Ahmed are on their feet and both have their hands in the air. When the Principal doesn't see them the mother says, loud enough for our whole row to hear, "Excuse me, can you talk a little about how you address the particular needs of the exceptional child?" She crosses her arms as if to deflect an inadequate response and her little boy does the same. The Principal navigates the stairs down from the right side of the stage sideways, leaning heavily on the rail.

Upon her arrival near us, she announces in a raised voice, "We are ideally equipped for the gifted. You might say that's our norm given the results of the state achievement testing for last school year. Can I show you the numbers? Come. Let us take a peak. They're in my office."

Despite the lure of Brownie Bites and two trays of bakery butter cookies, I can't escape fast enough. Dragging Ted by the hand, I weave past a handful of parents who've stopped at the refreshment table. The first floor hallway is animate with parent race-walkers trying to outpace each other with silent jockeying to be in front. To be the first to the room. The forward momentum is both palpable and contagious as if the first to arrive at the classroom will strain through a finish ribbon, have a paper cup of water shoved into their hand, and get a free backpack teeming with school supplies draped over their shoulders.

At the classroom entrance I'm surprised and embarrassed to find myself standing in the doorway. Behind and around me parents crowd and bunch, though no one is willing to break the spell of the room by actually entering. I cower, mindful of those behind me who want a view. Inside all the rudiments of early learning; alphabet displays,

123's, computers, weather graphs, calendars, books and games have landed in a floor to ceiling display in an upchuck of primary colors. The woman, Peggy, whose son is still in diapers, has followed on my heels. I feel her breath on my neck. Before I realize what she's doing, she pulls out an impossibly small digital camera and starts snapping pictures of the room from over my head like a desperate paparazzi. Taking in the darling room, my eyes sting with tears of nostalgia. I'd been this way, unmoored and unhinged, since we'd decided to move. And in this instant I want nothing more than to regress to the wonderfully carefree time when someone zippered me, put a cookie in my hand and sent me off to play.

Behind me, the perky teacher is touching each of the parents' shoulders and chirping "Hi, hi, hi." I can so clearly see her bending in those smart, calf-covering leather boots to zipper Emma's parka to her chin and pull her fleecy cap down over her ears. Instantly and ardently I know I want her for my girl. I also realize I'm not alone. Three deep parents surround her, jostling to be recognized and favored by the newly crowned celebrity in our midst.

There's so much to see that after half the parents have gone and I've downed the last four melt-in-your-mouth Brownie Bites from the refreshment table, it's hard to leave. Ted examines two long tables crowded with popsicle-stick creations. Closer inspection reveals the handiwork to be the winning fifth grade bridge projects. Each one is more spectacular in design than the next. There are cantilevered bridges and arched bridges and solid long planks of layered sticks under ropey layers of dried hot glue. Ted puts his nose deep into them like they're tricked out Corvette convertibles parked on the street with their tops down.

For me the bridges don't pertain. They aren't relevant to the immediate future of our child so they don't hold my interest. Besides, across the table the teacher in charge of the check-in table gathers up crumpled cocktail napkins and adds them to the banana peel in her hand. I beeline for her.

"Hi. I'm Jennifer Lansing." Careful and obsequious, I don the posture of the groveling, slightly slumped shoulders and a deferential smile. "My daughter, Emma, will be in Kindergarten next year. Anyway, she's young? She won't be five until August and she's a little shy? So I think a class away from the more boisterous boys would be good and perhaps a young and nurturing teacher. A perky sort of teacher rather than a disciplinarian teacher." I stop short before adding the part about Emma very much liking spiky black boots on a teacher, and to slow down, to measure my words, to speak as if these are all just casual conversation starters, but I can't. The things are tumbling out of my mouth so quickly, like a confession I've been harboring for years until I finally get an audience with this priest. I force myself to halt.

A brilliant smile crosses the woman's face. "That sounds good," she says with an encouraging lift of her eyebrows. It's enough to open my floodgates. More words tumble from my face. "I mean a hugger is what I had in mind. I hear some of them don't hug anymore because they're concerned about touching children, and inappropriateness, and charges being pressed, but I always really liked a hugging sort of teacher myself. Someone to just wrap you in their arms and . . ."

With a gentle hand on my arm the woman says softly, "I'm a parent volunteer. I can't help you with the teacher, but can I talk to you about joining the PTA?"

August 1st

Our new house is a small but charming place with cut glass doorknobs and a few arched doorways. You just have to look past the intrepid paint colors the previous occupants slathered over every wall. The same week as the move, Emma turns five and I book a job on an Old Country Buffet commercial. It's a two-day shoot in which I play a featured diner. No lines to say. I just have to react with pleasure and amazement over the completely tepid buffet of meats, noodle salads and pudding deserts the ad agency has assembled in a large, warehouse-like studio. In my business you take the work when it comes. And it always comes just when every other aspect of your life feels runaway and unmanageable.

I am still an actress. My mother added the *still* when we ran into a friend of hers outside the Chico's at the Crosstown Mall last summer. Since then I find myself using it too. Only now, at thirty-nine, I'm a 'real person actress.' I clarify because I know too well the look of disbelief that flashes across people's faces when I tell them I'm an actress. Some who lack a social filter have even said the next thought aloud. "You don't look like an actress." It's true, I don't. But neither do any of my friends in the business. That's what they mean by my category. "Real people." We are not ugly, just lacking in model beauty. We are proudly woman-next-door normal, with larger booties, and little makeup. We have unruly brows and we wouldn't think of coloring over the grays that have snuck into our hair. We are the people you see in kitchen testimonials raving offhandedly about the amazing strength of our new, flexing garbage bags. We are the disheveled ones on the street who seem surprised that someone has stuck a camera in their face to ask them about the Democratic candidate for Governor. We aren't surprised by the camera, though. In fact, we've gone through, on average, an audition, a callback, a rehearsal and some time in a canvas makeup chair to earn the privilege of saying the line, "I want a candidate who puts my kids' education first."

In other words, we work as actors because we can make you believe we're *not* actors. And because the trickle of money that comes in from the spots that I have airing now pays for the two burly men in sleeveless tees to unload our U-Haul truck for us at the new house.

My friend Nicole has a tiny emerald nose stud and persistently disheveled black hair and she books jobs all the time. We met at a Jiffy Pop audition four years ago. We were both lugging our kids, who were infants then, in matching car seats with those handles shaped like half a swastika. And we've been friends ever since. I'm sure you've seen her on TV. She's the one hocking free checking for National Bank while she loads broccoli from her cart onto the grocery store conveyer. Also she's on cable using a Black and Decker rotary tool to carve a spiral design into a chunk of pine, although because of the safety glasses she wears in that spot, it's hard to tell it's her.

Adam, Nicole's son, is also a summer birthday. He's six days older than Emma. They've played together since they were born, and throughout their early years we've remarked at how their interests and abilities have developed in tandem. Their uncanny kinship is like that of biological twins raised miles apart who both, as adults, meet unwittingly at a conference of animal dentistry specialists. Within days of each other this past year, Adam and Emma both became fascinated with Spanish, risked flushing, refused to wear hats, learned to draw faces with the nose and prefer chewy, over crunchy, multi-vitamins.

On the freakishly hot day in August after the movers have deposited us at 2411 Woodlawn St., Nicole drives up from her town-home in the city to help me unpack the kitchen. She brings Adam, and after returning half our glasses to the box they came from because there's no more room in the cabinets, we bail on the unpacking and take the kids to the park.

After we get the kids going on the swings I make the mistake of wondering aloud if I'm remiss for only having been inside Emma's new school the one time. Alarm spreads on Nicole's face. Inevitably her responses incline towards the dramatic, but she is also fresh off a fourteen-interview circuit to get her son Adam into the right, private Chicago school, which isn't even called a *school*. It's a *Learning Center*. I should have thought through her back-story before I asked.

"You didn't interview the Principal? Case the playground as the school day ends?"

"No. I drove past, but there weren't any kids."

Nicole sighs, shaking her head. "Me I have to smell the hallways in the morning. See if the classrooms are pigpens. If the rooms get sun?" The lilt that ends of most of her sentences leaves me squirmy, as if something like an answer is required of me.

"It doesn't help any child to be in a room that deprives them of D."

"But it's supposed to be a great school," I say. "It's in the top ten in the state."

"Top ten based on what? Achievement test scores?" Her lip curls. I can't answer her question for certain. But I've already bragged about Jefferson to half a dozen people from Cornwell, including my mother, as if I had personally participated in earning the school accolades.

"You could still check out some privates. Get wait-listed."

"Nicole, it's good. It's a public school. It's a *great* public school. It's like a beautiful park or a delicious drinking fountain in a park.

You get to just show up the first day and partake. There's something fantastic about that."

"Okay? So say it is one of a rare handful of good public schools. Then you at *least* have to make sure she gets the right teacher." Here she stares at me, inhaling through a toothy grimace as if I were morbidly derelict in my parental duties. It's the look you'd expect to receive if she stumbled upon your toddler, sucking the driveway oil stains, dressed only in a grimy tee and yesterday's Huggies. Over the top? You bet. It is the quality that captivates, though. Once she brought her yorkie in a huge canvas sack to a Puppy Chow audition. I chided her in the waiting room for going so beyond what was required, and all of the other actresses glared at the animal, but she got the job.

Our kids are busy on the playground equipment. Unlike Emma, Adam has not yet mastered the pump and glide needed to propel the swing. His feet jerk wildly back and forth to no real effect and we watch as he jumps off in frustration.

"What about Adam?" I persist. "Is he nervous about Kindergarten? Do they call it Kindergarten at his Learning Center?" The question leaves me as a fistful of mulch leaves Adam's hand.

Nicole's on it. She claps once and hollers, "Adam, leave the mulch on the ground!"

"Actually," she squints briefly at me then toes at the mulch with her shoe. "I don't know if we'll send him this year after all. He has some readiness issues. We may give him another year of preschool. You know, the *gift of time.*"

"The gift of what?"

"The gift of time. It means a delayed start."

"What? A delayed start is showing up forty minutes late on the first day. Waiting until the snow stops falling to dig your car out and deliver him ten minutes after the bell rings. You're seriously going to hold him back a whole year?" Nicole's face folds gently closed. She blinks slowly like a cat. This is clearly a touchy subject.

"He's very young, you know, Jen. He just turned five."

She looks off toward a red wooden train engine moored into the mulch. Adam has climbed on top and rides it like a horse with an undulating motion that is undeniably sexual. Watching the ground, Emma uses her toes to wind up her swing. Then she lifts her feet off the ground to spin.

"Right. Emma too."

"And there's some other things. Like in a group he prefers to be off by himself. And sometimes he uses one word when he means another."

"Emma too," I chuckle.

"And then there's sequencing stuff? You know he mixes up the order of things."

"Emma too."

"And the specialist we took him to thinks it might be a good idea."

Okay so she had me there. I have not taken Emma to a specialist. I have never even thought of taking Emma to a specialist. Should I take Emma to a specialist? I test in my head the question, a specialist of what? Nicole has told me that Adam has seen several chiropractors, an herbalist and a cranial-sacralist. Certainly this manner of assisted living should be enough to propel the boy three blocks down the street to his school, er, Learning Center in the fall. Here I've been going along content with the illusion that our lazy walk down the old neighborhood hill, Happy Child preschool, a few shots and some new dresses would be about all the ingredients required for Kindergarten. Never had I considered or doubted Emma's "readiness." What is *readiness* anyway? Other than a word that calls to mind the last baking stages of a banana nut loaf.

August 15

During our first week in the new house I study Emma's face for evidence of trauma. Before I fall to sleep at night I hold my breath suspended, waiting for Emma to wake in a panic of displacement. Nada. She sails through the transition like she does the cold that, when I catch it, waylays me for two weeks. On the other hand when my eyes fly open in the middle of the night, I cast about our new room for three menacing seconds in the dark. Frantically I fight to dispel the fear that I've been moved to a gay couple's outrageous guest room; carried off as I slept by a beefy, maverick stork that, rather than bringing new babies, rearranges sleeping adults. With its walls painted the crimson color of a Coke logo, and the lingering smell of the previous owners' cats, the place doesn't feel like our home at all.

During the day I drive to Chicago heading south now, instead of north, nostalgic already for the view of the city coming up on it from the other direction. I puzzle auditions in between Ted's networking meetings, and on the way home I stop at Target to buy more things that it strikes me should automatically be provided with a new home. Things like a Swiffer sweeper, a paper towel holder and an eight-foot extension cord so we can actually plug in a lamp in our purple living room.

The fourth day after the move, I'm leaving the Target waiting for a break in the traffic that whizzes by me in both directions, when I notice a woman in a paisley headscarf clipping roses from the bushy rise of landscaping that marks the entrance to the parking lot. With a cheery bundle of candy red blooms in her fist, she sees me staring at her, and her whole biscuity face crinkles into a grin. "Hi!" she calls swinging her hand back and forth over her head. It is a guilt-less greeting, as if I am the friend she awaited while standing in the Target garden stealing their flora. As if the clipped flowers in her hand were a gift for me. I smile back at her feeling suddenly bereft. And then, as if reading my feelings, she blows me a kiss. I pretend not to see and quickly pull out into the westbound traffic. Not be-cause it is the way I want to go. It is the opposite direction of the way I need to go, but because in that moment I realize how much I want a new friend. That's what I *really* need. Not a paper towel holder or the eight-foot extension cord, but a friend.

When I get the first piece of mailed correspondence from Emma's school the next morning I weep. Not at first. At first I call Emma into the navy entryway at the bottom of the stairs and attempt to elicit some enthusiasm for the envelope that came "from your new school!" I sing the last line, pumping it full of gold-star-sticker promise. She waits, scratching a mosquito bite on her neck, while I rip it open, but is gone, skipping back to Dora the Explorer by the time I extract the thick bundle of stapled sheets inside. The top page is a form letter and the remaining pages are the school supply list. I flip back to the first page. "Dear _____." The underlined space here demands a name. A name that is mine, but has been inadvertently left blank. It's not a sign. It's not a sign. It's not a sign.

"Welcome to Jefferson School. Please know that careful consid-eration has been given to place your child in a Kindergarten class and it is our policy not to switch a child once he/she has been placed. Your child, <u>EMMA LANSING</u> 's Kindergarten teacher will be <u>M. Slaughter</u>." I read the name again slowly, as you would when forced to masticate a marble.

It simply cannot be.

M. Slaughter is like choosing a pediatric oral surgeon named Dr. Wrench. Or a priest named Fr. Lusting. Tears bite my eyes and then overwhelm them. What about someone named Miss Honey like in the Roald Dahl book, *Matilda*, or a garden-variety name: M. Smith or M. Jones. Or Miss Barbey. I pine for the dulcet, "Hi, hi, hi," of Miss Barbey. Hell, a Miss Murder would be preferable to the brutality conjured by the word Slaughter. I sink to the top of a large unopened U-Haul Box. We stupidly packed books into the thing: Ted's old yearbooks, his hardcover crime fiction and his business manuals. Now we can't budge it from where it sits just inside the front door. The cardboard corner holds under my weight while I sniff and blink and read the rest of the letter.

When the eight-note chiming doorbell above my head sounds at a decibel that could crack the eggs in the fridge, I leap to my feet. It's the first time I've heard it, and I haven't exactly dressed yet. Meaning I have no bra on under my tee shirt – but a quick glance through the peephole reveals someone so similarly attired it is alarming and edifying at the same time. I wouldn't call myself a religious person. But I am superstitious and I believe you get what you ask for. And here on the other side of the door is what some might call my answered prayer.

"Hey there. I'm Temple. Temple Lee, I'm your neighbor lady." She talks matter-of-factly into the peephole with her head bowed, listening like it's an intercom, and I'm briefly thrown. Aren't you supposed to be invisible from the outside? How does she know I'm even here? I dry my eyes on my sleeve, and inch open the door. Before me is a woman who appears to be in her late thirties in gray sweat pants and a faded Brooks and Dunn concert tee shirt. Like me, she carries an extra fifteen pounds. And, like me, her brown hair is gathered in a sloppy ponytail behind her head. Her mouth hangs open in a grin and in her extended hand is a yellow package of frozen Nestle chocolate-chip cookie dough. "Hi, Jennifer," I say, opening the screen to accept the package.

"Temple," she corrects.

"Jennifer. I'm Jennifer," I say again, my hand to my chest. She slaps her forehead and gives a laugh that starts far back in her throat and is jazzy and musical.

"Oh lord," she says. "My caffeine isn't working yet, is it? Am I ringing your bell too early?" Her voice has the rolling cadence of someone from the south; Georgia I'd bet. That means she's a transplant here, too. And suddenly everything is okay. She is irreverent and normal and she is my neighbor. She belongs to, and reflects, the new house and the new me. She shares my desert tastes, my wardrobe and my street.

Eying the cookie dough as if she forgot she'd brought it, she shrugs and says brightly, as if the offering was really grand. "Found this in the freezer."

"This is great. Thank you. It's how we eat this stuff."

"You got your letter I see. Kindergartener?" I follow her eyes to the Jefferson School missive still in my other hand.

"Yeah. Her teacher's name is Slaughter . . ." I was only just starting down this conversational road but Temple derails me with her delight. Without waiting to be invited, she pushes inside and I step back, immediately kicking myself for not inviting her in first.

"Mine too," she hoots, unabashedly craning around to take in the house, her hand on her hips.

"The place is still a disaster, you know," I say.

"So what. We've lived here for four years, and so is ours, darlin'. We've got a girl. She's a Kindergartener too. Maxine. We call her Maxi. As in pad? She's got Slaughter too. They'll be in the same class." Here she raises her hand to receive my high five. "She turns six nine days after the cut off. Coulda made a scene and started her last year, but whatever. She can't wait for school to start. Who am I kiddin'. I can't wait." She chuckles and spins, examining the dining room and living room, both visible from where we stand.

"Whad'ya think of the paint colors in here? Crazy, huh? We came through at the open house and thought if it were us we'd do the whole place over ourselves in sage or buttercup or something right away. Doesn't the first floor bath just call for some bead board? Hell, we could tack that up ourselves if ya want. If you're into the DIY."

She was prattling on as if we'd left off just yesterday. My concern about the teacher's name quickly sinks under the wave of relief I feel at being suddenly situated. I have not only made my first friend but have provided Emma with one as well. We can all walk to school together. The whole companionable fall of burgeoning friendship set against a backdrop of sifting, golden maple leaves flashes before my eyes.

"We should get them together. The kids. What's your daughter's name?"

"Emma. Like . . . M&M. We should."

"Emmen." She clutches my elbow. "I love that."

I love her. I love her because she curses and brings cookie dough. And because she tells me that Mrs. Slaughter is new to the school and to Google her if I need to know more.

On Google what I find is that someone with the name of our daughter's Kindergarten teacher has a Facebook page and 182 friends, none of who appears older than seventeen. I also find that someone with the name of our daughter's teacher allowed three hits and a walk in a softball game against Mokena Junior High in 2002. And that one Marisa Slaughter is an expert in Vegan Campfire Cooking with three tomes on the subject to her name.

August 23

The trill of a ringing landline in a new home is a joyous sound. It means someone else knows you've arrived. That this is now where you can be located. It is an audible symbol of healthy connection with the outside world. Emma's napping and since it is most likely her last nap until she conks out in front of QVC when she's sixty-two, what with the Kindergarten being full-day. I'd thought I'd let her sleep. I thrill at the first ring but pounce on the phone so it won't wake her. The caller announces himself as representing the Auxiliary Police. He explains that he's looking for donations for their retirement fund. We don't yet have a retirement fund, I try to explain and the gentleman hangs up on me. I have visions of a burglar in a black hoodie slicing our side window screen with a box cutter as two uniformed officers watch and smoke – reclined against the squad car parked under the street light opposite our house. I call Ted on his cell and he sighs and says, "Jennifer, the *auxiliary* police? They weren't from the *main* police – don't worry about it."

The second call was from the breast cancer people. I hang up on them without speaking because I'd left the phone in the bathroom next to Emma's room. And then my new friend Temple calls to tell me she found out Slaughter is a transfer from another grade school on the south side of Lake Park: The only school in the district that failed the No Child Left Behind standards. We're not a minute on the phone, dishing about whether the option of transferring out of failed schools applies to the teachers and the call waiting beep goes off. I fall over myself in apology and click over, "Hello?"

"Yes, hello. Is this Mrs. Lansing?"

"Yes, it is. How can I help you?" Brisk, clipped quick. Had plenty of practice this morning. Wanna get back to my friend.

"My name is Marnie and I . . ."

"Well, Marnie. No thank you. We're not interested." And the phone is in front of my face – my finger poised above the flash button that when pressed will connect me back to my friend, Temple.

"Hello? It's Marnie Slaughter," comes the tinny voice through the earpiece.

Instantly my heart's a riot of beating. "Mrs. Slaughter? Hi! I thought you were . . . I'm sorry, can you hold on just one minute?"

I click back to Temple. "It's her! It's Mrs. Slaughter. Only she said her first name and when a teacher does that it's like the cashier at Kinko's handing you her breast rather than your change. Isn't it?"

Her jazzy laughter and then, "What is it? What's the name."

"Marnie."

"Good. Marnie's good, don't ya think? Call me back." And click.
I switch over again and spend some more time tripping over myself. The teacher wants to meet us. And quickly we land on a time.

After an excruciating silence she says, "Can I? Can I speak to Emma?"

"Yes. Of course."

If she would have instructed me to, say, climb to the crest of my roof and sing *Thriller* four times at the top of my lungs, I would've. And before I know it I am standing in Emma's dark room reaching the phone towards her sleeping face. It's wrong and the next instant I'm back in the hallway. "I'm sorry. Did I say, yes? I meant, no. I'm sorry. She's sleeping."

"She still naps?"

"Yes. No. Rarely. She won't. Don't worry. She won't in school." For the remainder of the conversation I coo and falter. Afterwards I sink to the top step and think back on our exchange replaying the tone and quality of her voice. The smile I detected behind the, "Goodbye." Emerging from my ten-second review, I'm convinced that she is wonderful. I'm giddy and relieved. She seems accommodating. Gentle but firm. Seasoned but not jaded: someone who can simply extend a hand and a smile and draw children to her. Forget the perky teen. My girl will do just fine with Mrs. Marnie.

"Exerpro is a company that caters to *real* people, not athletes," my agent, Blane, tells me. "The home gym market."

"I don't know any real people with a home gym."

"Come on. It says on the breakdown, 'Submit everyone.' I've got middle-aged men on this audition. All types. All ethnicities. You've got a real shot at it, babe."

I'm reluctant. We've got to get school supplies and I've spent the morning lugging half-full boxes to the basement. If I can get a handle on the disorder in my household world, I will miraculously be restored to a woman with an enviable sense of well-being. A better me.

"Blane. Do you know anything about thermostats? I can't figure ours out and it's ninety degrees in the kitchen. I'm disgustingly sweaty," I say to my agent.

"Thermostats. Eew. No. But the sweat thing is perfect! You're doing a treadmill. That's all, babe. No copy. Pretty please?"

"Okay."

"Groovy. Say 3:30?"

The second page of the packet from Jefferson School is a double sided excel spreadsheet that is the daunting list of school supplies. But I'm up to it, the task of gathering the crayons and pencils and the buoyant sense of new beginnings the list brings. September.

Month of renewed industry. Corduroy pants and shiny new loafers. Sense of purpose. The list, after all, is something to *do* to prepare for Kindergarten. I am much better with something to *do* than I am with something to think about. Emma, on the other hand, still shows zero interest in school. When I broach the subject she gets kind of starey and chews on her sleeve. So my little private pep rally: "You'll meet new friends! Yah! I'm sure there's craft poofs and pipe cleaners!" eventually sides off into the admonition, "Don't put that in your mouth."

I can't help thinking that the process of physically gathering the things Emma needs for school will grow her confidence and her internal sense of . . . *readiness* for the school year. So I stand outside the bathroom and cajole through the closed door. "Emma, listen. We have to get scissors and crayons and markers, pencils, a disposable camera, and forty-three other things. It'll be so fun!"

There's a pleasurable grunt in response. I pray she's pooping. Emma has, in the last two weeks, discovered the tantalizing business between her legs. The developmental books say its normal. So I'm being casual. Casual as lawn furniture, when I find her fingers wandering. "Private, honey," I coo. When she emerges here, I follow her skipping self down the upstairs hall.

"I don't want to come," trails her like a comic thought balloon.

"Honey everyone is getting their supplies! All the other kids are doing it."

Really soon I'm going to stop using that line so that I can credibly sell, "Just because your friends are doing it doesn't mean you have to!" But I'm a little desperate given the time crunch before my Exerpro audition, and the line works. She comes with. And we go to CVS for school supplies. And then we go to K-Mart for school supplies. And then we go to Walmart along with every family from Rogers Park to Winnetka. There she insists on tie shoes for gym because they light up when she steps. I buy them even though she has no idea how to work the laces.

At home I find a pair of decades-old shorty shorts that make my legs look like pork sausages stuffed carelessly by the new deli guy. Richard Simmons would like the shorts. They curl up at the side of the thigh, as does the white stripe that runs along the bottom. It looks like the shorts are slit on the side so they can accommodate and accentuate the thigh bulge. Mine is not a business for the faint of heart. It's a business for prostitutes, comes the instantaneous, follow-up thought. For people who'll trade their personal integrity for a slender paycheck and a two-cycle airing on cable between reruns of *Ask this Old House* and *Mission Organization*. I pull on a pair of sweat pants over the short shorts and resolve not to take them off unless specifically asked to by the director. Here we are not one-day friends and I call on Temple to take Emma for two hours. She's not only willing, but goes on and on about how Karla, her oldest, loves little kids and needs the practice watching them. When I bring Emma to the front door, Karla answers it.

"Hi there. You must be Karla!" I cultivate enthusiasm to mask my surprise at what a real-life eleven-year-old girl looks like. Being so entrenched in the preschool and under set, I haven't actually seen an eleven-year-old girl up close in a while. She's gorgeous and lithe. A long skinny tee shirt rises over two pert breast buds and descends to cover whatever, if anything, she has on underneath. Adding insult to injury, from beneath her shirt flows a twin pair of impossibly lean naked legs sunk into a pair of fur covered flip flops. In her hand is a red lollipop glistening with saliva.

"Hey," Karla says as if she's welcoming the Orkin man for the monthly termite inspection. Without once lowering her eyes to Emma, she turns and sashays to the kitchen where she leans against the counter twirling her lollipop in her mouth. The room seems in progress. Next to a four slot toaster is a stack of mottled granite squares. A book of wallpaper samples lies open on a banquette table. Through the bay window I can see into their backyard and the weathered cedar fence that separates it from our own.

"Oh lord, don't look. It's a mess." Temple enters and immediately begins tidying. The wallpaper book is snapped closed. From the table she scoops up a crumb filled plate.

"You done with this?" With menace, she shoves the plate under Karla's nose.

"Uh, yeah?" the girl says, as if it were obvious, which it sort of is because the plate is empty. I have the impression the girl was supposed to take care of it herself. Then Temple realizes there's someone behind me. She sets down the plate.

"Why hello, li'l darlin'. Who's this cutie?"

Temple's got Emma by the arm and she's successful in coaxing her out from behind me.

"Em, can you say, 'Hi?'" Of course she won't say, 'hi.' This is a futile routine. I don't know why I persist. Like one day I'll arrange the words in precisely the right way, and out she'll pop; a whole jack-in-the-box explosion of greeting. For now, Emma says nothing. She just locks her arms around my leg. It doesn't matter because Karla stares blankly towards her like I've assigned her extra algebra homework and Emma is the textbook.

Beside me Temple squats. "Emmen, Maxi is just your age and she's working on a Lego City Airport in the family room. Come on, darlin'. I'll show you." Then she turns to Karla and scolds, "Hey, Kar. Did you say hello to Emmen?"

"Yes. I know. You don't have to tell me," sneers the girl, dropping her lollipop to her side as if this is the last straw.

"Hello, Emmen," she exaggerates.

"It's Emma," I say.

They're running late at the audition. I sign in and squish myself into a folding chair between a sinewy marathoner and a dark skinned man twice my age wearing Hanes sweats that match mine, and a Chicago Bears stocking hat. As we all make small talk and wait for the door to the audition room to open, all I can think is Crayola

Classic Markers. Emma needs two packages of them and every store we'd covered had only generic brands left on the shelves.

Inside the audition room, the casting director cracks his gum by way of greeting. I've known this guy for years, and while I've aged in his mind from an eager college girl to a harried middle-aged mother, he's remained twenty-seven. He's always worn purple tinted John Lennon glasses and, being a man of few words, doesn't even ask me to remove the sweats. Instead he fiddles with the camera and points me towards a treadmill that's been set up against the mottled blue background wall. The treadmill is white. The color is something new. I'm no expert, but I've never seen a white treadmill. This must be why Exerpro is making a new commercial. He shows me how to start the thing in a weary drone gesturing vaguely to the series of controls. I should have said, "No." That's all I can think here. I don't run. I've never run. I find it jarring, and it makes me out of breath. And that's just when I hoof it to chase Emma to make her laugh or to prevent her from being flattened by the hurtling brown UPS truck as she beelines for the street.

At a gathering-speed-jog now on the rubber tread I realize that I was so focused on the shorts it never occurred to me to wear a sporty bra. I can't imagine that the sight of my ample twins bouncing on a white treadmill would encourage anyone to purchase one. And as soon as I have this thought, many seconds before the churning mat under my feet has even reached full speed, the casting director says, "And, thank you." He turns off the camera and, already huffing, and slightly panicked I search for the button that stops the runaway tread.

An hour later at the Target on Chicago's north side, the back to school aisles are a battlefield after the conflagration. Thirty plaid backpacks adorned with skulls have collapsed their hook and are strewn about the floor. Their akimbo straps block the plundered aisles like the limbs of dead soldiers. Carts are stacked up at the end of the row that's supposed to hold a wide variety of markers and crayons including the Crayola Classic Washable Marker 10 Pack.

Weary parents face the empty shelves with lists in various stages of crumple fused to their hands like spent, ineffective weapons. Nada. Zip. There are only Rose Art Markers: many packs of them next to hooks bearing multi-colored protractors. Another generic. And then I see them. Not one, but two packages of Crayola Classic Washable Markers in a deserted cart parked in the queue behind the dead soldier backpacks.

"So I stole them." That night the fingers that did the lifting still sting a little. In my life I've never done anything like that and now I'm purging to Ted who gulps a green healthful drink after his run. A run that has accentuated the long loafy muscles in his legs. It is a confession meant to absolve me of the residual guilt.

"You paid for them, right? So it isn't stealing."

"But I took them right of someone else's cart like a thief would. Just plucked them out and dropped them in my cart without knowing what came over me."

"Why didn't you just get the generic?" Ted asks, showing me his green, particle-laden mustache. I am ready for the query. Producing the school supply list I unfold it in front of him and iron it flat with my hand.

"Look at this. It's crazy," I say, pointing down the list. "I had to go to Office Depot after a woman who had four kids with her lunged in front of me at Target and cleared the shelf of Elmer's."

"Elmer's. I see." I check him here for mockery, then plow on.

"'Elmer's glue,' 'Crayola Markers,' 'Fiskar Scissors,' 'Ticonderoga pencils.' You can't just get generic."

"No. *you* can't get generic." He leans in to kiss me with his green mustache. I duck.

"Okay. Say I do. Say I get her generic to bring to school. Then I'm not following the directions am I? It's the supplies. The first impression. And what's the teacher gonna think about Emma? Here comes that cute little girl who won't be able to follow directions."

Ted shrugs and sets his glass in the sink. I shouldn't complain to him. He'd never say it, but I know he's worried about business. His firm has yet to land a client and we're plowing through our meager savings at an alarming pace. The $94.00 I just spent on school supplies didn't help.

"Maybe the cart was for stocking and you were free to take what was in it."

"No, Ted. It belonged to someone. It was full of school supplies and Purex and an economy pack of small cans of Friskies flaked-style cat food. I feel bad about this. Let me just feel bad about this."

"You want me to make you a smoothie? It'll make you feel better."

"I don't feel that bad," I say, blasting the green flecks off the side of his glass with a stream from the faucet so they won't fuse there.

August 26th

"It's okay to be a little nervous, Emma. Everyone gets nervous meeting the teacher the first time. Just be yourself and you'll be fine." She ignores me. She skips and walks in fits and starts staring down at the sidewalk on our walk to school. I'd braided her hair and changed her out of the "My parents went to Taos and all I got was this lousy tee shirt," tee shirt, lest it convey a bratty, wheedling temperament. Suddenly she shrieks, "Mom!"

"What!"

"Mom you're standing on it. It's bad luck!" she says. My heart in my throat, I look down and move my foot off the crack in the sidewalk to the center of a square. "Better?" I ask tucking my hair behind my ears. My stomach somersaults as we make our way up the steps of the school. I turn to Emma. "How do I look?" The ridiculousness of the question pops out like a cartooned conscience character to jeer at me, and my query goes unanswered. There's a doorbell next to the school's double front door. Emma sees it first and pushes it repeatedly before I realize what she's doing.

"Don't *do* that with the bell," comes a bellowing admonition from within. A square speaker screwed high onto the brick is the source of the voice. When I locate it, the voice commands, "Name?"

I give it and hear a soft click of the door unlatching. Inside the first floor hallway smells of fresh paint. At the top of the stairs a beefy woman with four thousand braids, each no thicker than a vermicelli, guards a sprawling lobby of terrazzo. One foot is jutted out as if to trip us.

"Hello." I say. Emma scoots behind me and hides her face in my rear. The she-guard doesn't answer, but stays there watching as we sidle past her and make our way down the hallway. There's an aura of suspense in the empty bulletin boards bordered with their wavy contrasting colored paper frames, in anticipation of all the craft and toil they'll get to display in just a week. Less than a week. Six days.

Two teachers stand chatting outside their open classroom doors. Miss Barbey, the chipper young one I recognize from last year's Kindergarten Information Event, spots Emma first. She lights up.

"Hi, hi, hi." She scrunches her hand in an enticing little wave like a carnival barker who's desperate for you to try for a stuffed squirrel at her shooting gallery.

Emma realizes she's being spoken to by someone over three feet tall, and beelines again for my rear. Me and my human bustle say, "Hello," and excuse ourselves on down to Mrs. Slaughter's room and Mrs. Slaughter herself standing sentry at the door. I take her in, in scrutinizing gulps. She isn't young. Her black hair is gathered into a loose ponytail captured at her nape and a thick band of silver hair frames her face on each side like draped garland. Her dress is loose, a leopard print rendered in lavender hues. And she wears a fanciful pair of readers with pink and white striped frames on a chain, of what look to be espresso beans, around her neck. When she sees us she clasps her hands together and tilts to one side to see around me. I take a deep breath and stick out my hand a good ten feet before we reach her.

"Mrs. Slaughter, So nice to meet you I'm Jennifer Lansing, Emma's mom. I've got a lot of questions for you!"

Relieved, suddenly, that I wore pants, I feel Emma's nose pressing against my right butt cheek and the teacher sinks in front of me and addresses Emma through the space between my legs.

"Hello!" she says right to the zipper at my belly. "Is that Emma Lansing I see? Come out, come out wherever you are?" It's too much. I turn, grasp Emma by the shoulders and switch places with my daughter pinning her in front of me. Mrs. Slaughter, still on one knee, gasps and brings her hands together again. "You are as pretty as a picture, aren't you? I have crayons and markers inside. And I'd love for you to draw for me inside your new classroom."

Because I tower over the scene, I am cloaked in invisibility and from this lofty position, I hear what is unmistakably my voice booming down over the two of them. "That's great cause she loves to draw, really. Don't you, sweetie. Why right before we came here she drew the most amazing picture with our whole family and even a miniature poodle . . . "

Mrs. Slaughter has Emma's hand and in one muscular swoop she stands and tugs. Her eyes are still locked on Emma's face. "Em. Can I call you Em for short?" she asks.

" . . . which is funny 'cause she wants a dog but doesn't have a dog. Behind us in the picture is a rainbow, and the clouds in the sky of course . . ."

"Can you say goodbye to your mommy for just a few minutes while I show you around inside your new classroom? I love your dress. Do you like to wear dresses a lot? Me too."

The soft click of the latch silences my tongue and I realize, staring at the blond wood surface of solid door, that I've been ditched. Dumped. That's fine though. It's fine . . . because there's a little glass rectangle in the door and if I squash my face against it I can see them. I can see them and hear them a little. I press my cheek against the cool wood of the door and watch. Together they sit in tiny plastic chairs at a little, low table. As soon as she's down, Emma buries her face in the comfort of her elbow. "Come on. Look up, sweetie," I whisper. Mrs. Slaughter sneaks an orange crayon into Emma's fist and gazes patiently at her, her chin in her palm. Through the door I hear the teacher ask Emma to write her name. And for a while no one in our strange triad moves.

"Come on, Emma," I whisper to the pane of glass in the door.

As if hearing me, my baby lifts her head and . . . shakes it back and forth. It's not a defiant, "No." But a, "no," like, *name? What name? Nobody ever said anything about a name before.*

"Come on, Emma," I coax loudly. My heart is pounding. Everything else but the little meeting on the other side of the door has fallen away. I might as well be in there. She'd be writing her first and last name now if I were in there. My hand encircles the knob. But I know that turning it would brand me one of *those* parents. No, I can't push myself in on the meet-the-teacher day. There'll be then an invisible *H* for *hovering* on my back and each time I entered the school I'd have to live up or down the perception.

"You can do this!" I squeal. My fingers squeeze into tiny fists.

Mrs. Slaughter leans close to Emma and says something. And after a minute, a smile creeps onto Emma's face. She likes her! Relief cleanses me. They stand now and tour the room holding hands. Mrs. Slaughter gestures to a low bookshelf and then moves on along that wall and out of view.

"Hello?" It's an urgent voice from behind that startles me. I feel instantly like I'd committed some crime, spying here. Whirling around I see before me, pacing, the suited woman who sat next to me at the Kindergarten Information Event. Today her suit is eggplant. Its hourglass shape is secured at the waist with a large button. It seems too tight, and too much to ask of any fastener working alone. The look is completed with a skirt, hose and black wedge heels. I feel suddenly slovenly in jeans.

"Hi," I say, extending my hand for the second time this hour.

Her eyes fly to me and when she turns I see the earpiece curled around her ear like a metallic snail.

"Not you," she whispers, wagging a finger in my face.

"Hi. I'm here," she says briskly, lowering her chin. "No. I'm just going into a meeting now. Have him shoot me an email and I'll get back to him later, 'kay? Thanks."

It's been silent in the hall until now and her voice pierces through that peace like a ceramic blade. She pushes some buttons on her Blackberry then shows her teeth briefly to me in a smile prepared earlier in the day. It's wilted, slightly spoiled now when she pastes it on.

"Sorry, Mrs. Slaughter," she says to me, while her fingertips tap at tiny phone buttons. "I'm Duncan's mom. And this is my son, Duncan." She extends her hand to me. I take it and endure one firm, chilly pump. Then she turns to the small antic boy in a red polo shirt whose hand is lost down the front of his khakis and spits fiercely, "Get your hand out of your pants!" The boy screws his face up at her – but removes his hand. I'm resolved not to shake it. Even if that's what his mom directs us to do next.

"Hi. I'm not Mrs. Slaughter," I say. "I'm another mom. I'm Emma's mom. She's in there with Mrs. Slaughter."

Duncan's mom clearly has no memory of me, so we proceed along as if we've never seen each other before. She looks down at her son and says, "Duncan you and EhEhEmma must be in the same Kindergarten class. EhEhEmma's name starts with a what, Duncan?"

The boy's face screws up into a stormy expression that broadcasts equal measures of effort and disgust. "I don't know." He stomps around as he answers as if he's holding in a liter of pee. "An 'A'?"

"No honey, an "E!" You knew that. Didn't you?" The mother's hands are on her hips. "Dashenka worked with you on "E's" didn't she?

"Is that a giwl in there?" Duncan whines and huffs. "Are there boys in my class too? Can I go in?"

And he does! He turns the knob and walks right on in there hauling his mother. They nearly collide with Mrs. Slaughter and Emma who are coming toward us.

"Emma, do you have any questions about school?" Mrs. Slaughter is bent again, oblivious to anyone taller than a dwarf or a five-year-old.

"Yes." I am crouching to catch some leftover crumb of her attentions. "I do. I have a question. What time does school start?" It's out of my mouth before I can catch it. Pushed out, no doubt, by the other, better questions crowding behind it.

Mrs. Slaughter ignores me. It's not a bad thing. I want her to be attentive to my child; I just had no idea it would be at my expense. She looks Emma in the eye. I'm folded to their level, and still, she doesn't see me. "8:55 is the first bell. So you have plenty of time to take off your coat and wash your hands before the 9:05 start. You know what they say about the early birdie. Do you like to get woken up early Emma?"

A hosed leg lands squarely in front of me and then the whole of Duncan's mom eclipses my view of the teacher. The hand of Duncan's mother swims in the air like a conductor's, and she sings, "Excuse me, can we get going here? I've got the 2:30 time and I've got to get back to work."

Temple's husband, Denny, runs camera for a Travel Channel show. He also always has a Bluetooth device curled around his ear and simultaneously talks on a hand-held phone to someone else. He travels a lot and is fond of wearing tracksuits. I suppose he has to be ready to leap onto a flight at a moment's notice. He probably has a packed overnight bag in his trunk like a very pregnant woman. When he's home I never know whether to converse beyond a wave when I see him gathering the paper or pacing for a signal in his front yard.

On the Saturday before school starts, we invite their family over for pizza. Karla and Maxi arrive first. Maxi and Emma have, over the one earlier playdate, become fast friends. Maxi is a mysterious child with thin, dark hair that lays flat against her head, and will always lie flat against her head despite the later life efforts of curling irons and volumizing conditioners. She cocks her head to look adults directly in the eye, and breathes solely through her mouth because of some persistent nasal constriction.

"You wadda pop the heads off your Barbi dolls?" she says right to Emma's nose with a conspiratorial grin and a snuffling mouth breath. Emma's in with a nod, and holding hands, they quickly disappear upstairs. Maybe this new, bolder kind of child will awaken a sense of daring and adventure in my shy girl. This is what I tell myself to fend off the forward thinking vision of Maxi passing a smoldering roach between the cedar pickets of the fence in the back yard. Karla has come over in her pajamas; loose flannel pants imprinted with cartooned monkeys hang in a roll from her hips. They completely cover her feet so that the bottoms are in tatters from being walked on. It's still August for goodness sake and she'd be boiling if it weren't for the white, strappy camisole she's stuffed into on top. She casts around the living room for a moment and then turns with a despondent sigh and follows the two little girls upstairs.

Temple and Denny's entrance is loud and friendly as if we've been friends for years. They've brought a bottle of wine and even though Denny still has his earpiece on, he shakes Ted's hand warmly and gives him a shoulder squeeze, which in its generosity tells me that the husbands will be friends as well. When the four of us are accessorized with drinks and settled onto the living room furniture I uncross my legs, back out of the conversation for awhile, and listen while our neighbors share stories about Karla, who'll start sixth grade at the middle school, and her after-school juggle of violin lessons, hip-hop class and travel soccer. After our first beers, Temple's husband, whose face is animate and rubbery, commands the room with a mean impression of Karla's math tutor, Jaquan, who reinforces multiplication rules with rap rhythms.

"And now the *eights*!" Denny says, crouching, his hands on his knees and his eyes bugged out. Then he points and dips the top of his head to the left chanting, "Eight times one is eight, uh!" The last grunt comes with an uninhibited pelvic thrust before he starts the pattern again. I'm amazed at the staying power of his earpiece and then I worry that maybe he's left it on and some VIP on the other end is hearing the show as well. Once on a commercial shoot I left my microphone on while I went to pee and toot and when I came back to the set, the sound guy took the headphones off his ears and said out of the side of his mouth, "Everything came out okay, I heard."

"Eight times fo is twenty-fo!" Denny is on his feet now. With the fingers of one hand splayed on his pelvis he gyrates his hips and circles his other arm above his head. It's quite a show. They must be the kind of couple that takes advantage of the free Salsa lessons in the space over Affordable Portables on Tuesday nights. We should do that too. Ted has a smile frozen on his face as he watches from the couch. Temple smiles but covers her eyes with her fingers and mutters, "Oh lordy. Sit down, Denny."

"Not yet. Eight times five is forty. Uh!"

"Dad. What are you doing?" Karla is halfway down the stairs watching her dad. Her hip is thrust out, her head is pressed back onto her neck and her mouth hangs open in disgust. Caught out, he slinks to the couch.

"Nothing, Kar.," he says with a wink to the rest of us. Temple slaps his leg and hides her snicker in her hand. Karla broadcasts a tight smile to the room and announces as a question, "There's a little problem with the nail polish up here?" I accompany her up the stairs. She comes up to my breast, and she fills the climb with alternating apology and excuse in a manner that is childlike and darling. The "little problem" is a royal blue puddle the size of a Big Mac on the floor just inside the bathroom door. No one will cop to the spill. The little girls compete with each other, echoing the phrase, "I did not do that." So an audience of innocent children watches me mop up the stinky lacquer with a paper towel. Given the company downstairs, I hold my scolding tongue. I am, in fact, a picture of reassurance, of taking the spill in stride. It is the opposite of the response I'd have if Emma and I were alone and, I'm aware as I clean, my often-inconsistent response in such scenarios is a prime example of what the books would call, "uneven parenting." This realization, and what impact my behavior will have on my child, bothers me deeply keeping me awake nights. Particularly in the week before my period.

When I return to the living room Ted is apparently mid sales pitch. "Seriously, let me go through your garbage." Temple and Denny look to me baffled. "Everything okay up there?" Temple asks. And then she adds, "Karla loves to do nails. She does a good job, too." And she waves the magenta tips of her fingers at me. Ted turns to me, giddy with the anticipation of getting hold of the neighbor's stainless kitchen bin, potato peelings and all. I put a hand on his shoulder.

"Ted's in Identity Theft," I say. "He's a consultant. He has his own business." I look at Ted. "You've got to tell people that first, honey, before you ask for their garbage."

"Nah." He shakes his head. "It's not as powerful then. The impact of the request gets diluted. But when you ask for garbage without the explanation first," He touches his forehead here with one finger, "That's when you're gonna get their attention and keep it."

Here his sales pitch ramps up and he turns to paint the picture for Temple and Denny. "See, that's where it all happens. The garbage. Get a hold of that and you can steal at least four people from there. Social's, Visa numbers. Heck just a name and address will get a good thief started." Buoyed from his pitch he points at each of us, "Beer? Beer?" Nods all around and he goes off with a jaunt.

"So. Identity theft, huh," Denny says to no one in particular, but something in his tone invites an explanation.

"Ted spent years in accounting. His old boss was a little off. He loved tap dancing. Used to close the door to his office and practice his shuffle step on a piece of plywood. He also had these eyes that gazed off in two different directions. It drove Ted crazy trying to have a conversation with the guy. He never knew which eye was the working one. Where to look. You know?"

"Well," Denny says. But he stops here, and a silence chokes the room. Temple brings her empty bottle to her lips and tips it back for the foamy dregs.

"Not that that's why he quit. He's just not wired for a nine to five. You know? He hated that." I haven't done a very good job of conveying Ted's promise. This is a man so resourceful that even if there weren't any more beer in the fridge he'd come back cradling four cold ones.

"Four years ago Ted had his identity stolen by some woman who used his good credit to buy thousands of dollars of anti-aging serum."

"Thousands? Really? Anti-aging creams cost that much?" Denny asks.

"I guess the ones from boutique companies do. They hire deep-sea divers to harvest the exotic ingredients from mollusks 250 feet below the surface."

"No shit. I'm in the wrong business."

"The police weren't very helpful so Ted took it upon himself to catch the person."

"What about the serum?" Temple leaned forward, an elbow on her knee.

"It took Ted months to track down the store that still ran credit cards over those inky little carbon papers. But the whole experience turned out to be a blessing in disguise. Now he's going to make his living protecting other casual consumers from the same experience." I shouldn't have said *going to*. Like he hadn't started yet, when he had. I'd made it sound like he's embarking on some pipe dream. When that isn't it at all.

"What about the serum?" Temple is stuck on this point.

"They caught the woman. Which is so rare."

"But did you get to keep any of the stuff?"

"No."

"Too bad." Temple curls back into the couch.

"You'd be astounded, what people throw away," Ted says as he doles out a fresh round of Bud Lights. "Like those credit card solicitations. People toss them in their garbage unopened. You know all a thief has to do is check 'yes' send me the card, change the home address field to their own and bingo. Some sleazebag is loading up Wiis and flat screens at Best Buy on your good credit."

It was powerful, this spiel.

"That's what I'd take. Electronics," Denny pipes.

"Nah. The cream. That's brilliant," Temple says. We all sip out of our fresh bottles.

"Do you guys shred?" Ted asks.

They look at each other and Temple says, "I just pour old yogurt or whatever's grown mold in the fridge over the trash inside the bag before I close 'er up. Or did you ever let leftover kidney beans go so long that they grow that white furry fuzz? That is one hell of a stench, my friends. No one'll ever go lookin' to steal a person from my trash cause they have to pick off those babies first."

September 4

On the afternoon before the first day of school, I read to Emma *Countdown to Kindergarten*, *The Night Before Kindergarten* and *Miss Bindergarten Gets Ready for Kindergarten*. Emma still seems nonplussed about the start of school. She's satisfied, simply, to go to a room that has its own poofs for crafts. Then my agent calls to tell me they've invited just a few people in to audition for a public service announcement on homelessness and I was requested by name. I'm not sure that I believe him but I'm flattered and say I'll go. There's one line to learn. "A dollar a day." It's to be delivered in a plaintive appeal to the camera. Another, "young ethnic male actor with in-your-face hand gestures" according to the commercial breakdown, will finish the sentence with, "Is all it would take to get us off the street."

I kick myself before I'm fully awake the next day, because it was my plan to devote one hundred percent of my energies to my daughter for the getting ready hours and instead I race around trying to feed and clean everyone while a quiet voice inside me repeats, "A dollar a day," like a mantra. At eight-fifteen, despite the fact that Emma was up at six, we're running late to get to school. I holler upstairs for her. When she bounds down the stairs at fifteen minutes before the bell it is with a tiny Polly Pocket doll and a plastic magenta dress sized to fit a cricket. "Mommy, can you put this dress on my Polly Pocket?"

"No, honey, there's no time. Put your things in your backpack."

She peers out the kitchen at the leaning tower of Target bags in the entry.

"How?" she asks plainly.

"Not that stuff. Those are your supplies." My mind is flipping through my inventory of clothes. It wants to land without looking on an ideal ensemble for season-less homelessness. The wardrobe in commercials is always season-less. Long cotton sleeves. Light layers. That way they can air it all year, in warm climates as well as cold.

"You know, a pencil or some Kleenex. Stuff like mommy has in her purse."

"Candy?" she says, hopefully.

Ted's bare feet pad down the stairs behind her. He's clutching an inadequate green hand towel in front of his junk like a loincloth. The naked whole of him stands there dripping.

"I thought you did the laundry," he says.

"I did. It's clean. The towels are in the basket outside the dryer."

"Candy? Can I bring that?" Emma asks heading towards my purse.

In addition to being irritated at the lack of toweling, Ted is a mostly silent critic of sugary foods. And he has no idea that I've got two different kinds of M&M's in my purse.

46 "You're gonna give her candy to take to school?"

"No," I say, to Ted.

"No, no candy." I catch Emma just before she delves into my purse. "No candy, honey. I packed you a lunch. A healthy lunch. It's on the counter in the Barbie lunchbox! Put that in your backpack. And other stuff like Kleenex and maybe a pencil like Mommy has in her purse."

"In the basement?" Ted asks.

"Yeah."

"That's not done. It's not done until it's put away."

"Done is dry." I call to my husband who's already pounding down the stairs to the basement.

Five minutes later, I'm dressed in my oldest pair of jeans: jeans that have gone tight at the waist and threadbare at the knees, and a flannel shirt that I've layered over one of Ted's yellowed undershirts. "Smile," Ted calls to us. He has our old Sony video camera, a thing the size of a four-slice toaster, pressed to his eye. Frowning then, he holds it against his chest and fidgets with the controls.

From the dining room Emma calls, "Mommy where's my pink headband with the thingies."

"Honey can you find the Sony manual for me?" Ted asks, fidgeting. "I know there's a way to put a title in here." A red light on the camera comes on and Ted swings the thing toward me again. I take the lens and point it down toward our daughter who gallops in from the dining room, the headband dangling from her mouth like it would from the jaws of a golden retriever.

On our front steps Ted juggles cameras. While I sneak on some bright red lipstick as a surprise for Emma, the video camera gets swapped out for the still camera. And he clicks away while Emma reaches around to catch the straps of her new Strawberry Shortcake backpack. She is impossibly small under the thing. It protrudes from around her back and over her head like a turtle's shell. While Ted arranges her for his picture, it gives me a moment to observe her objectively. It's still unmercifully hot, and the school isn't air-conditioned, so Emma wears a summer dress, ankle socks and sandals. She does the best she can to muster a smile for her dad, but Emma has never had a regular smile, preferring instead to jut out her lower jaw and expose her small bottom teeth. It's the strangest expression, and until this moment it has never occurred to me to comment on it. Like so many of the other peccadilloes of our five-year-old they've just seemed like darling and unique little gems of character. But now it occurs to me that in the public sphere of the Kindergarten classroom maybe someone will mimic her strange grin, or call her out for bringing her finger to her nose to smell it after she sticks it in her ear. Maybe someone will ridicule her. These thoughts roil around inside me and

I corral her with a fury-driven passion when they're done. Kneeling, I hold her hands and flash my ruby red lips at her.

"Em," I say softly, "I'm going to give you a big kiss on your tummy, 'kay? It'll be our secret but you'll know my love is with you, today. And if you miss me, you can just look right here at my love." Lifting her shirt, she recoils as I press my lacquered lips onto the soft skin of her belly.

"Stop!" She twists away, wiping the imprint of my lips into an angry red blur.

We load our fourteen plastic Target bags into the trunk. Our family could be poster people for the recycling industry. Some green neighbor will snap our picture and reproduce it surrounding us with a circle with an angry diagonal drawn through it. We'll be featured as the "Don't" people in ads next to the "Do" family who've brought their items in reusable canvas sacks with leafy trees stenciled onto the side. As we finish, Temple's door flies open and she shuffles out in a men's black watch flannel robe and fuzzy slippers to collect her paper at the end of her walk.

"See you there!" she calls groggily, as if there were hours to spare.

At Jefferson School, I follow twenty other dads wielding video cameras up the steps. Ted has narrated our entire journey into his camera. "We're walking, still walking, now turning the corner, accompanying the lovely Miss Emma . . ." Inside he squats, shuffling backwards down the school hallway. "We're walking into the Kindergarten room on the first day. Can you wave, Emma?" At the classroom door Mrs. Slaughter has to step aside for him to pass and he swings the camera up into her face.

"And who's this? Your teacher? Hi, teacher." He sticks his hand into the frame and waves close to her face. My hand is starting to cramp now with the force of Emma's grip around it. We work our way around a mammoth infant-car-seat stroller-system parked inside the classroom door. Leaning against the rear wall is a phalanx of camera-equipped fathers, like a rag-tag documentary crew awaiting instruction. As we pass them they stare at us and the fresh smell of musky aftershave from the gathered photographers assails me. Together, the three of us make it to the sign-in table and, with her free hand, Emma picks up a pencil and scrawls an 'E" while Ted narrates from above.

"What we have now is Emma drawing a . . . you're signing in! You're writing your own name!" He gapes at me over the lens. "Honey, did you know she could write her name?"

Our daughter's been writing her name for a year. He must've known that. I handle his observation as if he was kidding – with a little jab of my elbow and an aren't-you-hilarious smirk. Many parents crowd the classroom now like mammoth trespassers in the land of Lilliputians. We tower over the small children who are, literally, half our size. They sign in and, with the aid of their entourage, migrate silently to the story rug. There each child's name is written on a bit of masking tape affixed to the carpet. One by one they find themselves and sink, cross-legged. They eye each other suspiciously, as do the parents. Emma releases my hand and sinks on top of her name. She is wide-eyed but determined. And at the sight of her pale, knobby knees that stick out from her skirt when she folds them, something inside me blooms with melancholy pride and affection. I squat beside her for a moment, tearing open the left knee of my old jeans in the process, and give her shoulders a squeeze.

"We're going to go, Emma. Just have fun, today. We love you . . ." Her arms encircle my neck.

"I'm not scared," she whispers gamely into my collar, as if saying it would make it so. The moment overwhelms me with the urgent need to not only stay, right here on the story rug, but to be made invisible and subsumed into this tiny child of mine. Right now I love her in the kind of drowning way that I only experience when I have to leave her somewhere strange. And for a fraught second I'm quite certain that I will howl out in a manner both feral and completely against my conscious will.

At that moment Duncan broad jumps onto the story rug. I am so grateful because he's stolen my impending (and potentially mortifying) scene. His sneakers land on the fingers of a freckled girl with tight braids. She promptly bursts into tears and flies into the legs of her impeccably dressed mother who wears a silken dress of deep purple. One of the woman's arms shelves a sleepy toddler draped over her shoulder. His minute leather shoes dangle by her hip. The mother comforts the girl while holding her teary face at arms length to preserve her outfit. The girl presses her whole body forward to get closer and, after a glance at the accumulating audience, the mother gives up, and the girl sinks her streaming face exactly into her mother's crotch. Then she shakes her head back and forth to wipe it there, while shrieking for her mother to take her home.

An urgent poke on my shoulder startles me to standing. A sheen of sweat glistens on the upper lip of Duncan's mom above a smear of fuchsia lipstick that is exactly two shades brighter than her maroon suit. Holding the suit together at the waist is a single, straining button.

"Hi, Emma's mom. Duncan's mom." She touches my arm and then her chest to illustrate the players here as if, in the interval since our last meeting, I might have become a deaf mute. "I wanted you to meet our nanny, Dashenka." She extends a hand like Vanna White would when introducing a pair of "D"s, and steps aside to reveal a round-shouldered woman with a bulbous nose and a full head of moppy yellow hair. "She'll be bringing Duncan most days, because I work." She brings her hand to her chest and with this last word her eyes dart downward to take in my ripped-at-the-knee-jeans and nubby flannel. Let me just say that, when I have to costume myself for work it is a relief. Someone else has picked my clothes for me. I fill these outfits, even the homeless person one, in a way that I don't the clothes I choose for myself when I'm not working. These clothes.

These *costumes*, lend definition and purpose to my being. They are an essential part of my job and, as such, fill me with purpose and confidence. That said, I'm wearing rags now and it is only in this moment in the room full of so many suited and coiffed adults that I realize my own covering is shit.

Dashenka is pumping my hand earnestly. When she speaks it is with a thick, guttural Slavic accent, chunky with consonants. "Hullo!" she bellows. Before I can respond she stills Duncan by catching his shoulder in her grip. "Duncan, get your hand out of your pants!" And then with a curl of her lip she says to me, "Is good having meet with you."

"Shoot. Gosh darn it." The buttons on Ted's maddening camera hold his focus and provide a reason for our exit. I'm pulling at him with both eyes on Emma. The color has drained from her lips, but that is the only sign of nerves on her. Even when a freakishly large boy dressed in a tent-like tee shirt and lime green pants that end at his ankles plops down next to her. He waddles back and forth on his rear to smush himself in between two children half his size. His entry is accompanied by a definite waft of White Linen by Estée Lauder. Mysteriously, the mother arrives after the scent. She is round faced and wincing with apology through a ready grin. After her mammoth boy lands, she buries both her hands in her son's hair. It gives the impression that she's pushing down on him to help him fit. While smoothing his curls she turns and announces to no one in particular. "We red-shirted him, and he's big for a six-year-old, but . . ."

"Seven!" The boy scowls up at her.

"*Six*-year-old. Really." She giggles and her whole face crinkles into an apologetic smile. The boy stuffs his thumb in his mouth and sulks sullenly. "Not seven for some time," the mom squeals in a high voice. She hugs her son roughly under one arm, not even needing to bend to do so. "Okay Henry?" She lifts his chin to see his face. Henry the hulk, I think. Henry Hercules. Will have to pay for an extra seat when he flies United. Then I see the panic in the boy's eyes and feel an immediate rush of guilt. Of course he's scared. They're all scared. We're all scared. Here they are at the start of the academic slide. Once they push off there's no turning back; and no telling how or where they'll land at the bottom, or rather, the top.

I blow Emma one last kiss.

"Freeze," Ted shouts. The assorted scenarios of farewell on the rug all oblige for a bizarre, static second. Even Duncan lands on one foot and holds the pose. And then as if by mutual agreement, life moves on. "Hang on, Jennifer" Ted speaks to the camera. "There's a way to fade out with this thing and that would be really super while you're saying goodbye."

"We're done," I say. "It's over, Ted. Honey? It's over."

"Amen," the woman with the soiled silk concurs sadly. "It goes like that doesn't it?" She snaps her fingers. "One minute they're babies, and the next they're gone." She shifts the toddler on her hip and waves once more at her little girl. The mother is oblivious to the slimy stain down the front of her dress that has congealed to form what looks like a peace sign.

In the hallway the school bell rings. Temple, in yoga pants, gym shoes and a loose hoodie, rounds the corner at a clip, hauling Maxi by the wrist. The girl has on pink shorts and tee shirt emblazoned with the words "I Love My Hamster." I know the outfit because she wore it at our house yesterday.

"Crap, Maxi, we're late on the first day." She gives her daughter a little push and gently slaps her rear, "Get in there, girl. Have fun."

Maxi marches up to Mrs. Slaughter who stands with her back against the door.

"I brunged these for you," she says, holding out her fist.

Mrs. Slaughter cups her hands to receive the acorn tops that fall from Maxi's hands. It is as if they were Tiffany earrings. "Oh my. These are wonderful," she says, stroking them gently with one finger.

"Where are her supplies?" I ask, taking in Temple's empty hands.

Temple rolls her eyes and waves off my question. "We don't do the supply thing anymore." As if the gathering of supplies were passé. Something she used to do, but with time and wisdom has outgrown. Like thumb-sucking.

Ted leaves to walk home. I shoot Emma one last glance. She doesn't see. She's cross-legged on the carpet. The fabric of her skirt is stretched tight over both knees and the whole top of her is folded over into her lap.

Temple lifts on one toe to see Maxi through the door, offers a final thumbs-up to me, and squeals, "OOOEEE! Free at last, Jennifer. Both kids in school and I'm going to the nine-thirty Bikram. Gonna sweat 'til I smell like rubber."

In the hallway other mothers are huddled together in clutches of crying and consolation. From the words and whimpers that rise from their commiserations, it's clear that some career mothers turn in their last of their many children and grieve this day. The first floor hallway is dotted with groups of casually clad mothers huddled in a collective state of profound disorientation over the denouement of the full-time parent thing. After the drop-off, all day presents not six-and-a-half hours of opportunity, but a chasm of loss and expectation. Loss of the Kindergartener to the grade school and the expectation that on the walk home you'll carefully reconstruct the self you were before kids, complete with a six-figure income and personally rewarding hobbies. Suddenly my homeless ensemble doesn't seem so bad. I may not have the career I'd envisioned: meaty lead roles in new plays by Pulitzer winning playwrights; losing myself in the delicious lives of broken women who are crazy or terminally ill or, ideally, both. I do, at least, have a job.

Plastered against the rectangular window of the closed door to Miss Barbey's Kindergarten classroom is a petite mom with layered blond hair that's tangled in an ethereal poof at the back of her head. She is alone. A keening sob, as from a wounded seal, draws me to her. Her face is contorted in grief and running with tears. I touch her shoulder gently and introduce myself. Maybe her child is hurt or sick and the cheery teacher has forgotten how to open the door. "Hey. It's okay," I say. She turns her running face towards mine and sputters a sob. "Hi." The woman's nose is cherry red; her eyes are swollen.

"Can I do something? Can I help?"

She turns back to the window, gasps a little and wails, "This is going to be so hard for my Becca." The whole front of her is pressed against the door. If sheer will could counteract the solid properties of maple, she'd pop through there by now, and be tucking her hair behind her ears in the back of the classroom. "She is not at all good with separation," Becca's mother wails. With a hand on her arm I try to pull her from the door.

"Come on. Let's go get some of that coffee the PTA people are offering new parents." I tug on her a little harder and she takes one step backwards with me. "Come on," I coax.

"Okay," she sobs. Then at the top her of voice she wails, "Bye, Becca. Bye, honey! Mommy loves you!" She turns and begrudgingly walks alongside me as if the gallows were just ahead. Then she lifts her chin, turns a game face to mine and sputters, "I think I'll come and get her in a few hours. Full-day Kindergarten is going to be too much for her."

The PTA coffee is in the gym. Printed signs with hand drawn arrows direct us down the stairs to the basement. At the door, Becca's mom gets sucked in, literally clutched at and then consumed by three moms with pens and clipboards. The same wide-eyed camps of mothers from the upstairs hall have relocated to the gym and are now sucking on their conciliatory coffees. On the opposite side of the room a series of tables run the length of the gym. On them sheets with hundreds of volunteer opportunities beckon. Standing behind the tables, loyal mothers pitch their causes and I can't help but recoil. These commitments demand I know something about them as well as my own proclivities before I commit. Am I a silent auction type or does my persona scream wrapping-paper fundraiser? Set-up? Or Clean-up? Committee co-chair or lackey? The panoply is daunting.

I leave the gym quickly, suddenly struck by the fear that someone will see me trying to make a run without committing to anything and send a team of wolfen dogs after me. But I have less than ten minutes before I have to head downtown for my audition and I'm feeling shell-shocked. Like I've accidentally left an appendage inside of Jefferson School: a whole foot, or the indispensable right hand. It rained while I was inside the school and now the sun is out. Everything feels new. Sharp and glistening. Our car is parked opposite the playground. Childless, I head towards it. Inside it smells the way it always has; sour and a lot like feet. I'm grateful for the familiar. Then I catch a glimpse of my face in the rear view and am instantly mortified to see the red lipstick I applied earlier smeared from my lips onto the surrounding skin. It looks like Ted and I went to town in the back seat before the bell. Why didn't he tell me? The combination of lip smear and homeless garb was the two-pickles-shy-of-a-sandwich impression I left in there for all the new peers to remember me by.

From my purse I retrieve my two kinds of M&M's and I pour a combo of them into a flannel bowl fashioned in my lap from my shirtfront. Four peanut-butter and four regular M&M's make the perfect anesthetic mouthful for whatever ails. You knock the candies around for a while to work away at the tough outer shell and, ultimately, they grow rough as it melts. What follows is a delicious amalgam of peanuty-chocolate flavors. With my mouth delightfully loaded, I turn my focus over the wet playground to beam good wishes towards the first floor window I'm fairly sure is Emma's classroom.

After filling my mouth with a second combo. I see a woman coming towards me in my side mirror. Furtively, I shove more candies into my mouth. The woman is older than the most of the mothers I left inside. A shock of pure grey hair sticks out from the hood of her black sweatshirt.

"Hey," the woman says, in an inadequate greeting that implies a prior encounter. I study her, racking my brain. Her face is colorless, absent of life, and her whole head lists to one side as if it's too heavy to hold erect. One hand is hidden behind her back and a steady curl of smoke leaks from up behind her like a rank fart made visible.

"Hello," I say through my mouthful of chocolate, peanut butter sledge. I'm unable to place her.

"How ya doin'?"

"Good. Have we met?"

"I'm Margaret. You new?" She talks at me through my window. Her greeting comes without any expression whatsoever. No smile. No variation in inflection. No warming of the eyes. Nada. She stares at the pile of candy feed in my lap. And I have the urge to conceal it. To slip my hands over it. I can't yet speak coherently. My mouth works urgently; a piggish symphony of chew and gulp.

"Yes I am. I have a Kindergartener. She's in Mrs. Slaughter's class." I insert the name at every conversational opportunity – seeking the jaw-dropped response I had when I first heard it. Instead Margaret gives a single, laconic nod, takes an unabashed drag on her cigarette and blows the smoke towards the school.

"Margaret, twins in sixth," her droning response. "Also a third grader." She presents some fingers through the two-inch crack at the top of my window. "You wanna get involved here?" she asks, and again her eyes land on my remaining candy. I have a flicker of guilt for not sharing.

"Yes. Absolutely," I say. "I do. Yes. PTA. Whatever. There's so much to choose from. I'm just trying to decide. It's a whole volunteering festival in the gym. You know, at the coffee?"

"You went to that?" Her brows shoot up and down so fast I question whether they moved at all.

"Yes. Who knew how many jobs there are!"

"So you're picky about volunteering. Like when you buy a new rain coat."

Not it at all. That's what I think. But what I say is, "Yes, I guess."

"Don't you think sometimes the salesperson knows best? And you just have to go for it?" She sucks again on her cigarette and continues exhaling smoke filled words. We're speaking in metaphors that's clear – but the point eludes me.

"You into candy?" she asks.

"I am. I am. Who isn't?" What kind of a question is that? And why do I feel caught out. Like she's sliced me open and emerged to hold aloft the gilded treasure box containing my rabid vice. Here smoke curls out from both of Margaret's nostrils. I can't help but rub my own nose. Doesn't that burn?

Margaret examines the end of her cigarette and can't find an answer there. After a silent moment she says, "Did you hear?" She squints as she draws a last unabashed pull and drops her cigarette on the ground. "We did PTA clean up on the playground yesterday. Know what we found right next to that yellow twisty slide?" She pauses here to grind one booted toe onto the butt on the walk. Then she fixes her lifeless gaze to me and says, "Condoms."

On the way downtown it occurs to me that for the first time in her young life, I have absolutely no idea what Emma's doing right now. For all I know she's gone AWOL from the rest of the class and is splitting leftover desserts with the janitor in some basement mop room.

On Lake Shore Drive I rout around in my bag for my cell to call Ted and after a minute or two of groping, come to realize that I don't have it. I must've left it on the counter, or on top of the U-Haul box by the front door. My day has soured into a collection of leaving behinds. I feel far-flung and scattered. And then I think of the story I've heard Ted tell; the one about how he left Kindergarten on the first day because he was bored. At five, he walked nine blocks home by himself. He crossed two major intersections. When he popped in the back door at 10:30 and piped, "Hello!" he nearly felled his mother who was, at the time, loading a tuna-noodle casserole into the oven. In the car I indulge the fantasy of gathering Emma from the school and setting her down inside her new jumbo-crib, complete with age-appropriate Sponge Bob bumpers, to read her a Junie B. Jones. I miss her fiercely. This feeling works for me, though, at work in the audition room where I have to elicit empathy. In response to my "dollar a day" line, a whole couch full of casting people turn to each other and discuss how well I've done. I pick out the words "plaintive" and "forlorn" from their conversation. It's clear they're impressed and the approval, along with the certainty of pay booking the spot would mean, buoys me.

We make it through the first day. We do. After school I present Emma a juice box and a Go-gurt and I ask her a little about her day.

"What was it like? Do you like your teacher? Did she like you? Was she nice? What did she have you do? Do you get to play? Did you go outside? Did you play with Maxi?" She blows into her plastic yogurt sleeve.

"Mommy, this boy Duncan gotted yelled at. And this other boy, Rico lost his tooth." She shoves her fingers into her gum. "This one. Right here. He pulled it like this."

"Did you get a snack? What did you eat? Did you go potty honey? Did you wash your hands? Did you use soap? Did you remember what parts are private? Did you remember to use the Purell I put in your backpack?"

"And it bleeded onto the Brown Bear book!"

"Emma, honey. How do you feel about school? Do you like it?" A need-to-know hysteria nips at my heels like rabid dogs. I lean over the counter in anticipation of her response.

She shrugs.

"How did you feel in school? Were you happy there? Can you tell me, sweetie?"

She sticks out her lips, rubs at her nose with her whole hand and says, I felt . . ."

My fingers are crossed because how she feels now about school will portend how she feels later about school. It stands to reason that if she likes going now, she'll do well. She'll want to go. And in middle school she'll tackle her homework willingly, without a struggle. At college she'll choose a more difficult major because she gets a kick out of a challenge. She'll resist the friends who tempt her with an invitation to a progressive drinking party between frat houses, because it would interfere with her work ethic. The ethic that (ready, set, go) as of just today she's begun to cultivate.

"Yes Emma. I'm listening, honey. You felt . . ."

"Hot."

"How did it go?" Ted asks, hours later, after Emma's asleep.

"I have no idea. She's not exactly forthcoming with information. I asked her detailed questions like the *Kindergarten 1 2 3* book said to, and I still have no idea if she likes it, if she likes Slaughter, what she did all day."

"Not Emma. You. How was your audition?"

"Alright. They said I was plaintive and forlorn."

"That's good."

"Have you seen my phone?"

"What, you lost it?"

"No. I just don't know where it is. Nicole was there. At the audition. She said to say, 'Hi.' She reeked. Like actually smelled. Don't know how she achieved that. Maybe she rolled around in her compost. Plus she dragged in all these ratty Hefty bags stuffed with old clothes. It was a nice touch. She even found this decrepit old backpack at Goodwill." The one word catches on something in my head. That's it. I bolt from our bed and pull on my sweats.

"What's the matter?" Ted's up on one elbow.

"Her backpack!"

It's in the entry on top of the box of books where Emma plopped it after school; Strawberry Shortcake, recumbent and inviting on her cardboard chaise. Hello Strawberry, with your corkscrew curls, inflated bonnet and forthcoming face. A face that says, *I'll tell you anything you'd like to know. Try me.* I'd walked past the thing four or five times without even thinking to look inside. Sitting now on the U-Haul box, I cradle her in my arms for a moment feeling a special reverence for her heft and promise. Hello there, friend, I think. For she is my new friend. My liaison with the school. My voyeur. My Strawberry Shortcake. I unzip the main section. The compartment is bulging. It's like Christmas morning, for the potential of the thing and its contents. As the zipper rounds its way home I peel back the flap. Strawberry is crammed with information from Mrs. Slaughter and Jefferson School! My heart gallops around my chest and I can't help but spin her around in a worshipful dance. Together we twirl in the moonlight that shines in through the slender windows alongside the front door. "Hello, dear friend!"

In the backpack today:

A school calendar

A class snack schedule

A form to be filled out regarding volunteer opportunities for parents. These include: cutting out at home, taking dictation from students, before school writing enrichment, sharing about cultural or religious celebrations, helping with holiday parties, volunteering at the Fall Festival, pull-out reading helper, field trip chaperone, pull-out math helper

A welcome letter from Mrs. Slaughter

A packet from the Picture People with an order form for school pictures due back by Friday

A lunchbox containing a half a peanut butter and jelly sandwich, crusts removed, an unopened single serve applesauce and plastic spoon

And, a PTA membership form

September 5th

The next morning, Mrs. Slaughter stands bent over at the class-room door to welcome the children. She's wearing a long brown crin-kle skirt with a matching top. The outfit looks a lot like a sari. She has one hand on her chest to keep her readers from swinging. The other is clamped around a loose bunch of envelopes and forms. A string of tiny topaz chunks dangle from a gold wire through each of her ears. Despite the welcome letter that said parents shouldn't come in after the first day, I caught the side door before it closed in a coffee-fueled bit of bravado, thinking they couldn't be serious. They're five and Emma had her vice grip on my hand. I couldn't bring myself to peel it off. "Hello," I sing to the teacher. "Morning!"

"You've come in with her," Mrs. Slaughter announces when she sees me. She rises to her full height, disapproving, and that surprises me. My presence here illustrates my interest in my child. Isn't that a good thing?

"Yes," I say because there's nothing else. "Here I am!" Suddenly I feel too large and my breath tastes inordinately sour. I dally there, watching Emma after she's admitted.

"Do you have the form for me?" Her hand is extended to me, but her attentions are on two boys spinning each other around on the reading rug.

"The form. Yes. The volunteer form. Go ahead and sign me up. I'll do anything you need."

"Okay, put that on your form and sit down, Henry!" It's a singular sentence that throws me briefly. "You can go, you know," Mrs. Slaughter says, her eyes on Henry, her hand on the doorknob. "She's fine."

"I know. I'm just watching." Watching Emma scrawl her name on the sign in sheet and give shifty, wide-eyed stares to any child who passes within three feet of her. Watching her slumped shoulders and silently telepathing bales of confidence in her direction. The wooden door swings in front of my face in its arc of closing.

"She's fine," Slaughter says again as the tide of voices from inside the classroom spills out into the hall and a set of twins zip into the room just before the door closes. These are the words uttered, but the translation is, "Get out." I know it. Like I'm one of *those* moms. There're two of them in Miss Barbey's classroom across the hall. They're camped out in collapsing chairs from Dick's Sporting Goods sipping vanilla lattes from Starbucks like you would at a soccer game. At regular intervals one pops up to peek at their offspring through the little window in Miss Barbey's door. Then she takes her seat and sibilantly summarizes her findings to the other.

62   I scurry back down the hall like a shooed squirrel. At home there's an urgent message from my agent, Blane, on the answering machine. "Jennifer. Babe," he says. I've left a thousand messages on your cell and finally talked to some rude woman who answered, it. What's up with that? I have good news!" He pauses here to build suspense then continues in a rush. "You're the homeless mom! But I've got to confirm you for the job because it shoots Wednesday. I know it's fast. So call me back, babe. Bye."

"Gimme your cell number," Temple says. Thick plastic glasses make her eyes look like tiny black bugs today. We're standing in her kitchen an hour after drop-off examining little samples of Formica countertop material. "Some kid probably lifted it out of your bag when you weren't looking. Maybe even one of Karla's friends. Maybe even Karla." She finds her phone and pulls her mouth down. "Really, darlin'. You never know. That's all they care about. iPhones. Touch screens. New apps. After the fifth grade they completely lose the ability to talk to their friends. They just text or IM whatever they need to say."

Searching for a beverage in her fridge, I reel off my number. "You won't get anyone. I tried that last night and got my own voice mail." Temple, it turns out is a Dr. Pepper person; another tie that binds. My mouth waters as I pop the tab.

Temple pushes my cell number into her phone and, with it stuck on her ear, returns to squinting at the oatmeal countertop tile. She raises it to new light over the sink.

"I like the little flecks in this one, but . . . Hello?" Her face lights up and she snaps her fingers at me.

"Hello?" she says again into her phone.

"Who is *this*?" she asks. Then she frowns and her head snaps back on her neck. Instantly the shade drops on her good humor. "Never mind who I am," she barks. "I asked who *you* are, bitch."

Then the color drains from her face, her beady eyes close and before I fully understand what's going on she tosses the phone at me, and hisses as it sails through the air, "It's Principal Otis."

There wasn't a choice about retrieving the phone. It was something I had to do. And though I seriously consider implicating Temple in the name-calling. I can't figure out how to say it without sounding petty. *It wasn't me. I didn't say it. It was my friend. She did it. She's the one who should be in trouble.* She's the one who should have to endure the smirk on the face of that sassy secretary to whom I have to announce myself, first outside the school, and then in front of her reception desk. Ms. Gravely, the secretary, makes me wait as she sucks a cheesy orange coating from her index finger and, after examining it thoroughly for errant residue, presses a button. Then she swivels in her chair, turning her back to me, as if, "She's here," is a deeply intimate thing to say into a mouthpiece.

The Principal's office is redolent of Chinese food. So much so, that I stand in the doorway scanning the room for white cardboard boxes with thin wire handles. Principal Otis motions me in with a quick gesture from behind her desk, and pushes her chair back as if she's going to stand. My mouth falls open and I feel a ball of words ready to fall from it, but then before it does, she tells me to wait while she finishes an email. She is a paradox of styling with the spiked hair and her penchant for pastel-hued suit jackets. Compared to the rest of the building that holds in the heat like a pizza brick, the main office is cool. A clanking window unit churns out billows of freezing mu-shu beef infused air. As she types, she watches her fingers dance on the keys, not the message they're composing on the screen, and it occurs to me for the sixth or seventh time that day, that I'm in trouble not even forty-eight hours into the school year. Between us on her desk sits my cell phone. She's using it as a paperweight on top of a thick pile of Illinois State Achievement Tests. I'm drawn in by the little tic-tac sized circles next to each question on the top page. In front of that pile, a brass nameplate engraved with Mrs. Otis's name stares at me. It starts a Bette Midler going through my head. "Miss Otis regrets she's unable to lunch today, Madam."

It's a rousing melody, if not exactly applicable given that *this* Otis was obviously was able to lunch. Egg rolls, maybe some Pad Thai. The Bette Midler song is one I love. Principal Otis must love it too, I think, and without even realizing it my jittery nerves have me tapping on my knee. "And the minute before she died she lifted up her lovely head and cried, Madam. Miss Otis regrets she's unable . . ."

"Excuse me?"

Was I humming aloud? "Nothing. Sorry." My palms are wet. I feel color rise in my neck.

The Principal drops her head over her keyboard and types at a furious pace. Hands dancing on the keys like Liberace. On the wall behind her desk is a framed series of enlarged Sun Times articles featuring the top grade schools in Illinois. There's 2009 and 2010. I'm squinting to find Jefferson on the list when Principal Otis says, "Okay." She hits 'send' with one finger like it's a high G and squares herself to me. She's a pin person, a gold stick pin in the shape of a daisy graces her lapel and gives me hope and also an idea for a Christmas gift down the line.

"I think we understand the main infraction here," she says, steepling her fingers under her chin.

"We do. I do," I stutter. The Principal is younger than me and she's wearing a coral pink pantsuit. Despite those reassuring facts, she intimidates me.

"I didn't send it with her. She just took the phone to school. Emma did. Really I had no idea. I told her to bring stuff like I have in my purse to school . . . in her backpack." I pepper my speech with remorseful pauses that clearly invite interruption and mercy. Then under the pressure of her austere response, I crack. "I mean, at least it wasn't a tampon, right?"

"Well," the Principal clears her throat. "We don't think it moves our ball as a community of learners to pass blame."

"No." So much for telling her it wasn't me that called her a bitch. She lays a finger gently on my phone and looks up at me.

"This rang many times from your daughter's cubby. It caused a lot of disruption for us on a day that is challenging enough, particularly for our new-bee Kindergarteners."

"We understand." I am nodding. Obsequious. "I'm sorry. Really. It won't happen again. Next time I'll make sure she has it on mute." Ha, ha. The cool blue eyes of the Principal narrow.

"I'm sorry. It was a joke. Silly. No time for joking. Understood."

"Now. We did answer the phone once we recovered it from Emma's cubby." Oh god. That would've been Blane.

"And, that being said. We can understand your embarrassment over your . . . situation. But really homelessness is nothing to be embarrassed about. At Jefferson School we're a community. We protect our own." Here she rises and brings two shopping bags filled to the brim with canned food from around her desk. Two family sized Campbell's Chunky Sirloin Soup cans peek out of the top of one of the bags. Del Monte Peaches sprout from the other.

"Can I have Al help you get these to your car?" Her face is softer now and for that alone I am infinitely grateful.

"Okay, yes," my voice says. Mercifully, the whole tenor of the moment travels from bleak and judgmental to empathetic in a split second. She holds my phone out to me, and a small smile filled with pity seals her thin lips. But before I can take it from her she clasps it back to her chest and says, "We need many parent volunteers to proctor our State Testing in March. I'm assuming that because you don't work, you are available to help us?" I do work. I 'm working later in the week in a spot for the Indiana Lottery.

"I do work."

She looks relieved. "Well that's a start then. What do you do?" she asks, extending the phone once again.

"I'm an actress."

"Well that must be fun for you." That's what she says, but the look on her face is the same one she gives to second graders who want to be astronauts but are years away from finding their spaceship.

66

"You can spare a day or two that week, then?" Her grip is tight on my Nokia.

"Yes. I'm sure I can manage that." They are the magic words. Her fingers spread and suddenly my phone is mine again.

In the backpack today:

A worksheet on the letter B with a red star and very good from Mrs. Slaughter

A practice sheet on lower case 'b' and 'd' to be completed at home and returned to school tomorrow

A red leaf glued to pink construction paper along with three blue cloud puffies

A letter from the nurse that begins, "Dear Parent/Guardian, Someone in your child's class has developed conjunctivitis . . ."

Emma's lunchbox containing an unopened single serve apple-sauce, plastic spoon, some other child's gummy-gushing-fruit-snack wrapper and a leaking Go-gurt sleeve

And a reminder . . . Wednesday is picture day

September 14th

I'm going to the first PTA meeting because Ted can be home with the kids, because I have no idea what the PTA is, and because the meeting takes place in the faculty lounge. Place of intrigue and mystery. I've never been *inside* a teacher's lounge. Although I keenly remember cigarette smoke and laughter escaping into the hallway every time a teacher emerged from the FACULTY ONLY door in Junior High. I'm utterly convinced that through the FACULTY door is the interior of Jeannie's bottle; complete with a circular lavender sofa, relaxing mood lighting and maybe even lava lamps. Instead when I follow the voices, I'm met with overhead fluorescents and laminate chairs that render the enigmatic place indistinguishable from the break room at Walmart. Posters of mountains and meandering streams with words like EXCELLENCE and VISION in bold at the top followed by cursive lines of inspirational text are tacked to the walls. I am briefly saddened that teachers of my child might duck in here between math lessons to seek fortification from such a poster. Clusters of women locked in conversation occupy most of the tables and I slink into a chair at a table near the door and take in the other parents at the meeting. They are mothers, all. Not one male. Among them I seek the tell tale lanyard of a teacher, the 'T' in PTA, but excepting the Principal, there aren't any of them either.

The governing body here is the three women from the first-day-of-school coffee. They operate in concert, working from the front of the room like a six-tentacled organism, fixing us to them and their commitments with reaching waves and fully extended gestures. The women all wear stick on nametags with their names followed by "Co-President." Apparently the duties of the president are so crushing, they have to be portioned off into thirds. If it were possible to stretch a smile and hook it over each ear with a thin piece of elastic like a mask, that would be the expression on the face of the PTA co-president occupying the center seat. Her hair is white blond and she sports a ski jump nose. Her nametag reads "PIPPA" and at the end of each letter line she's made a little ball; her own personal font. She stands now to address room. First she names the officers flanking her. Her thin arms extended, she claps in the general direction of each person she introduces. It's a noiseless gesture, an imitation of a clap, because her palms are joined at the heels. Next to the three Co-Presidents is Principal Otis whom, when she's introduced, receives a robust burst of applause and a hoot from someone on the other side of the room. Then Pippa searches the crowd mugging, a hand on her hip and the other in a salute over her brow. "I'd especially like to welcome our new Secretary – Treasurer. Where are you Lana, mother of Connor in fourth. Stand up! Stand up!" Each phrase is attended by a flowing movement of hands, suggesting a childhood of dance lessons. "I love the new bob!" Her hands cradle her own Nordic bob. "Super. It looks just super on you."

Her eyes flit about the room and land on another woman. "Come on Shelly with Silent Auction and son Charlie in second. I see you!" A crouch and point. "Stand up! Stand up!" Her arm arcs in a manner that harkens the Price is Right's, "Come on down!" Here more bursts of applause follow as each committee chair smiles and stands bashfully when their names are called. This meeting is sort of like an awards show with the prize being all the time and energy you get to donate throughout the school year.

At this point the co-president on the left looks past the center PIPPA to the co-president on her right. "Name loop?" she asks.

"Name loop?" they ask of each other. Agreement brings the co-president on the left to her feet. And she looks directly at me and says, more definitively, "Name loop."

I'm thinking they're bringing their suggestion to the floor, so I nod. "Yes. Okay." And I'm aware now of mothers around me tittering, lowering their heads and sharing tight smiles. The color begins to rise in my chest and my heart pounds against my tee shirt.

"What is it?" The Pippa woman has her cupped hand extended to me, like a beggar woman awaiting my coin. She tosses her head again so that her white blond hair swings, catching the light.

"Nothing! I'm fine."

"Just say your name," the woman next to me whispers. I've avoided looking at her, because she's been breastfeeding an infant under a baby blue cloth since I sat down.

"I do. I have one. Just had to find it, Jennifer. My name's Jennifer. I have a Kindergartener, Emma." My fumbling produces a chuckle here. And then the breastfeeding woman is announcing her own name while simultaneously performing a deft, veiled reattachment.

I follow the name loop around the room. And it occurs to me that this is where all the student council people come when they grow up. The very ones who scrawl their name in poster paint on banners in middle school and try to get you to elect them President of the seventh grade, all end up in this meeting as grown-ups. Two persuasions of parent are represented here: the wide-eyed Kindergarten moms preparing to take notes and the veteran mothers of the grade school, who drape themselves over a chair, sweep up a bottled water from the middle of the table and grab a fistful of Jefferson School branded M&M's from the bowl. They are slower to settle to attention than the Kindergarten moms. They've been here done that, some of them for years and years on end because their children are each four years apart. They are the *Mothers Who Know*, the upperclassmen of mothers.

70

They have children who are in a grade with a number. Children who have long ago blown through size 6X, are long legged, zipping, buttoning, and in possession of all big teeth. These ladies are also a new mom's Cliff's Notes to all that goes on at the school. They can answer the, "What happens when…?" and policy queries whose answers are not readily uncovered by a cursory scan of newsletters and the crumpled disgorging of Rescue Hero backpacks. They can define "In Service" and know, without looking at the school calendar, exactly what time to collect the kids on early dismissal days. They've weathered their share of conferences, car-pools from extra-curriculars, and chaperone duties. They know the names of the janitorial staff and the lunch helpers. They are the mothers who head the fundraising committees and talk casually with Principal Otis, calling her by her first name, Deanna.

Through their casual command in the room this night, I realize who really run the school. It's these women. But they govern quietly, by stealth operations, phoning each other after the kids are tucked in bed upstairs, dishwasher churning in the background. *"Ring Ring, Have you heard?"* I've also seen them holding court after morning drop off on a corner couch at the Starbucks. Their caucus is how any major change at the school begins. Temple told me that the careers of new hires hang in the balance until they're officially approved of during a stealth November meeting of *Mothers Who Know*.

"Budgetary Considerations," is the first agenda item listed on the sheet in front of me. One of the women flanking Pippa reads down the list in front of us in a drone. This portion of the meeting is excruciatingly boring and not much different than a HOA meeting, except there's also this constant circling of clipboards. As I pass them I read, 'Please sign up to cook for the teachers' welcome lunch.' 'Please join the wrapping paper fundraiser sale committee.' I've already said "yes" to all the volunteer opportunities in the classroom, and I've committed myself for the state testing, so I accept one clipboard after another and pass them along. I soon realize, though, that everyone else is signing, so I dig urgently in my purse with one hand and continue to field clipboards with the other. A good seventy minutes later, the meeting has slowed to a listless pace. First with the question of exactly who and what was entitled to tax exemption at the Office Depot and then with the report from S.I.C.; an acronym for School Improvement Committee. Over the summer the two mothers that comprise the committee cooked up a plan that calls for the adding of a trickling mosaic fountain to the school lobby. Now they take turns making their case to the PTA from a script on note cards.

"Research has proven time and time again that the sound of running water is restful, it reduces stress and may even stimulate the brain waves responsible for learning." The skinny woman leading off is halting and nervous. She holds one finger in the air as she speaks. "Also there's the noise mitigation factor. Sounds like wailing or screaming can be masked by the soothing sound of running water."

"It'll just make my Sam want to pee all day," a heavy woman with a robust mustache and sleeveless blouse heckles in a loud aside.

"Also, we could get grant money and pro-bono design work from Pippa's husband, whom many of you know is a fabulous architect. That puts the project within reach of the SIC Committee's budget."

Before the woman speaking can resume her seat, another tanned, busty woman is up and charging ahead with her bit. This one's eyes glint with exhilaration. She's the instigator no doubt as well as the best salesman. "We've got a mosaic artist who can do a residency with the upper grades in the spring. We can let it be the kids' creation. Plus, no other school in our district has a fountain. It really would set us apart. Make a grand statement to all who enter."

Her ample chest juts forward in an impassioned shimmy. "Picture coming up the stairs and hearing before you see. A total sensory surprise – which is what elementary education should be. Don't you all think? The living proof that Jefferson emphasizes the needs of the *whole* child not just their test scores." Here she shoots a flicker of a smile, an invitation to speak, to Principal Otis.

"Yes. Along those lines, we love it! Don't we." Principal Otis looks out over the crowd. "Let's move forward." Here she pounds her palm on the table like a gavel.

"Is it functional? Can the kids get a drink from it?" The butch woman leans forward on two elbows.

"No. It's decorative." A finger in the air.

"Inspirational," corrects the shimmying saleswoman. Within seconds the room peels off into pro and against factions, whom entertain a lengthy debate over the strength of the terrazzo, the cost of the necessary plumbing and the construction time frame. I'm inattentive. They've lost me. My attention is on the list of faculty summer accomplishments on the white board behind the PTA leadership. At the top in looping, parochial-school cursive is the teaser: *I'm proud of. . .* Below the teachers have offered their own versions of "What I did over summer break:" *I built a wrap around cedar deck. I coached my son's lacrosse camp. I drove to my sister's wedding in Kearney, Nebraska all by myself. I completed a brown belt in Tai Kwon Do.* The accomplishments are confounding and captivating because they don't name the teacher who accomplished them. Also it's somewhat alarming that the teachers of my child have a whole host of pursuits that have nothing to do with their purpose here at school. And I realize that if I could, I'd deny them an extra-curricular life. Eliminate their own attention-sucking offspring with a brush stroke in order to consolidate their full energies on my child. Temple told me the teachers don't even supervise recess anymore. When I was growing up the teachers were out there with us in the thick of recess. Now they have special, other people that do it; people that don't give two hoots if Emma is smiling or making friends. If it were up to me, there'd be lifeguard chairs on the playground so the teachers could scrutinize my child's peer interaction out there and report back. When I tune in again to the fountain debate, the opposing factions have reached a consensus to proceed with a feasibility study and tersely agree to leave it at that.

After the meeting the three co-presidents line up next to the laminator with their clipboards. To get to the door you have to pass them. And even though I duck my head, determined to plow on through to the hallway, they are as determined as the Nextel phone guys at the mall to prevent me from doing so. Pippa is the last of the ladies and she stops me by smiling warmly, dangling the promise of her friendship. "Hi. Haven't we met before?" It's a pick-up line for sure, but I have to admit, my ego's stoked that she remembers me.

"The coffee on the first day?"

"Right." She taps her forehead. "You've got a Kindergartener." Never mind that I've announced this at the beginning of the meeting, her attention lulls me into believing that she likes me, for me. Her clipboard is tucked under her arm.

"Yes. New. I'm new. My daughter, Emma, is in Kindergarten."

"Great. Great age." She nods vigorously. As we grow silent her tongue slips along over her teeth and I wonder if I can go. Then she reaches across her chest and whips the clipboard from under her arm aiming it at me like a saber.

"The Fall Festival is next month. This is the kids' favorite! Especially the Kindergarteners. Playground games, pony rides – but we need everyone to help!" A pen sprouts from her other palm and she points that at me as well. I sign, committed, and feel as Emma must have her first day. I don't exactly understand what I'm in for, but by signing on, I've shoved my eight-and-a-half-sized foot inside the door marked 'belonging.'

"Good to see you, again . . . " Pippa taps her head in an exaggerated pantomime of name recall.

"Jennifer."

"Right. Jennifer." She smiles broadly. "I knew that."

Outside it's dark and chilly. In front of the school I hear, "Hey. It's Jennifer, right?" from behind me. The sleeveless heckler has followed me into the night. She walks sideways alongside me in a kind of criss-crossing dance step. "You're not an advocate of the fountain thing are you? I saw your face in there."

"I wouldn't put it that way. It does seem kind of silly, but . . ."

"Exactly." She points some pudgy fingers in the shape of a gun at me. Her large teeth emerge here in the moonlight.

"Let's do an anti-fountain petition together. I'll cover the upper grades. You just have ta do K thru three. Whadya say?"

I'm too early in, to be anti-anything so what I say is, "Oh gosh, I don't know. And I told my sitter I'd be home an hour ago. So really, I've gotta run." What I don't say is, the sitter is Ted.

When I get home that night Emma's already asleep. I stand over her blanketed form in the dark room with the circling butterfly light. She breathes noisily from her mouth and the room smells deliciously of shampoo and spit. Her little head is resting on the freakishly large cheek of Dora the Explorer. We caved and got her the sheets last year so she'd stay in her own bed at night. She only takes up the first couple of feet. The rest of it seems a waste. Another child or two could sleep there at the bottom. I step around her animals gathering dirty tights and underwear from the floor to take down to the laundry.

Downstairs a second large cardboard box sits in the entry next to the U-Haul box o' books. It's smaller than the first, but not by much. The outside has no postal markings and no return address, so I open it. Inside I find several dozen smaller boxes of candy bars, ten to a box. Reese's, Milky Way, M&M's. It's a bonanza.

"Did you see? The U-Haul box got a friend," I say to Ted who's at the stove waiting for the water in the teapot to boil. That the U-Haul box is still in the entry is a sore point. I've asked him twice to help me unload it. Never mind that it contains all his books from his office. If I ask again, I'm a nagger; a branding I resist with all my being. My mother was a nagger. I don't think she ever called my father by his name. I think she always prefaced it with a directive noun, a reminder modifier: as in, "Garbage, George," or, "Hall light-bulb, George."

"What?" Ted says, failing to catch my drift. "What are you talking about?"

"The massive box of candy in the hall. What's up with that?"

He goes to the entry and looks inside the thing. "Wow. Don't know. I found it outside the front door. I thought it was something you ordered. It's gotta be a mistake."

"It's all the best kinds. Look there're even Fifth Avenues under the Reese's. You never get Fifth Avenues."

"Did you see the message on the counter?"

"No."

"Some sick woman called for you. I wrote it down."

In the kitchen I find the napkin that says exactly that. "Sick woman."

"That's it? That's all she said?"

"Yeah. No name. No number. Said she hoped you would meet them in the lobby in the morning."

Already I know that I will come downstairs after Ted's in bed and indulge in the creamy, peanuty crunch of a Fifth Avenue. My mouth waters with the thought of savoring it outside on the front steps; gooey goodness eclipsing, for a few moments the multiplying entry boxes, the question of the lobby fountain and whether I'm pro, or against.

September 20th

For days now Strawberry Shortcake has brought us reminders from the picture people; envelopes for payment, options on new green, blue or purple water-colored backgrounds to coordinate with the outfit. And despite the fact that my old school pictures are pressed into an album on the bottom basement shelf of my mom's condo in another state, my anxiety builds with each tidbit of correspondence. What if Emma writes on her face with purple marker before the anointed hour? What if the PTA lady assigned to help smooth the hair and clothes looks like Ellen Burstyn in *Requiem for a Dream*?

Emma appears, barefoot and twirling, at the top of the stairs in her Cinderella costume and tiara. While explaining the difference between dressing-up and dressing-up, I march her back into her room to put on the white corduroy jumper, pink tee shirt and striped tights we chose last night.

In two years I'll look back and wish I'd let her wear the costume. In twenty years I'll call Emma and tell her it doesn't matter what her daughter wears for school pictures. I realize this as I wet down the renegade cowlick at the crown of her head. Finally we're ready. At the end of the block, the yews that cover the first floor windows to Margaret's bungalow are already coated with nylon webbing in celebration of Halloween. It's September 20th. Could it be? As we pass, the side door opens and identical twin girls both wearing black lipstick and eyeliner emerge. They list forward to support the weight of their voluminous backpacks and one turns and locks their door with her own key. Without acknowledging us, they file onto the sidewalk ahead.

"What's that smell?" Emma blurts. Whether or not they've heard her, the twins don't break stride in front of us. Like Pig Pen in the Charlie Brown strip, the girls are trailed by a wake of body odor. We have no choice but to walk in it. Mercifully the guard crosses them first and holds his STOP sign on a stick to us so that a Suburban and two mini-vans can accelerate through the intersection next to the playground. The air clears.

While we wait for the crossing guard to signal us into the street, Duncan materializes in a full navy suit and shiny brown dress shoes. "Watch this," he says. And he high jumps into a puddle just off the curb. The crossing guard shoos him back up onto the sidewalk with his STOP sign. The boy stomps around then sticks his face in Emma's. I hold her by the shoulders ready to whip her out of the way.

"Sweetie, can you say, 'Hi' to Duncan?"

"I got waffle. Want some?" he announces. And I catch his wrist. (Slender, like a pencil. I could snap it in half if I chose to.) As he squeezes a doughy glob through his fingers, dangerously close to Emma's dress.

"Yes, I see that's waffle. No honey. Duncan, she doesn't want any. I do like your suit and tie though."

"Hullo."

Dashenka catches up to us and ignores Duncan when the crossing guard motions us forward. The boy stomps, for a second time, into the puddle next to the curb. Dashenka walks so close to me our shoulders rub. "I have this major zit," she pouts, her finger on a nasty, white-capped irruption beside her lip. "I should maybe pop it. What you think?" And she side steps forward to better my view.

In the last weeks I'd been buoyed by imaginary conversations with *Mothers Who Know* that I'd like to have on the playground. Each morning I see them. Having had a little time for themselves before school they've showered and applied a little rouge and mascara. They also know to bring beverages with them for the drop off. I can, in fact, spot them by their sleek, stainless steel coffee containers. In my dream they'd notice my entrance and wave me over, and their little circle would crack open like a clamshell or a Rockette's kick line (butts out shuffling backwards, jazz hands a flutter). Their stainless mugs would catch the sun's early rays and after I was admitted, after I had stepped in to complete the formation, we would all close up again. I have rehearsed this so often in my head, like a one-sentence commercial script, but nowhere, nowhere in my wishful indulgence is there a character named Dashenka aiming a volcanic zit at me. She's still stuck to my side as we arrive at the chain link fence that borders the playground. The knots of mothers deep in conversation are already established. There is no opening for my admittance. No shuffling backwards in a dance line, no cheerful waves.

"You should pop it, I think," I say to Dashenka. My diagnosis throws her. Her shoulders sink.

"Oh, that is big sucks for me," she says, shaking her head.

Emma is pulling at my jacket. I follow her to a little cluster of Kindergarteners from her class. I try to recall each of their names while they shyly compliment each other on their outfits. Casting about the playground, it's clear that other parents have sailed through these mounting weeks in apparent oblivion. Temple is in this category. She shuffles onto the playground with Maxi whose hair sports a rat's nest for bangs. When I ask, I learn that the black on the girl's nails is Sharpie, not polish. Other kids arrive to school in shirts scrawled with affiliations for last year's summer's camp and jelly on their chins. And for a moment I want to be the parent of one of them: the mom who recognizes that the schooling is more important than the picture of it. The mom who didn't try six times to put the part in the right place. The busty woman from the SIC committee is at work on her daughter's hair over by the swings. A comb is captured in her teeth as her fingers work fast to finish a braid. Temple's eyes narrow when she sees her.

"You met her yet? That one with the spray tan and fake boobs?"

Briefly we discuss the hallmarks of breast implants and then I explain about the SIC Committee from the PTA and their fountain proposal.

"I wouldn't give that woman a free spit let alone a fountain," Temple seethes. "Her older daughter's in class with Karla. That little bitch forwarded one of Karla's texts to half the girls in the sixth grade."

"Was it bad?"

"Forwarding it? Hell yes. You don't just forward on a *private* text to whomever."

"No, the text."

"Oh yeah, totally rude. It said something about this other girl looking like a tree frog. Which, by the way, she does. And believe me, I spoke to Karla about that. But she's not the one who *forwarded* the thing. That just crossed the line for me." Seething, she folds her arms across her own chest.

The bell rings. Sweeping Emma's hair from her eyes, I kiss her once and can't resist saying, "Quick. Honey. Show me your smile!" I tried, after her bath last night to get her to practice picture day into the bathroom mirror so she could, perhaps, observe the lower teeth issue and refashion it on her own, without me telling her to do so. When I finally suggested she show her top teeth, her lips curled back into a grimace so frightful I let the whole matter drop while she was still dripping.

After Emma disappears into the school with Maxi and Temple, who it turns out is the Picture People helper, I scurry back across the street. I have to get downtown and back this morning to pick up a check for the Homeless Coalition PSA. Because it's a Public Service Announcement it doesn't pay well, but we desperately need the money. I'm a block from our front door passing

Margaret's house when I hear, "Did you get the stuff?" from behind me. Trailing me is Margaret herself who walks with her arms crossed in front of her and her black hoodie pulled up over her hair. Dragging around her feet is a long black skirt. The ensemble is positively witchy.

"What stuff?"

She brings her puffy, expressionless face so close to mine that I can smell the stale tobacco on her breath. "The candy," she breathes out of one side of her mouth.

"Oh, the candy. That was you! Yes I did." I'm kind of relieved and kind of sad. I'd been eating a bar a night since it arrived, knowing that when the mistake was realized, the box, its contents, and my nocturnal pleasure would vanish.

"Yeah. So listen. You can't tell anyone about it. What we do, is we wait until the recess supervisors are ready to line up the kids up to go back in the school." Her mouth moves to emit her drone of voice, but the rest of her face is mordantly still. And she locks eyes with me unblinking, in a way that disarms me. "You'll know, cause the supervisors will clump together by the door and finger their whistles. That's when you come in alongside the soccer field fence with as many bars as you can stuff in your pockets. It'll take the kids awhile to trust you – but after a week or so they'll be handing over a buck a bar like nobody's business."

Here she steps back. I quick fill my lungs with fresh air.

"You got a long coat with lots of pockets?" she asks, surveying my fleece.

"You want me to sell candy to the kids at recess?"

"Yeah. It's important. We've got to do something to get the sugar back in the schools, don't you think? It's childhood. Besides you'd be surprised how much money you can make." Here she holds open one side of her hoodie. The inside is sewn with special candy bar sized pockets. From the tops peaks an array of the same sugary assortment as in my entryway box. "This pays for my twins' tutor," she drones. Then she casts about for onlookers and crosses her arms back over her goods.

"What're you doin' hangin' out with her?" Temple's eyes sparkle as she delivers her question. In her hand is a piece of paper with figures on it. I want to tell her about the whole selling candy proposal, but I haven't yet figured out Margaret's position in the school and I don't want to be labeled a rat so quickly into my grade school career.

"She wants me to do some thing for the . . . PTA. You know."

"Oh," she says. She seems disappointed but her response might be to the electrician's estimate for installing pendant lights over her fantasy kitchen island.

October 22nd

Fall goes by in a snap. It turns colder, the radiator in our bedroom emits a continuous bronchial wheeze-clank, and the green outside begins to lose its authority to the colors of autumn. Temple and I take turns walking the kids to and from school.

The next time I see Margaret, Emma and I have stopped to take in the display in the side yard of Margaret's house. Over the past three weeks, in a small plot of grass no bigger than a picnic blanket, she's crammed a skeleton, several bats, three tombstones, and what looks to be a man stuck head first into the ground. Only his jean-clad legs frozen in a cycling pose are showing. It's this planted guy that disturbs Emma. Every time we pass, she asks how he breathes with his face buried in the ground. So now I must demystify him, to show her he's not real. I peel back the guy's jeans where they meet his boot and pull out a handful of straw. As my fist emerges, Margaret steps from her house and turns her back to us to lock her door.

"Hi, Margaret." Immediately I explain, "Emma was scared of this man in the ground which, by the way, is so, so clever . . ."

"I'm not scared," Emma pipes from behind me.

"She said she was. She was scared so I removed some straw to show her . . ."

"No!" Emma insists.

Margaret doesn't seem irritated. On the contrary. She seems especially buoyed by the season. One corner of her mouth has a little upward lift going on. Now that the weather has turned colder she's moved on to a woolen ankle-length coat. As I shove the straw back into the buried man's jeans, I fight the urge to ask if she has any Reese's Cups on her. Her eyes shift up from the sidewalk as she talks to me about demand at the middle school being up, particularly among the sixth graders.

"They all like the Wonka Bars," she says.

"But the sixth grade doesn't come without its dilemmas." She glances at Emma. "I've got two boys just shy of wet dreams both begging for Salem Lights. I'm not sure what to do about that."

She is dispirited; genuinely stuck in this predicament and her neck shortens now, like a turtle's. Who knows, with the right conundrum her head might disappear entirely into the top of her coat. She squints off into the street as a bit of wind sends a golden heap of fallen leaves clattering.

"Maybe I'll sell 'em as a one time thing around Christmas." She lifts her shoulders in a heavy shrug. "We'll see."

Emma spins circles around me holding my fingertips. She is puzzled each time my arm reaches full extension and she has to let go, let me unwind and grab it again. It is my turn now, to provide an update for Margaret. And I shrink under the beacon of her gaze when it returns to me. The truth is I have never once gone to the grade school at recess. Okay, well, I did once, but that was only to see that Emma really was wearing her jacket. I parked across from the playground when they let the kids out. I *viewed* the recess once. And one other time just to make sure she was socializing. Each night though, as I enjoyed my Fifth Avenue/Reeses/ Snickers Dark, I'd rehearsed this encounter. And I am prepared. From my rear pocket I take a twenty and hand it over. Margaret takes it and folds it in half, then in half again, before slipping it into an inside breast pocket.

"Mom. Mom. Mom," Emma pipes loudly from my side. "Pull his jeans up. His leg will getted cold."

And I do. I adjust the denim so that it covers the top of the boot. "He's good," I smile down at Emma.

Here she squats and hollers at the earth, "Have a good day, man!"

Tuesday is our snack day. That's my excuse to get into school at drop off to check in on Emma's classroom. I like coming here. Particularly as the temperature outside sinks. It's cozy, colorful and warm. I've lost two jobs in a row, Ted has yet to land a regular contract, and coming to school with Emma gets me out of my own concerns and reminds me of what's truly important. What's that phrase, "Today may be a better day if I have made a difference in the life of a child." Temple has it on a magnet stuck to her Frigidaire.

Now, in hopes of gathering Mrs. Slaughter's attention I stand inside the classroom door at her desk towering over the rest of the pint-sized people that surround her. "Good morning, Mrs. Slaughter," I say. I turn and coax Emma from my rear by telling her gently to go and wash her hands.

"Mrs. Slaughter, I'm the snack mom today." I feel that my having an armful of snack should be the currency I need to gain access to the room I hear so little about. What I don't address is my costume. I'm wearing a black blouse and a pair of sweatpants because I have to be a mourner later in the morning. My black skirt is already hung in the car. When I get downtown I'll climb into the back seat, because our rear windows are tinted, rip off my sweatpants and emerge moments later in head to toe funeral fare. And passerby, as they always do, will slow when I climb out the back door and they'll stare, waiting for the dude to follow. They won't move on until I press the remote lock that sets off the horn and they're convinced there's no one else in my car.

Now I set my snack bag down on the sign-in table next to a gaggle of children in constant motion. They are goofy, loud and animate, like a singular organism, as they make their way to the story rug via a locker, the pencil sharpener or their friend's table place. On the rug they roll and bounce. I suspect that the most difficult challenge for this age would be to hold utterly still for even a second. By my side, Emma grips my sweatpants so tightly I feel them creeping down over my hips. Behind Mrs. Slaughter a mother in tight jeans with a bloom of embroidery on the rear pockets sets clumps of Q-tips atop black construction paper at each child's place.

"That's perfect," Mrs. Slaughter says to her, taking in the project preparation going on. The mother beams. Her hair is cut into a sharp variation on a bob. It hangs fashionably longer in the front than the back. A piece catches in her lip-gloss and she removes it by tossing her head.

"How is it going?" I say plopping my bag down on Mrs. Slaughter's desk. The space in front of me empties as Mrs. Slaughter bends to tie Aubrey's shoe. When she returns to standing, she addresses a natty boy in a too small red sweatshirt who pats her gently on her side, just under a belt of multiple strands of wooden beads. "One minute, Rico."

Mrs. Slaughter surveys my snack, frowning at the bag. "What have we here?" she asks raising her eyes to me. What we have here

is pretty obvious, I think. The Rold Gold pretzel bag is transparent, revealing the pretzels inside, and just in case you were still mystified, the bag clearly says, Rold Gold Pretzels on the front.

"It's pretzels. For the snack."

Rico pats the teacher's side.

"One second, young man," Slaughter says quietly. Then addressing the class, she says, "People, let's find your name on the rug." At my snack, she tsks with dismay. "This is the snack. Well, I understand. Given your situation." Emma lifts her face to mine.

"Mrs. Slaughter . . ." Rico begins.

She turns full to him and says, "Yes, Rico." He reaches around her waist again to pat her side in the same place. "You're squishy here." He blinks up at her. His nose is running a clear stream down to his lip.

"Thank you, Rico," Mrs. Slaughter says graciously, as if he'd just handed her a signed permission slip along with the correct lunch change. With a tissue from her desk, Slaughter pinches the snot off his nose.

"Our situation has improved, so much," I say. "Immensely. We're all good. Snug as a bug in a rug, at *home*."

"Oh!" Her face brightens. And then she looks again at my pretzel bag and with renewed dismay shakes her head from side to side just enough to swing the miniature dream catchers hanging from her ears.

Having completed the preparation for her project the trim, volunteering mom joins Mrs. Slaughter behind her desk.

"You know. I can bring something to the Halloween party, if you still need that," I offer. Mrs. Slaughter's face flickers with promise and she gestures to the trim mother behind her. "Talk to Jack's mom. She's our head room parent."

"Hm? What?" Jack's mom snaps too, as if she previously wasn't listening.

"I'll bring something for the Halloween party. Hi, I'm Emma's mom."

"Hi. Jack's mom." She points across the room, "He's the one in blue."

"Polo shirt?"

"Right." And we shake hands giggling at the formal gesture that doesn't transfer well to the Kindergarten.

"Let's see," she says, turning to draw inspiration from the classroom. "The committee already met; we have a committee to partyplan the class celebrations, but I'm sure there's something. Oh, there is! Something pumpkin!" She snaps her fingers. "We've got most everything but we did agree we could use something with pumpkin." Mrs. Slaughter has taken a high stool at the other end of the room in front of the story rug. "Good morning, boys and girls," she calls over the low hilarity on the carpet in front of her. Rico drags the bottom of his shirt across his face, a girl in braids opens and closes a zipper that runs down the front of her dress absentmindedly. And Henry the hulk sucks his thumb and rocks quietly. It's lunacy this picture. Age everyone in here by twenty years and it'd be a morning meeting in the day room at the asylum.

Mrs. Slaughter has gone on with her day and moved completely past me and my snack contribution in the process. My whole Halloween volunteerism was designed to offset my failure with the snack, and now even that gesture goes off course, totally missing its intended target.

Downtown Nicole has the audition time right before mine. She wears a simple black suit and dark sunglasses. A moist, lace hankie is balled in her fist. I should have thought of that. You can tell it goes well for her. She comes out of the audition room trailing laughter from a joke she'd shared in there with the client and the ad agency people. Afterwards, I park at her house, change back into the sweat pants and we go together in her car to pick up Adam from his half-day Kindergarten. His Learning Center is housed in a red brick building on a street of old factories in various states of conversion. There is no parking, except in the church lot across the street, so for pick-up, parents stay in the car. The teachers escort their students outside and into the waiting vehicles. Perfect for the winter, I think. As we wait Nicole changes the XM channel to Radio Disney. A hip DJ screams at a caller who's also screaming because she's won a chance to see a Jonas Brothers concert. During the ten-minute wait we inch forward behind a Jeep Cherokee with four circular magnets proclaiming affiliations to the school, the Y Swimmers, Travel Baseball and the Y-Guides.

Nicole hawkishly watches a school bus squeeze past us. It misses her side mirror by centimeters. Then she explains how the

Learning Center's green committee has a new mission to eliminate bus idling in front of the school. I'm about to ask about how this affects the twenty cars idling in the car-pool line, but Nicole has spotted her son. As cars collect their kids and peel off from the front of the line, we inch closer. I don't hear it ring, but just short of the clot of waiting children, Nicole digs for her cell and clamps it on her ear. That's it. It's probably Blane to tell her she landed the funeral commercial. I'm sure of it. My spirits sink. I'm replaying my own failed audition in my head, when both passenger doors open. Adam's backpack sails onto the back seat followed by Adam himself. Simultaneously, a grim looking adult without a coat ducks her head into the car over me. Her ear is three inches from my nose. The bottom of her lanyard, strung with a school ID and a whistle, dangles in my lap. Wind whips her hair into my face. I can smell spearmint gum.

"Mrs. Renowin," the woman addresses Nicole, "Adam will tell you he got another check today, Mrs. Renowin." Here she reaches across me, and taps at Nicole's leg. She is brisk and efficient, but the way she's bent over me to get to Nicole clearly reveals her breasts down her blouse. I don't know where to look. Nicole ignores the teacher. Her eyes are wide, frantic and her palm goes up to silence the teacher without ever really looking at her.

"No, doctor. That wasn't one of her symptoms. It wasn't . . ." Here a sigh of exasperation as she's interrupted by the person on the other end. "No. It was an all-over pimply rash? With a tremendous amount of itching around the groin?" She has her palm pressed to her cheek and her finger in the ear that doesn't have the phone. Her face is a contortion of worry. Who is she talking about? Clearly irked, the teacher in my face dimples up her chin as if she's going to curse and then, finally, extracts herself from the car. "Here," she says, throwing a piece of paper onto my lap. I feel the car begin to inch forward as the teacher hollers, "She needs to sign it and send it back tomorrow. It was *not* a good day."

"You can't give her that, she's allergic!" Nicole yells into the phone as the door beside me slams shut. We peel out into traffic with a lurch that pins us against our seats. The raised middle finger of the woman in the Jeep is the last image I see as we pass her, fleeing the school.

"Mom, I'm not buckled!" Adam hollers from the back. I twist to help him, and by the time he's secured the phone call is done. The thing is mute and inanimate on the console between us. I don't even recall a goodbye. Nicole screeches to a halt at the corner and suddenly, it's as if the last moments haven't happened. No teacher, no doctor, no pimply rash, no itchy groins.

Nicole is smug. Her mouth is screwed up in a kind of grin. Casually she tosses Adam an organic strawberry fruit leather and a small bottle of lavender hand sanitizer.

"How was your day?" she asks into the rear view mirror before twisting around for his response. The Jeep follows just inches behind Nicole's bumper. The face of the woman at the wheel is contorted in fury.

"Fine," Adam says attacking the fruit wrapper with his teeth. The Jeep woman lays on her horn.

"Who was on the phone?" I ask.

90 "Bitch?" Nicole says into her rear view. She stops the car and doesn't move.

"The phone call," I shout over the Jeep's horn. "Who were you talking to? Who were you talking about?"

Nicole shrugs. "I don't know. No one? Anyone, except Adam's teacher. She's got it out for him? Yesterday I pretended to have the Director of the Learning Center on the other end. That one really got her. She gave up like that." She snaps her fingers and inches the car forward.

I unfold the sheet of paper in my hand. "This says he licked Amelia Veracruz three times at lunch."

"Oh, please." She rolls her eyes.

We're driving now. The sound of the horn recedes. There's a city park a mile away where she takes Adam to blow off steam after school. Nicole raises her voice over a boppy Hanna Montana song. "Adam, honey. What happened at lunch?"

His response is mumbled through a mucky mouthful of organic strawberry fruit leather. "Mom. Turn it up."

Nicole raises the XM volume and her voice. "What happened at lunch today, Adam?"

"Nothing."

She lifts her brows at me. "See?"

At the park the only available bench is occupied by several long legged au pairs who jabber a runaway stream of French into their cell phones.

"So despite his teacher, Adam's doing really well in half-day," Nicole says after we spend a moment rehashing our audition. "It was the right thing to send him to Kindergarten this year after all. Between us, I think it's the fit ball. They use those instead of chairs in his classroom. It keeps the kids' cores engaged? Helps the overall concentration."

At the playground equipment in front of us, Adam fights the stirrup seat of the swing instead of swinging on it. He hurls the thing towards the bar from which it dangles, and then clears out so that it doesn't hit him on the way down. Nicole stares towards the scene without seeing him.

"What in the world do you bring for snack at your school?" I ask her. "I think I failed with pretzels today."

"Oooo, don't even get me started about the snack." She crosses her arms. "At the beginning of the year Adam's teacher assigned letters of the alphabet to each family – like the 'A' family had to bring in a snack that starts with the letter, 'A,' the 'B,' 'B' etcetera.

"That's a good idea." The twiggy au pairs lazily move on from the bench to follow their toddlers to the sand pit. Adam attempts to climb the swing chain. He is raging with effort. We can hear his grunts from where we stand.

"Yes, well it started out really well? The 'A' person brought Apples, 'B,' Bananas. But by the time it came around to 'H,' we started to get things like Gummy Bears and Ho-Hos." A shiver of revulsion travels her spine. "All sugar, fat and hydrogenated oils."

"Mom. Mom. Mom. Mom," Adam bleats from the swings.

"What, Adam?"

"I said, can we get ice-cream on the way home?"

"No, honey, we cannot get ice-cream on the way home." She pauses here for a moment. I can see her improvisational wheels turning. Then a flash of brightness and, as quickly, her face falls. "Because . . . ice-cream stores are against the law here. They don't have them. Anywhere." She spreads her arms as if she's searched long and hard for them on some prior occasion. She wilts then and brings her hand to her chest in an expert look of profound regret. "I'm so sorry." Then Nicole turns back to me, her perkiness restored, "So, you know what I did for 'R,' our letter? I brought in my pressure cooker, plugged it in by the teacher's desk and prepared a nice tasty treat of brown rice."

"You did not."

She nods smugly.

"Are you serious? What did his teacher say?"

"What can she say? It's a private school. We pay out the wazzoo for things like, oh, let me think, her *salary* so we get more say." Here a sly smile crosses her face. "I was at school yesterday for a meeting of the zero garbage lunch committee? And I overheard the Director saying they're replacing the new KW teacher already. The parents warned him to stop playing dodge ball; such a vicious sport. But he didn't listen. Kept right on playing it only he changed the name to Sniper. Sniper, can you believe that? So that's the price you pay in private."

"What's KW?"

"Kinetic Wellness. You know, gym. Why, what do they call it at your school?"

"Gym."

Later Temple says, "Yeah, the snack thing. When Karla had to bring Kindergarten snack for the first time I spent like $50.00. I peeled the clementines and brought little cocktail napkins in the school colors." She chuckles. "Maxi's day was last week. I found an open bag of Ritz in the closet, tossed in a roll of toilet paper and called it a day!"

October 25th

"Don't tell me. Don't tell me." During the elaborate pantomime of name retrieval I wait. Pippa the PTA president points at me then taps her head. "Is it Julie?"

"No it's . . . "

She silences me with a frantic wave of her hand. "Don't say it. Let me find it." She moves her pen down her clipboard. She's wearing long khaki shorts and a pink turtleneck. Eventually she finds my name. "You're Emma's mom, right?"

"Right."

"Oh, you're the pony ride with me! This is the kid's favorite you know." She puts the clipboard aside and starts rummaging through a large canvas bag marked PTA. "Let's get you set up."

Today is the Fall Festival. Strings of tossing games manned by parent volunteers in fall sweaters and sweatshirts line the perimeter of the playground. Children of all ages adorn the playground equipment in the center like zoo chimps. On either side of the monkey bars, the pro and anti-fountain people call out for signatures on their respective petitions. Other than the kids who cling to the monkey bars, no one ventures near them.

The boy scouts, who've strung up a rope bridge between two trees, commandeer the adjacent soccer field. Next to the bridge is the pony ride. It consists of one cloudy-eyed, saddle-backed mule tethered haphazardly to a stake in the ground. We eye each other warily. The day has proven to be pristine: abundant sun and temperatures in the high sixties. Already the kids' coats are off and accumulating in piles next to the twisty slide and outside the flap door to the jumpy house.

"Here's a plastic bag for you." Still bent over the PTA sack, Pippa reaches back towards me with a Wonder Bread bag in her hand and waves it at me like a hankie."

"This is a bread bag," I say, taking it from her.

"Right." She faces me, tossing her hair. "Do you have a dog? It's the same principle. Now I'm going to lead . . ." She steps forward unwinds the pony leash from the stake, and whips it over her shoulder like a boa. Then she finishes her directions with a balletic sweep of her arm, "and you can just . . . follow!"

In seconds a tiny Asian girl I recognize from Emma's class is by our side holding up a paper ticket. "Hello, little one." The PTA president exaggerates her words. Every consonant gets its own time in the sun. "Ticket please." She feeds the girl's ticket into a coffee can with a slit in its lid and hoists the girl onto the saddle. Given that some of the fifth graders are huge, I'm relieved not to have that task. "Ally oop! And we're off."

"So do you work?" the PTA president asks when the pony begins to saunter forward.

"I do. I'm an actress."

"Really," she says with the mix of curiosity and suspicion I'm accustomed to. "Where do you act?" I think she expects me to answer, "My basement. Pa's barn."

"TV. Commercials mostly."

"Ooooo. That's glamorous. I read somewhere where people would cut off a finger just to be on TV."

"Hmm," I say. "Those people are crazy."

I shot an Adventist Healthcare Systems spot the day before. I spent four hours standing next to a kitchen counter on a freezing set made to look like an office break room. Just before we started shooting, a production assistant handed me a mug containing dusty tap water. Before I could complain, the PA said, "It's just a prop. Don't drink it." Five minutes later the director told me to sip it while I took in my coworker, "Doris," played by the other actress in the spot. She had red hair carved into neat bangs, a gravely voice and kept the crew in stitches with her impersonations of Sean Connery and Star Jones. So it went like this. Sip dust and then my line, "Wow, Doris, I thought you had to be off a full eight weeks. And here you are, back at work, so soon after your fibroid surgery." She then, with a smug, healthy smile unencumbered by fibroids, got to reach across me, take a glistening glazed donut from a fresh, open box on the counter, toast my dusty water with it and take a delicious bite.

Now at the Fall Festival I walk in a slow circle, letting the pony set the pace. Every so often he stops and drops a steamy load. I wait. Then I gather it as quickly and as regally as possible into my bread bag. It seems most of the school has turned out on the playground. The place is raucous with children under the age of ten. Some rule requires them to move from place to place by running. They hurl themselves chest first, arms flailing behind them, towards the next activity. Fathers gather in loose groupings on the basketball court, surveying the mayhem from the sidelines. Occasionally a firm handshake ensues when two of them roust up a conversation. Most of the Kindergarteners come and take a ride on the pony. The huge red-shirted boy, Henry, who is not seven, rides four times, slouching, his back a 'C' and his thumb jammed into his mouth. His mother wears a Sox baseball cap and Dansko shoes and watches him from the sidelines. After two turns his mom moves in to walk alongside me. She's one of the few people not wearing sunglasses and she squints at me in the sunlight. "Hi, I've seen you in Mrs. Slaughter's class. I'm Henry's mom. Can I ask you a question?" She hesitates here as if worried about the impression her question will make. "Is your daughter getting teased at all in school?" She asks me the question in a teeny high voice that reminds me of a cartoon character I can't quite identify. An apologetic smile consumes her face. She's clearly eager for my response. Studying me now she waits, wincing.

"No," I say. Then, "Should she be?"

"No," the woman giggles.

I like her more because she laughed at my joke. "Henry is, though. I was so worried about his size. Kids calling him Shrek, or Lurch or Ord."

Did I think those things? I think I did, the first day, before I knew better.

"But that's not happening. It's his thumb sucking. Some kids are calling him a baby."

"God. That's horrible. I'm so sorry. Which kids?"

"Oh, I don't want to say." Her squinty smile drops off here. "Not yours! Gosh, Henry likes Emma a lot. But I don't think he's ever even heard Emma speak. She's shy, huh?" She dips her head here and watches me for a response. I nod. Silence nestles in the conversational pause. After Henry's sliding, oafish dismount that lands him in a heap on the ground, his mom continues as the boy lumbers off towards the jumpy house.

"I think all this is my fault. He was so freaked out about starting school. So I sprayed the inside of his wrist with my perfume, a little White Linen the first few days so he could smell it and be reminded of me. The parenting books said to do that, to make the transition easier."

"Lipstick," I say. "Kissed Emma's stomach. "Thought I'd leave a clean imprint. She rubbed it around so instead it looked like we clubbed her in the tummy. Then I forgot I was wearing it. This super hideous shade . . ."

"It was. Yes. I remember you. Anyway, I must've sprayed too much. He got teased about that too." This is the first mother that's overtly referenced the books. She'd fit right in to our Cornwell Lamaze group. Maybe we could start something like that here.

My wheels are turning. This mom is without Temple's ballsy confidence and I love her for her insecurity. She's silent again for a moment. The pony paws the ground and whinnies.

"It's not any of the girls." She waits politely while I squat to collect the mule's business. When I stand up she has clearly regrouped her outrage at the bullies. She giggles and speaks softly, but her hands knot into fists and work the air, "It makes me want to jam their Fiskars up under their toe nails, you know?" She smiles again at me and adds, "The little fuckers."

I am proud that I can name most everyone in Emma's class who comes to have a circle around on the pony. But now, with my bag heavy with mule shit, all I want to do is take a steel wool loaded with antibacterial soap to my hands. Here Henry's mom asks how I got this job. Wonder and empathy settle on her face and I answer quietly pointing my head towards Pippa. It's during the forming of this response that I realize I've been hazed. Not Cuervo Gold shots in the basement of Tri Delt hazed. But hazed nonetheless. Prime jobs like taking tickets and stopping and starting the music player for the cakewalk were all snapped up by *Mothers Who Know.*

The line of kids wanes at the end of our shift. Suddenly Pippa, who's been gazing off, sucking the stem of her sun glasses in her own little-leading-a-pony-world, takes a deep breath leans her face toward the sky and says in a voice so loud it startles me, "What a gorgeous, gorgeous day!"

Emma complains at the prospect of walking home, because her legs are worn out from three hours in the jumpy house. But the whining subsides as she counts her steps. "Eleven, Twelve, Fourteen, Fifteen, Sixteen." It's a new phenomenon this counting display and Ted is especially pleased. He walks backwards, facing us. "I see a developer here," he sings. "She already knows which floor to skip." Ted spent the entire Fall Festival talking football with a group of dads over by the Boy Scout bridge at the periphery of the playground.

"Why don't you ever come to my school, daddy?" Emma asks plaintively.

"I just did, sweetie."

"No for regular."

"Because Mommy gets to," he says. I shoot him a look that he mistakes for a plea. "And she's very good at it."

"You should, Ted. You should take her more. See what goes on. It's not the grade school of our youth, that's for sure."

"No thanks," he says with equal emphasis on the words, as if the invitation was to clean behind the little boy's toilets there.

Then to Emma he amends, "It's not that I don't want to, it's just that the dads are, what's the word – marginalized. It's sort of like when you breast-fed. Your little dyad there between you and your mom was complete. There's really not a place for me." He switches around now so that we can each grab one of Emma's hands.

"Some would argue," I say, "that, in terms of the school, it's a choice you make not to get involved."

"Some would argue that there's too involved." He says this staring straight ahead, and because Emma is between us, swinging, I let it drop.

In the backpack Monday:

A skeleton made out of Q-tips glued to black construction paper

An orange sheet explaining trick or treat safety

A white sheet explaining the timetable for the classroom celebrations for Halloween and what provisions have been made for those children whose parents are against the festivities

The typed lyrics to the Penny Nickel Dime song

Three drawings of assorted sized pumpkins under rainbows

A lunchbox containing a napkin streaked with jelly and an unopened single serve applesauce and plastic spoon

An envelope with Emma's school picture containing two grimacing 8 X10s and 200 grimacing, wallet-sized Emmas.

A letter from the nurse that begins, "Dear Parent/Guardian. Someone in your child's class has developed streptococcal throat infection . . ."

And the field trip permission slip

They're going to a farm. And I check, "Yes," for a prepared lunch, "Okay," I have read the statement about proper dress, and, "No," I cannot be a parent chaperone. The bottom requires my signature. Then we're supposed to send it back to school with nine dollars in an envelope marked "Field Trip." Something bothers me about adding my John Hancock; my tacit approval for a total stranger to hurtle off with sixty five-year-olds including mine in a ratty old bus. What about all those news reports where the sleeping kid gets left behind curled on a vinyl seat, as the temperature inside the bus soars to 140?

Ted wanders in, opens the refrigerator door and stands there, silently gawking at the contents. "Ted, look at this form." Joining him in the chill, I hold the paper in front of him. "What of this driver who comes only occasionally for field trips? What does he do the rest of the time? What's his real job? How could he hold one and still have time to drive the bus? And how do we know he's not a con?"

"If he's a con, he'd be in prison." He takes the paper from me.

"You mean an *ex-con*. Ex-cons have already served their time." He hands the paper back to me. For him the subject is done. Handled. He moves a container of greek yogurt aside to see behind it. Inside the fridge the temperature has probably already risen by ten degrees.

"You think they're ex-cons?"

"I didn't say I thought . . ."

"Maybe you're right. Maybe field trip bus driving is community service. It's occasional. Requires little in the form of regular responsibility. Shuttles the driver away to some place like . . . a farm for the day. Someplace where he surely couldn't get into any trouble." Ted rolls his eyes and grabs an apple from the drawer. His apathy is unnerving.

"Really, Ted, this is the first time in her five years I don't know anything about who's driving our daughter!" He turns from the open fridge and I bang the door shut with such force the bottles inside jingle. Ted gets the almonds from the cupboard. He's big on nuts. The apple gets retired to the counter and he shakes a fistful of almonds his hand like he's readying dice for the winning role. Then he pops one into his mouth. Between chews he says, "Honey, please. I'm sure the drivers are responsible. They do background checks when they hire them. And they have bosses they're accountable to."

He's right. Of course he's right. He closes the cabinet, grins at me and says, "Although I think they call them probation officers."

Emma survives the trip, comes home, back arching with the weight of the free pumpkin it takes both hands to carry, and announces that it was her best day at school yet. I don't know. She seems intact. But the next one – I'm gonna chaperone.

October 30th

The Halloween party in the classroom occurs on a day when I'm downtown for an audition in the morning, so on the way home I stop at Sam's Club and purchase a twenty-four-count box of cupcakes with a candy corn pumpkin atop each one. At home I quickly change and grab the bag with Emma's costume to take to the classroom. From nowhere, two weeks ago, came her announcement over dinner that she wanted to be a cheerleader for Halloween.

"Absolutely not!" was Ted's rapid-fire response.

"Why?" I asked.

His weary expression told me it was a stupid question. "Because, she's better than that." He was at the dining room table wearing latex gloves to examine the contents of someone's garbage in preparation for a breakfast meeting of Rotarians (AKA small business owners. AKA future clients). He'd offered to give his spiel for the Morton Grove Thursday breakfast group. Spread out in front of him on a vinyl tablecloth were unopened business envelopes covered in coffee grounds and what looked to be ketchup. The collection smelled a little too, like turned chicken. It was a bountiful haul. But somehow the latex finger he pointed at Emma's chest to drive home his point, lost something when played against the background of refuse.

"She doesn't want to be a *real* cheerleader," I lobbied. "She wants to wear the costume for Halloween."

"Yet." Ted's latex finger was in the air again. "She doesn't want to be a real cheerleader *yet*."

He took an envelope from Newsweek Magazine and sliced it open with his finger. Then he held it up.

"The slope's too slippery with stuff like that, Jen. No cheerleader. The Lansing kids are doers. They *make* stuff happen, we don't just sit on the sidelines and cheer other people on." I knew better than to argue when he employed a plural for our one child as if the good was greater than our singular girl.

At Jefferson the cupcake box is unwieldy and the grocery bag containing Emma's costume swings wildly from my right hand so I head directly to the classroom after being buzzed in. At the classroom door I'm nearly bowled over by the twins dressed as two pirates as their sword fight spills out into the hall. Mrs. Slaughter follows the boys. She is encased, head to toe, in a furry, black and white skunk suit. The costume coordinates perfectly with the garlandy strips of grey hair that drape either side of her face. Her chunky readers are low on her nose today. In order to address anyone she has to peer over them, her chin on her chest.

"People!" she barks in a voice sharpened to a point. It's the first time I've witnessed a true disciplinary moment and her penetrating tone causes something inside my womb to turn to chill liquid. "No weapons." She straddles the doorway, exerting her command over those within and outside of her classroom. In the hallway the reprimand has no effect. The two boys zig and zag, clacking their swords together around a steady stream of second graders headed to the bathroom to change. The tick, tick of the colliding plastic blades is audible above the Monster Mash song playing on the CD player and the excited chatter the holiday brings. Around the teacher mills a gaggle of partially costumed children. These are the in-need-of-help kids. Each clutches a problematic item; lace-up boots, an expensive but impractical gown that buttons up the back. It's obvious from their unfazed jostling that it's not the first time they've seen Mrs. Slaughter yell.

"Surrender your weapons. Please!" Slaughter's words are clipped and bitter and to no avail. As the boys in the hall continue their giggling duel, one is forced to his knees alongside the drinking fountain. Slaughter makes her eyes wide now and she has a hand/paw on her hip and I think three thoughts at once; it's too bad the lame bushy white and black tail affixed to the butt of her costume doesn't swish. It would be such a compelling effect now. Two: if it's *she* who will get in trouble with Principal Otis if her class shows for the Halloween Parade brandishing their swords. And three: if the sassy yeller before me is a regularly featured part of her persona when there're no parents in the room to be appalled.

"Young men. Get back in here, now." She barks this over her shoulder as she kneels to tie a glittering princess sash on Maxi. I zip around her and into the classroom. In addition to Jack's mom, the head room-parent, I recognize Henry's mom across the room. She has a mouth full of safety pins that she's using to close the back of the too-small Superman costume over her mammoth son. At the front of the room, a low table has been draped with a plastic cloth sporting cartoonish ghosts and skeletons. On top of the covering is a punch bowl filled with orange juice, a platter with sliced apples, a bowl of grapes, two bowls of plain popcorn and a tray of grainy looking baked globs. I steer my way through a low crowd comprised of a cowboy, two Belles, an Ariel, a Batman and Elvis. Emma threatens to tug the bag containing her costume right out of my hand and upset the cupcakes in the process. All the kids are out of their chairs and in various stages of changing. Some are on the floor trying to pull on tights or plastic boots. Two witches, a fifties girl and a bride return from the bathroom, their regular clothes spilling from plastic CVS bags. They veer around a kneeling mother who draws whiskers on her black cat daughter.

"Hold still," she hisses at the girl.

"Excuse me." The voice travels the room and the high chatter subsides for a moment. As a one we turn to the door where Principal Otis stands dressed as Little Bo-peep. On her head is a white lacy shower cap and she's drawn an egg-shaped oval of pink lipstick over the center of her mouth without any regard for the god-given lip lines. A three tiered baby blue dress with lacy white pantaloons and frilly ankle socks complete the look. Other than the pastel palette, the get-up is a complete departure from her no-nonsense manner of rule. In her hands are the two previously dueling pirate swords along with a staff I presume is her own.

"You," she says, ditching the weapons on Mrs. Slaughter's desk. Then she turns and faces me directly. We lock eyes across the room. Could that be? I shift away. She follows. My face burns with mortification. The CD player sings, "It's now the Mash. It's now the Monster Mash."

"Yes you. May I see you?"

Emma clutches my hand and from somewhere by the STORY RUG / TAPETE I hear, "Awwwwww," in a pitch-climbing, rubbing-it-in chorus. I leave, with what I imagine to be the snickering boys collapsed in the corner, their hands clamped over their mouths and the Rescue Hero symbols on their stomachs.

In the hallway Principal Otis says, "Follow me, please." And she turns quickly so that the petticoat under the layers of pale blue skirt twirls and raises in a circle above her pantaloons. As she walks she taps her staff alongside her and I, follow her . . . sheepishly. The turn into her office is executed with another twirl. The office secretary wears devils ears and I bite my lip to prevent the *Weren't you all supposed to wear costumes today?* thought from escaping as spoken word. From her cold glance it's clear that she's the source of my summons here and sure enough the Principal stops in front of the woman's high desk. (It has to be high I realize, so that when parents hurl stale snack items at her, she won't get hurt.) The Principal peels off a visitor's label from a spool of them atop the counter.

"We take security here very seriously," Principal Otis says. "It makes our job, it makes Ms. Gravely's job, infinitely more difficult when parents don't stop here to sign-in and collect your visitor's tag. She is, after all, our gatekeeper." Her face is scolding – her brows above the half moons of blue eye-shadow, furrowed. My grin won't be suppressed, "She's the gatekeeper?"

"Yes."

"Isn't the devil the gatekeeper of . . .?"

Both women are unflinching and humorless.

The visitor tag adhered; I escape back to Emma's classroom leaving multiple apologies in my wake.

"Do you have the pompoms?" Emma is beside herself at the door. The pompoms were under the bag on the kitchen chair and I didn't bring them.

I went to bat hard for Emma and we won. I had to promise Ted I'd shred the *real* cheerleader application when it comes home her freshman year of high school, but, for now, we won, and she looks adorable in her pleated skirt and "W" letter sweater.

"Let me see you!" I hold her at arms length. "You look great, honey."

"Do you have the pompoms?" It's louder than the first time and if it weren't for Henry whose costume has split down the ass, and who has thrown his head back and wails hoarsely at the ceiling, and also for the six superhero boys who keep bolting for the door, we'd be the scene.

"Em. Look. This way your hands are free."

"Mommy!" She stomps her foot and crosses her arms.

"I left them at home. So that they wouldn't get ruined before trick-or-treating, Em."

"You look fabulous, Emma." Henry's mom has deserted her boy and made her way to my side. The compliment reduces Emma's disappointment to a silent sulk and for that I'm grateful.

"This is madness," I say out of the corner of my mouth.

Without loosing her warm smile, Henry's mom turns her face so Emma can't see and says, "I'm gonna fucking kill him." But it's also clearly killing her to be across the room from her son in all his despairing glory. She turns her back to him now, as his fit grows louder.

"The books say to ignore the tantrums." She takes a deep breath and exhales slowly. "You know, respond to him only when his behavior becomes more appropriate." She bites her thumb and sneaks a peak back at her wailing son, who has collapsed between two chairs. Laying there, he bangs his flesh-toned, strap-on stomach musculature on the floor. Next to Henry another frowning mother is completing an elaborate bow in her daughter's hair while steering the girl's eyes away from Henry. She repeatedly turns the girls attention back to her by placing a palm on top of it and twisting. It's the same gesture that closes the peanut butter. Only now, surveying the room, do I realize that none of the orange plates littering the tables hold cupcake wrappers.

"Fuck it." Henry's mom bursts and marches across the room to her tantruming boy. She speaks to him through clenched teeth and has a grip on his arm that's sure to leave a curving pattern of finger bruises. She must be threatening him. It's what I would do. And this outburst of Henry's mother fills me with a sympathetic and twisted brew of gratitude and relief.

"You can take the cupcakes home." The room mom speaks to me. "We put them up on top of the cabinet." I follow her eyes to the CABINET / ARMARIO. "Sorry. Thought I said something pumpkin. We have too many gluten sensitivities for real cupcakes."

November 7th

On a Tuesday early in November, a brutal freezing rain begins to fall just as Emma, Maxi and I arrive to school. I am emboldened by the shit weather and slosh my way down the warm hallway in a moist sea of people half my height.

Inside the classroom kids and parents crowd Mrs. Slaughter's desk. Here limps Aubrey the five-foot Kindergartener waving a paper. "My mom says I can't go to gym because my ankle is stained."

Duncan broad jumps into the room as Dashenka shakes out her clear plastic rain bonnet onto the hallway floor. Behind her Principal Otis, today in a pale green turtleneck with a turtle stick pin, gasps and grabs the dripping plastic right out of Dashenka's hand.

"We can't have this liability in the hall." Principal Otis holds the dripping wrap away from her and cranes around, straddling the puddle Dashenka has made. "We need Al here, and the mop." She makes her announcement over the heads of two tardy boys shoving winter gear into their cubbies. Not understanding, Dashenka lifts her shoulders and says what sounds like, "I like eat. Eat slides off the rain from my here."

Duncan has latched onto my jacket in order to hold up his bare leg. His jeans are bunched up around his thigh, which is the slender diameter of a wiffle-ball bat.

"Smell my leg," he challenges, pointing his nude knee at Mrs. Slaughter. "It smells like waisins. Go ahead. Smell it."

Rather than obliging, Mrs. Slaughter cups Duncan's chin briefly in her palm and then sinks to her knees, setting down her clipboard, to tie his shoe. From the floor she addresses the assembled masses. "Okay everyone. Listen up. Here's what I have today. First, someone gave me two little dollars. Who's are these?" She waves them in the air. "Okay, now lets see." Another boy with a streak of what looks like chocolate, or poop, on his chin unfolds his fist over Mrs. Slaughter's desk and an assortment of coins spills out and rolls every which way. The teacher reads from the clipboard in her hand, pointing vaguely in the direction of the children she's addressing. "Rico is going home with Duncan. Becca, you're leaving at eleven for the dentist. Aubrey isn't going to gym cause her ankle hurts. Maxi's mom is going to be late picking up today. And, everyone, remember, today is report cards!" Then she turns to the churning children to order them. A feat that seems like coaxing sparrows on a freshly seeded lawn into neat and tidy lines.

Report cards! It comes back to me. Behavior evaluations. Will Emma's report card be good? Will I be the kind of parent who praises her for effort, has one eye trained for the areas that ignite her curiosity? Will I be the parent whom holds little stock in grades, tossing the thing away like so much recycling? Or will my attention catch (and tear) on the one substandard mark? And will that "Not Meeting Grade Level Standards" form the kernel of a lecture Ted and I will deliver every marking period for the next thirteen years?

After school moms gather on the playground to wait for the bell. I look around for someone to talk to. Hugging the periphery feels a little like the seventh grade dance. All the *Mothers Who Know* each other are already chatting in little groups. Except for Margaret who works the crowd passing out a leaflet. One mom has the courage to swing. Sunk onto the middle stirrup, she flies back and forth with gusto as two flanking preschoolers on their own stationary suspensions stare at her. A shock of pink dye runs town through her bangs and her denim jacket is studded with purple rhinestones down each sleeve. She is far from the door and it occurs to me that she must be high. Probably keeps her stash on the basement shelf between the Tide and the Downy. She's sucked down a furtive one hit next to her dryer before heading off to meet the bell. Maybe that's why she's able to stay and watch her kids play on the playground for an hour or two every day – entranced by the graceful swing of a six-year-old navigating the monkey bars. I see her wave and then realize she's reacting to my staring at her. I am overcome suddenly by the fear that she'll ask me to push her. I wave shyly back and turn away.

I can count the mothers whose names I know on one hand. And I still cleave to the chain link separating the playground from the sidewalk. Cold comfort. Literally. But I find safety on the outskirts. More parents arrive pushing monstrous double strollers or pulling back against large dogs straining on leashes.

Dashenka materializes at my side. "Hullo, Emma's mom." She seems almost cheerful.

"Dashenka. Hello."

"Emma is so shy, no?" She turns and stands facing me. The distance between us could at this moment be measured in millimeters. The zit is gone. Her back is to the school.

"Hey." It's Henry's mom on the other side of me. Her hands are jammed into the pockets of a brown parka and she wears a grass-green knit hat with a felted cherry for a tassel. I'm so grateful for her appearance here. I have the urge to lay down and hug her Ugg clad ankles.

"Hey. It's freezing," I say instead, bouncing on my toes. "Report cards today. Did you hear?"

"Are you serious?" She rolls her eyes and shakes her head slowly in the direction of the school.

"Yeah. Not that Emma cares. I imagine going over her grades with her but of course she doesn't read on her own yet, she pretends.

And she hates when I try to read anything out loud to her anymore. You know what I mean?" The door at the top of the stairs opens and releases two fifth graders in orange crossing-guard vests who race each other down the stairs, taking them two at a time.

"Henry's reading. He has been for awhile." It's not what I meant and she just dumps her freighted words out there on the four-square court on which we stand, like the private contents of her purse. "He probably should have started here last year, but my husband was a cornerback for Notre Dame." She shrugs and lifts her brows as if that explains a lot. A toddler's scream from the bottom of the slide causes us both to turn and study a girl of about two who's landed hard on her bottom. From twenty feet away, her mother swoops in and gathers the girl in her arms like a set of sheets fresh from the dryer.

"Hey." Margaret is here suddenly, pressing the paper handout on us.

"This is important," she drones before moving on. The sheet reads, "Public Act 94-994 entitles us to know that information about sex offenders is available to us online. Please know that the law states that sex offenders are not allowed to be on school grounds or be within 500 feet of school property unless the offender is a parent or guardian of a student attending the school and the parent or guardian is conferring with the school personnel about the child's performance."

Now I don't feel so bad. Even the sex offenders are worried about their kid's performance in school when, presumably, their list of things-to-worry-about is much longer than my own. In a really strange way the note pushes me further into the 'normal' column.

Henry's mom has already crumpled up the note. "Anyway," she says. "My husband thinks that if Henry is bigger than the other boys in his grade he'll have more confidence on the field in high school. Be a better blocker. Like his Dad." Briefly her apologetic smile lights her face then fades as she stares down at the pavement.

The bell rings, and seconds later Miss Barbey appears at the top of the concrete steps sparkling like a beauty queen. Her chunky sweater has a garden of primary colored flowers knitted onto it. And it's paired it with a white corduroy mini-skirt and some durable waterproof boots covered in yellow smiley faces. Her arm shoots straight up from her shoulder and she scrunches the high hand at the gathered crowd below. "Hi, hi, hi." Behind her trails a rag tag line of Kindergarteners who pick their way down the steps. One hand of each child ends in a manila envelope. That's it! There they are. It's no longer simply a card! It's a whole envelope of progress reports! There's a visible lurch towards the goods on the part of Barbey's parents: a press forward that catches the rest of us in its momentum. As the last of Miss Barbey's class exits the school Mrs. Slaughter emerges with her class in tow. She's got on a long knit sweater, dark hose and three-inch heels. Another adult in a North Face three-quarter-length parka walks alongside her. Excepting the occasional handled lunch box, the kids that follow, do so with empty hands. No envelopes. She must've concealed them in the backpacks with the rest of the school mail.

At the top of the steps Slaughter crosses her arms against the cold. She's deep in conversation. And as they move to permit the exodus of Kindergarteners the parent is revealed to be Temple. In her hand is a stack of what look to be CDs. She spreads her arms wide and says something that makes Mrs. Slaughter's face crinkle in laughter. Then there's a quick grab of the teacher's elbow, a leaning in for a private joke. A quiver of jealousy spurs me on and I take a step upstream against the departing Barbey traffic towards them. Some of Barbey's parents have already ripped open the envelopes and are hunched over their down-encased children clapping their thickly coated backs in praise. I find a route through the people but the strollers and baby backpacks trip me up, pinning me in place after two steps forward. A toddler in one of the backpacks removes his fist from his mouth and reaches for my hat. It's a conspiracy I think. I've no choice but to stay put. Over the heads of the throng, I watch as Temple hands over the CDs like cash to a maître d'. Jump Start First Grade computer games is what they are. Mrs. Slaughter regards them as a bum would a fifty and then with her free arm draws Temple to her in a robust hug. In a final bit of choreography Temple reaches around for Maxi's hand and the two of them sashay down the stairs together. Emma, who carries her lunch box and her backpack in her arms, follows them, scanning the assembled crowd for me. She is knocked aside by a boy who takes two steps at a time. His hand-me-down pants and parka are too large and covered in oily grime. Emma frees a hand to wave goodbye to him in a tight gesture performed inches from her chest, The boy sings, "Bye Emma," in soprano response, revealing a wide gap between his front teeth. Then as he reaches the bottom of the steps he hurls his backpack high into the air and, when it lands, jumps on it with both feet.

On the walk home Temple waves the teacher gift off like an offensive odor. "They were practically giving them away at Office Max. Seriously, they were like a couple of bucks. There were stacks of them in some clearance bin." The girls pair off in front of us. The whole way I am forced to follow Emma and my friend Strawberry riding piggyback, her coy grin taunting me with what is concealed inside her.

Both girls disappear into Maxi's house and I have no choice but to follow. Minutes later I just want to get home and I've lost track of Emma. Maxi is laying on the kitchen floor picking at a logo adhered to the bottom of the fridge with her finger. She's entranced and very cute, breathing adenoidally through her mouth; a constant sort of snore that's compounded by her effort with the appliance.

"Jennifer did I tell you, we're this close to a countertop decision?" Temple's eyes flash with delight and she runs her hand along the emerald Formica next to the sink, imagining. "Course it's complicated by the backsplash which you gotta consider at the same time."

"I love your kitchen." I do. Temple's kitchen looks fine to me. It's quirky: a kind of retro country with a little wooden fence that runs around the top of the caramel cabinets. A fence for reigning in knick-knacks. Hummel plates and wicker containers of all heft are artfully arranged in the space, along with the occasional pile of cookbooks. If she revises her kitchen with materials quarried and sleek, it will alter, even if only slightly, my impression of her. No longer will she be my cobbled together, determinedly messy friend. Also, if she ramps up hers, I might have to reevaluate our own kitschy kitchen.

"Shit!" Temple's hands fly to her head. "What time is it?"

"It's a quarter to four," I say.

"Is today Tuesday?" she says eyes bulging with panic. She's already pushed her arms back into her downy North Face.

There's a momentary lull in the room. Maxi snorts and raises her head as we both successfully identify the day of the week as Wednesday at the same time.

"Whew," Temple says shedding her coat. Karla's at A Village but it's not my day for pickup.

"What's A Village?"

"Tutor. Only they don't like that word. It's support for composition, comprehension. All the girls in her class go. We carpool."

"I thought you used the rapping guy."

"Is Jaquan cobing tonight?" Maxi pipes from the floor.

"Not tonight, Max," Temple says.

"We do have Jaquan, but he's just math."

"Awwwww." From the floor.

"Maxi *loves* him."

"Cause he's mide dow. Seben tibes two is foteen. Uh." Temple pulls down her mouth and whispers to me, "Cute, huh. She has no clue what it means." Then she looks to where the countertop meets the wall. "Maybe we'll do a glass tile thing on the backsplash. I would love that."

"Frrrrigiiidddarrreeeee," drones the writher on the floor. Without missing a beat, Temple spits in the direction of her daughter.

"The 'E' is silent. 'G's like 'J.'" Then excitement transforms her face. "Wouldn't granite be just fabulous!" she says, her eyes twinkling.

From the floor Maxi says with more confidence, "Frrrigidarrre. Frigidaire!" As she gets the word: the whole of the three-syllable word, so do I. My mouth goes dry.

"Temple, Maxi's reading?"

"Yeah." She rolls her eyes as if her child's feat annoys her. "She reads a little."

She says, "a little," like I've just asked if Maxi's nose is running. "A little," is so much more than I've thought about at this juncture. "A little," is knowing the sounds all the letters make and combining them to form a word. I can't believe she didn't confess this. Rather, she let me discover it in an ostentatious display of sounding out. Temple is my friend. It seems a thing too large to keep from a friend. Right up there with a pregnancy or a breast lump. Wow. I should have known. I should have spotted the warning signs. In my head I'm pacing now, sucking on a Marlboro Light. "I can't believe you didn't say anything."

"Oh, darlin', it's a second child thing." Again with that flick of her hand and the accompanying eye roll. "Karla's in sixth grade, remember? Anyway," her excitement returns, "you heard of quartz? You don't have to seal it apparently."

"Quartz. Yeah . . ." I realize here that Emma is MIA. As I go hunting for her I notice, for the first time, the educational aids in mocking abundance. In Temple's dining room four boxes of letter and number flashcards the size of bricks are stacked on top of the Apples to Apples game. And then in the living room there's the corner of, what is that? *Phonics is Fun* under the *Real Simple* on the coffee table. Visions of a whole house morph dog me. I think that when I leave Temple will clap her hands, calling the girls to a rigid, hands-crossed-in-your-lap, after-hours home-school. It is essential now to escape this place and get my hands on Emma's report card. As if she read my thoughts I hear my girl's trademark huff from inside their half-bath. When I push the door open I find Emma on the potty, her legs spread and her head down between them. Hair falls upside down from her scalp revealing a narrow strip of white neck. "Em? You still going potty?"

"Yes," she says in a pinched voice. There is no tinkle sound.

"Honey, what are you looking at in there?"

She lifts her red face to me, grunts softly and spreads her legs. "Is that my 'gina?"

I haul the corners of my mouth up into a nonchalant smile. "Yes, that's your vagina sweetie. It's private. Come on. That's enough. You've been in here a long time."

This is what I say to her, but what I think is: *My girl is discovering her vagina like a two-year-old while Maxi the genius brushes up on the vowel sounds.* Thoughts and fears multiply in my periphery like floaties. What if Emma never reads? What if Emma is . . . stupid? A life consigned to deciphering fast food menus for my adult child isn't exactly what I've envisioned.

"Everything okay?" Temple is at my side and from the kitchen we hear Maxi's voice, "Mob. Mob. Mob. Combe here. If you pull on hard on theb, these letters combe off."

.4 seconds later, we're in the safe confines of our entry and I'm pawing through my Strawberry's contents before Emma can get her off.

In the backpack today:

A turkey made from a painted handprint on construction paper

A worksheet on writing the numbers from 1 - 20

A reminder that our parent teacher conference with Mrs. Slaughter is tonight at 6:00

A sheet that says, I am thankful for _____ Emma has filled in "jele beens"

And her report card

Pouring over the cryptic contents my heart sinks. Her progress on this page is so sketchily illuminated, I don't know whether to be elated or despairing. Ted is in the dining room working a jam out of his paper shredder with the scissors I use to trim Emma's bangs. I can't help but assail him. "Ted, I think there is some mistake because nowhere on here does it indicate the inborn excellence Emma exhibits at home. Everything from, 'Knows letter sounds' to, 'Can count from 1 to 35' is marked *Meets Grade Level Standards*. Isn't that another way of saying, 'average?'"

Ted takes the paper from me, "Whoa. Calm down," he says. "Let me see. I think it's like a 'C' right? 'C's aren't bad."

"Yes they are."

"I got 'C's, Jen. It's fine." He hands the grade sheet back. "She left the whole section about, 'Contributing to class discussions,' blank."

"I know. I need more specifics." In the intervening hours before the sitter comes I add to the list of questions for Slaughter I started this morning in between rounds of Arthur's Memory Game.

At five forty-five that night, Jefferson School is ablaze with light against the black November sky. Inside each classroom, adults in groups of two and three huddle in collusion. Through every door parents and teachers engage in fraught analysis of their child's progress. We can't help but spy Mrs. Slaughter outside her classroom saying goodbye to the father of the twins who had the conference time before us. The dad, with his tousled curls easy, buttoned down smile and casual corduroys, is clearly very pleased with the results of his conference, and we wait and watch as he clasps Mrs. Slaughter's hands warmly and says, "We are very lucky to have been given you as a teacher for both our boys. Twice blessed." And then he hugs her! Folds her in a warm embrace. I think this is brilliant, this moment of open homage to the teacher. I will vary it a bit and use it somewhere in our conference if things turn sour.

Mrs. Slaughter's face is flushed. She's clearly smitten and thrown by the gesture. Ted and I wait as she watches the twins' dad leave. The expression on her face is one of undiluted adoration. I wonder if she's married. If it's happy. If she's imagining a better life for herself in the arms of the twins' dad. "Bye now," she calls. "Please do tell the boys I said, 'hello.'"

I widen my eyes at Ted who coughs on cue. The noise wakes Mrs. Slaughter from her swoon, and she says briskly, in a voice quickly emptied of warmth, "Mr. and Mrs. Lansing please come in." We follow her into the classroom and stand there along the wall with daffy smiles on our faces breathing hard with anticipation. We are like ice dancers awaiting our marks from the judges.

I am confident that if nothing else, Slaughter will look right at me for the first time all year. Meet my eyes and soften at the good intention she finds there. "Okay." Now she's wandering the room lifting up canting piles of papers. "Where are Emma's assessments? Yes. Here we go," she says. From three different piles on the low table in front of her she selects a thick accumulation of test papers. Without looking up she asks, "Are you working on the shoe tying with Emma?"

"No," Ted chuckles.

"Yes!" I cover quickly, jabbing his side.

"Okay good." She turns and notices our height. "Let me just find you somewhere to sit." She pulls out two diminutive chairs. The seats are formed of red plastic in the shape of a child's butt. They rise not even a full ten inches from the ground. She plants these chairs across from her then she sits in her own, full-sized, desk chair set alongside the table.

118

"Please do sit down," she mumbles. Her head bobs up and down as she studies the papers in front of her from over, and then through, her rectangular reading glasses. Ted is game for the theatrics of sitting. Grinning he hitches up his jeans and sinks into the chair. His arms are between his knees, which end up flanking his chin. He is all gangly angles. After several aborted tries at landing gracefully, I crash into the tiny chair, bottom first, causing the knobby feet of the thing to screech across the floor.

"Oh my." Mrs. Slaughter winces at the noise. I feel like a frog crunched up onto the little seat and, reading my mind, Ted leans over and whispers, "Rib-bit," into my ear. Finally here Mrs. Slaughter looks me straight in the eye over her readers and her face crinkles into the smile I've sought for three months. "Now, what does Emma tell you about school?" She lowers her chin onto her fist to gaze at me over her lenses. A fledgling grin is at play on her thin lips that are lacquered tonight in ruby gloss. I grip my list of questions tightly in my sweaty hand. Her query takes me completely by surprise. Aren't we supposed to ask the questions here? The truth is, Emma has told us very little of late and this realization comes crashing in now like a pop-quiz nightmare. Okay and maybe I haven't been so great at asking. What has she said? In my head, I'm choosing between, *Duncan got sent to the Principal again last week and Becca threw up the raspberry cookie snack on Tuesday*. I say neither, but turn to Ted to bail me out.

"Ted, honey." I shoot him a look of private intensity. "What does Emma tell you about school? Go ahead. You talk." Regret teems in me and all I wish in this moment is for Mrs. Slaughter to stop staring at us. Ted rubs his face with his whole palm and a little explosion of air escapes his lips. Suddenly I am dealing out words, sloppy and haltingly like a four-year-old deals Uno cards.

"We are . . . very lucky to have been given you as a teacher for Emma . . . Blessed."

A frown crosses Slaughter's face. She straightens her papers. "Does Emma tell you about show and tell?"

"Yes, yes, she does." This I can answer.

"We often talk about what she'll bring together like those colored ball hair things. Her doll that she named, 'Baby.' I know there was that one time when she brought my ATM card, but I swear I didn't even know she had taken it out of my wallet. Like that whole cell phone, misunderstanding thing."

In trying to produce a hearty laugh here, I hoot, like a cloven animal. Then I cough raucously to cover for the feral bleat that just escaped my depths.

"She really loves show and tell. Doesn't she Ted." I jab him again. He shrugs and smiles bashfully. My cute mute.

"Well," Mrs. Slaughter takes the glasses from her face and lets them dangle from her leopard chain. "I left several squares blank on her performance evaluation because Emma has never said anything in front of the class at show and tell or at any other time. She'll raise her hand, but when I call on her, she just hides in her elbow like the cat's got her tongue. She's never really talked to me. At first I thought she was intimidated. There are a couple of readers at her table. But now, I don't know." She shakes her head here and stares down at her papers. "It's going to be a problem, with our testing. If I can't test her, we won't know what she knows now, will we? And we want to have them all counting, exceeding the math standards. And of course, there's the DRA. They really should be between a two and a four by the end of the school year."

"The DRA. What's that mean?" Ted asks me.

"Their Diagnostic Reading Assessment." Mrs. Slaughter answers. It measures Comprehension. Fluency. Phonemic Awareness. Actually, Mrs. Otis wants us to aim for a six, but, between us, that's a bit unrealistic here."

I pray for Ted's silence. I can palpably feel the blue humor rise in him and I squeeze his hand.

"Ow," he says. But he gets it. "Wow," he amends to the teacher. Here she smiles, as if the scenario of my mute child staring back at her request to count backwards from ten contains some latent comedy.

Last night Emma wanted to play school in our basement where we set up a little desk and a blackboard on a Berber rug remnant for a play area. It's her new thing. I play the student and she plays the teacher, complete with tiny clacking heels and pink sunglasses that she rigs on a pink ribbon to dangle around her neck. I snuck from the small desk to put a load of whites in the washer while she went upstairs to use the bathroom, and when Emma clomped back down the stairs she took one cross look at me, spread her arms and hollered, "WHY ARE PEOPLE STANDING? SIT DOWN CLASS!" And then she turned and walked over to her stuffed Pooh bear in the corner by the furnace and screamed at him with a menace I didn't know she possessed, "Duncan, I am NOT going to tell you again. DUNCAN!" And she clapped her hands together loudly right in front of Pooh bear's face. That moment explained many things. I understood instantly why Mrs. Slaughter doesn't like parents in her classroom. I also got that my daughter is a fantastic mimic and, hmm, let me think for a moment. Oh, yes. Here it is; Mrs. Slaughter is a yeller. A screamer. An intimidator of children. No wonder Emma won't talk to her. I don't want to talk to her anymore either.

"I wouldn't worry just yet." Mrs. Slaughter closes her pen. "But if this continues you'll want to talk to the social worker, Mr. Klein. He's wonderful."

Many competing anxieties caucus in my head. I'm not sure where to go or what to say. It must be visible on my face. Slaughter pats at my hand. She's wearing the dream catcher earrings. Perfect. Little leather webs that capture and squelch the ardent ambitions of whomever she faces. "Don't worry. You know what I'm going to say to you." She's trying to be consoling. I want my hand back. She's going to say something glib and patronizing. I can tell. She's going to tell me that Emma *is* only five. That she's very well-behaved. And that her wide-eyed shyness is kind of adorable.

"What I am going to say to you," Slaughter smiles in a way that's meant to be a comfort, "is do not worry. That's my advice. There's a college for everyone."

She gives my hand a final pat then releases it. Mrs. Slaughter and Ted push out of their chairs. Everything she's just revealed about Emma washes over me in an overwhelming tide, taking with it all of my questions about her reading and math skills. This is the first time

I've thought of Emma's shyness in school as a problem. I catch my breath and realize that Ted is speaking for the second time all night. He's excited. I gather the papers we're to take home from the table and rise from my infantile chair to join them.

"So you've got a son at Purdue!" Ted is saying. "Does he play ball? They've got quite a team this year!" I hug Emma's papers to my chest and take in the room: The bilingual labels, the mail cubbies, the three old teal-colored iMacs. And the word wall. Underneath the heading are subsets of small words in alphabetical order. The longest up there is 'the' and 'hat.' But I find them crushing in importance and expectation and have to look away. Just as I did from the Logic syllabus doled out on the first day of the first quarter of my freshman year at Baylor.

Stroking his chin, Ted chats with Mrs. Slaughter as if she'd just shared a weather report, not a progress report on our baby. Both seem to have forgotten my presence by their side. The colorful classroom with the eau-de-guinea-pig smell closes in on me. And as I move to leave I'm hemmed in by the criss-cross of clothesline draped across the ceiling. From the strings dangles 23 indian headdresses, 23 cornucopias, 23 pilgrim people. Everywhere I turn I butt art with my head which suddenly feels grotesquely large and awkward because it's trying to hold all the things we're supposed to work on with Emma: Counting to twenty by twos. Counting to one hundred by fives, the "Penny, Nickel, Dime" song. Retelling stories in their proper order. Phonemic awareness. Bigger smaller. Lesser and greater. And already I've dropped something from my list. Everywhere are bold numbers and stick drawings and rainbows and chicken scratched words and those loud bilingual labels telling me what things are. SINK / LAVBO, TABLE / MESA, SCISSORS / TIJERAS.

"Come on, Ted," I whine. "I'm tired." I tug at his sleeve. "This was hard. I want to go home and have a snack."

What I end up having is a Bud Light. I race for it, like an alky who has held her thirst at bay during a three-hour meal with recovering friends. Emma is already asleep. Ted pays our teenaged sitter on the way out the door to drive her home.

"She's a good kid," the sitter says. It's a bland observation that holds no real weight or consolation after the teacher provided assessment. At the door the girl pauses while zipping her North Face vest. She bites her lip, removes a pink cell phone from her pocket and says, "You know, I tutor too, if she needs any help, you know, in school." Is it that obvious I think? Can this tween discern from watching Noggin programming next to Emma for an hour that the only sight word my Emma knows is "McDonalds?" The sitter is paused at the door waiting for my response. I don't know what to say. Part of me wants to lie at her feet. *Yes. Yes. Just stay. Move in with us, and work with her at the special little project table from Ikea; the Svala we bought for her room. Please tell us it's not too late.*

"I mean most of the kids I work with are younger, like in preschool." Her thumbs are at work texting as she speaks to us. Then she snaps the phone closed, looks up and says, "But she's cute. It'd be fun."

"Preschool? No way," Ted blurts. His car keys are in his hand.

"Yes, Mr. Lansing, really. It sounds sort of early but for private school, you know, the selective enrollment schools that are like K-8, the kids have to test in for Kindergarten. So everyone starts early. But Emma's sweet. If she's got some catching up to do I'd be happy to work with her." And now I'm affronted. Emma is my child, my apple from my tree. Her failings are mine. My doing, and mine to undo. Is there a more important job? I pull myself up tall.

"No thanks," I say. But my refusal cannot be sustained and I wilt. "We'll keep it in mind, though."

Later that night I listen to Ted give me a speech about a whole body cleanse. Something about hot water, lemon juice and Tabasco. How I should do it. It'd make me less stressed. He's rubbing my neck and it feels so inordinately fantastic that I'd listen to him deliver a whole speech on bio-math so long as he'd keep rubbing.

"I thought the conference was good," Ted says. He emphasizes the last word as if to convince me. "Her teacher lost me a couple of times. But I like her."

"I hated it. I don't even feel like she knows Emma." This feeling is the pits. I should've known better. Whenever I put someone up on this massive marble pedestal and revere them from below like they're the be-all-and-end-all, it's just a matter of time before something like this happens and they come crashing down.

"She was nice. She'll be good for Emma. Get her out of her shell. Hated the chairs but liked her."

"A lot of kids read already," I say. "Kids at her table. You heard her teacher. Shit, Maxi reads. Did I tell you that?"

"It's Kindergarten," Ted says.

"It is but it's not. Not in the Playdoh and pipe cleaner craft sense that we knew it. That's like preschool here." And then without my bidding them I feel the tears coming and I fall face first into the bed.

"Whoa, I should've seen that coming." His hand is gone, leaving a cold place on my back. "So . . . you want to move back?"

"What?"

"You want to move back to Indiana?"

"Who said anything about moving back?"

"You did. It's fine. Go ahead say it. You know you want to. It was stupid to move up here. To bite this off. Take on this much debt. Move two hours away from all your Lamaze friends and your mom. Right? Isn't that what you were going to say? I knew you felt that way." He's ramped up now, flexing self-righteousness. "It's about time you got it out." When the truth was, excepting a teary ooze, I hadn't gotten out anything. Last I noticed we were talking about Emma's conference and now, in the span of the weather segment of the TV news it's suddenly become a looming rant about the move.

"Well, I'm doing the best I can here, Jen. Every day I'm out soliciting clients. How many Rotary meetings have I done just this month? It'll pay off. It will. I can name three guys who are this close." Here a half-inch separates his thumb and his index finger. "I've got a lunch with Hale Neuson tomorrow. Did I tell you about him? He's in replacement windows, specialty doors; selling, installation. You name it he does it. And his good buddy, the guy who runs the meetings with him is Victor Smellet. Smellet's Plumbing? He's got a whole kitchen and bath showroom on Central. That guy's huge. They're gonna bite, they will. But it doesn't help if you don't support me. You gotta believe in this, Jen."

Passion drives him from the bed. He stands facing me now, both hands planted firmly on his hips in a position of absolute certainty. Some people don't require another person to argue. Some people can complete the whole thing on their own. They play all the parts. Antagonist. Protagonist. You just gotta sit back and watch. And as long as I can pretend that one of the characters isn't me, it's actually kind of funny. If I lie on the bed and stay silent, pretty soon he'll work his way around. But while he rants I can't help being swayed by the argument he's provided when he's speaking for me. Maybe I'm right. Maybe we should never have moved. And instantly I'm wistful for Cornwell.

When Emma was three, some of the more whimsical park district officials decided to flood the outdoor Rec. Center pool to provide a winter ice skating rink for our community. Along with the rest of the families in our town, Ted and I laced on skates, suspended Emma between us, and pushed off from the aqua concrete lip of the deep end next to the diving board. Under the lights used for night swimming, we had a glorious time, gliding and spinning over the lane lines we knew existed far below us. In the spring our winter ice rink became lore because the frozen water expanded the pipes. They burst. The cement fractured and the whopping cost of repairing our rink/pool in time for summer vacation required a special funding referendum on the county ballot. Of course, it being Cornwell, where pluck and good intention are, in themselves, their own modest reward, the initiative passed quietly and overwhelmingly without any pointing of fingers.

And, then there's Miss Ginger, the Kindergarten teacher in Cornwall. She still uses hot rollers every morning to set her hair and takes in the preschoolers when Miss Suzette is sick. I'm quite sure she's never even heard of a DRA. Still, as comforting as moving back sounds, we've journeyed to the other side. Walked barefoot in the greener grass. How in the world could we return now, knowing what we know?

"So now what?" Ted's at the window in his boxers and a tee shirt fiddling with the blinds. "You think that I'm being silly. Don't you? Well don't belittle me in that way. This is not about me. This is about you and your forgetting to even say, 'Hope it goes well!' when I'm running out the door. The least you can do is believe in me. That's the least." He is distracted here by the strings on our wood blinds. They only lower one side when you pull. "What the heck?"

"Just tug on the top with your hand," I say. He does. The whole thing comes down fast colliding with a slap on the sill. In the altered silence he pulls his shirt off over his head and carries it into the bathroom. Moments later he's back with a mouthful of toothpaste and a toothbrush in his hand.

126   "Like when you wrote that whole pitch for me to bring to Matt at True Value. That was awesome. Fantastic. And the red striped tie you got that I would've never thought for a blue dress shirt. But it worked. It did."

Here toothpaste foam dribbles from his mouth. He leaves again for the bathroom. I hear him spit and rinse. "That was great. You were great." The bed gives as he returns, sits, and resumes his back massage. "Okay I'm done," he says. "Sorry." And he kisses the place between my shoulder blades.

"I would be horrible at home schooling. I'm not wired to do it. If I were wired to home school, I'd be able to play grocery store with

Emma for more than twenty minutes without being bored out of my tree. I'd be a whole different kind of mother."

"And we'd have to go to join a neo-conservative Christian Movement. Get a press-on Jesus fish for the back of the car. Wait a minute. Who's talking about home schooling?"

"I am."

"That's a little harsh. Isn't it?"

Moments later I slip downstairs and chose a Twizzler from the candy box. He's right. So what if we don't home school or get a tutor? What if the freaky children who read at four are all aberrations? Maybe it'll turn out to be like smoking. Twenty years down the road they'll determine that early reading can be detrimental to your intellectual health. The argument gathers steam it my head. And then it seems crucial to know. I want to know who the other readers are. Just how many could there be? Were do they hang out? Probably in a little geeky clutch by the chapter book section in the library, comparing opinions on their favorite Junie B. Jones and Captain Underpants selections: like grad students in rumpled tweed sports jackets. No doubt some of the high achievers in that crowd have already made it to Number 22 *Revolutionary War on Wednesday* in the Magic Tree House series. They read it on their own in a quiet corner in front of a TV that's been dark since the PBS special on the Inca's Uprising aired in August. I can feel a chill wind seeping in around the front door and opt to chew my licorice in the navy dark gloom atop the book box in the entry. Upstairs, Ted's almost asleep. I nudge him and ask him to stop at Office Max and get a Jump Start First Grade computer CD for me on his way home from his business lunch tomorrow.

December 10th

In the backpack today:

A dreidel cut out of brown construction paper

A sheet listing the six essential components of a personal narrative

A sheet with 'Bat,' 'Cat' and 'Sat' in Emma's writing on it with a blue star sticker and an "excellent" from Mrs. Slaughter

A Christmas tree drawing signed by Emma

A connect the dots drawing of a menorah

A packet of number fun to be completed over the break

A reminder not to park in the bus loading area in front of the school

And a letter from the nurse with a clever little illustration running along the top

On closer examination, it's like a child's rendering of The Little Engine That Could. An upward slanting line with a plucky oval cab making it's way up the hill. The oval is labeled, "Le Huevesello." Below the drawing is a sea of Spanish words. "Le huevesello," must be the Spanish word for train. The letter on this side is addressed to, "Estimados Parents." It's clearly the word for, "esteemed." Perhaps I've been chosen for something. I flip the page over and see the drab, army blanket greeting: "Dear Parent/Guardian, One or more cases of pediculosis, head lice, have been identified in your child's class . . . "

"Head lice are insects about the size of a small pin-head. Adult lice are difficult to see but one sign is a persistent itch of the scalp often accompanied by infected scratch marks or what appears to be a rash. Closer inspection will reveal small, silvery lice eggs (nits) attached to the hairs."

My head, upon reading the last line, begins to itch ferociously. As if the letter in my hand not only contained the information, but hundreds of the gymnastic buggers who've already made the leap to my scalp. Emma is running in place on the couch eating an Oreo. Her mouth is rimmed in black cookie.

"Emma. Get down off the couch. Let me see your head." Frantically, I part and spread her thin hair. She twists to look up at me. Her face is filled with glee.

"Are there lice in there?" she asks with the same anticipation that precedes the discovery of bugs under a rock.

"No ma'am. Not that I can see. Did they talk to you about lice at school?"

"Aubrey brought a beehive for show and tell!"

"Emma your head. This letter says the nurse checked your head?"

"Josh lost his tooth in library. Right here." Her hand is inside her mouth. I'm trolling through her hair.

"It bleeded and he got a blue box from the nurse."

Nurse, is a period they failed to describe at the Kindergarten Information Night. Emma goes to *nurse* when they play dodge ball at inside recess. At *nurse*, she gets to color with crayons that still have their points and lie on a yellow, vinyl-covered bed. The bed is probably where they get the lice.

"He gotted ten dollars from the tooth fairy."

"No honey, the tooth fairy gives one dollar."

"No. Ten dollars. That's what Josh gotted. And twenty from his grandma."

After dinner, our front bell rings. It's Temple. Though it's freezing, she's coatless and her hair is gathered into a slick wet ponytail.

Her thick glasses rim her eyes. She blusters into our kitchen, both hands filled with chunky, square Corian samples.

"Do you like the sandstone or the tarragon?" She holds two little eased-edged squares up in our wan kitchen light as fog from her lenses clears. The previous owners of our house replaced what was presumably useful illumination with a octopusian fixture with adjustable tentacles that each end in a different primary colored glass cone. Some of our counters are awash in a golden color and others in a subtle arctic blue. I squint at the sample tiles in an effort of engagement. But the prospect of a full-blown renovation discussion makes me glass over.

"I'm thinking the sandstone would bring out the warmth in our cabinet color. Turns out they're raised-panel oak and if we keep 'em, it saves like thirty grand." Temple's ponytail has left a wet place down the back of her tee shirt in the shape of a tongue. She seems not to notice. In a kind of callisthenic she holds one sample up to the light and then the first again. Left. Right. Left.

"I've got to return these Corian samples to The Great Indoors tomorrow and I just can't decide." I take them from her and examine them. She watches me.

"These look the same to me," I say squinting at them in the fluorescent, under-cabinet light. Then I add, "How much does your tooth fairy give?"

"Depends on how late she is. Ours is busy. And forgetful. Especially on the weekends. She doesn't work then." It's as if we're discussing the maid service.

"What do you mean?"

"Well, she'll give an extra buck for each night she misses. So usually it's like two or three. Depends." She looks down at the samples and sighs. "Come on, Jen. You've got to choose." She checks her watch and rolls her eyes at the time. "Crap, I thought all Karla had was math tonight. She spent two hours watching cussing babies on You Tube. Then she announced twenty minutes ago that she has to build an Egyptian pyramid to scale tonight. It's due tomorrow, of course. And she wants to do it out of Rice Krispie treats. So, I'm off to the Safeway. Plus we haven't even started on Maxi's homework yet," she mutters.

"They don't have homework tonight."

"Oh yeah, Maxi does. She's got a book report for the Great Group . . . Great Reader Book Group. Something like that. I can't never remember the real name."

Reluctantly I ask, " What's the Great Reader Group?"

I want to hear her answer but I am also just a teensy bit outraged. What, then, do they call the kids in other groups? Is there a part of the morning announcements when Principal Otis reads, "Meeting at 2:00 in the library today will be the Slow Reader Group. Followed by the Give-It-Up Reader Group at 2:30. Please be on time!"

"It's some group Kindergarteners got picked for at the beginning of the year." Temple tosses this off with an eye roll like she's completely against the whole thing.

"They gotta read books like classics and prepare reports on them. But you got to do that part with them. It's kind of a pain in the ass." In other words this tedious endeavor, this colossal waste of time, would, in no way interest me, or my offspring.

"Hey did you read that lice letter today?" I coerce a change of subject because I can't help feeling like her complaining is bragging in disguise.

"No."

"You didn't? It came home in the backpack."

"Yeah, I don't never look in there any more." Her face moves within inches of her samples, now flat on our own Formica counter.

"It's disgusting. Did you know you have to use pesticide on your head to kill the lice? Just like the stuff for lawns. It's the same chemicals."

She turns to me. Behind her glasses her expression hardens and she lowers her voice. "Look. I know you and Emma haven't been over in a while but I should tell you, Maxi had some eggs." Her accent here is thick and roiling. "It wasn't really *real* lice, you know, just the *eggs* of the lice. But you have to wash everything just to be sure. Pain in the ass. Promise you'll tell no one." She grips both my hands so tightly my wedding ring gouges my pinky. Then she remembers the time.

"Crap. I gotta go pesticide my kid." And she's gone.

I close the front door behind her and holler upstairs, "Hey Ted, can you start Emma's bath? Make it really hot, okay?"

Lying in bed I think, Temple's secret will die with me, because I am disgustingly pleased by her revelation. It's only fair. Only fitting. After all, her little girl gets to read. Gets to be a Great Reader. The Great Readers should get the lice. Like all those celebrities with drug problems; this is the price of the gift.

The next day Ted arrives home from work with a Guatemalan cleansing tea for me in a little bag.

"Where's the CD? The Jump Start CD?" I demand.

"Whoa. I didn't forget. It was forty dollars," he says dropping a teaspoonful of powder into a cup. "I thought we weren't doing unnecessary expenditures right now."

"We're not. But that couldn't be. They were in a clearance bin."

"Nope. They weren't. No bin. No sale. Forty bucks."

December 19th

The day before the holiday break it snows. Temple picks up the girls and Emma leaves her boots at school and tromps home in her unlaced gym shoes. I think it's so she can run fast past Margaret's yard, where a discordant mixture of holiday fare has been tossed up in such a strange arrangement I've given up trying to decipher the scene. A crèche, as complete as the one in front of Fourth Presbyterian, commands the corner closest to her side door. It includes a baby Jesus waving his little fists from the manger.

"But doesn't Jesus come at Christmas? On Christmas Eve?" Emma asked when Margaret first put it up. Then, "Isn't he cold?"

"He's not real."

"Jesus isn't real?"

"*That* Jesus isn't real. The *real* Jesus is real." There are gradations of *real* one might say. It will have to do. And that's not the worst part. The worst part, lording over the whole crèche, is a five-foot inflatable Santa that is sometimes switched on. In this state he's pumped full of air, lunging in the wind. Other times he's a sorry, flat mound of flaccid red vinyl on the frozen ground. The Santa, when he's living, looms waving over the three Wisemen of the crèche like a jolly guide. It is an unforgivable blending of characters and stories. The alive Santa is menacing and snags Emma's attention on the commute to school every single day.

"Is that the real Santa?"

"No."

"But Santa is real, too, right?"

"Yes." A reluctant yes.

"Why doesn't he have a present for baby Jesus? His friends (the Wisemen) brunged presents."

Temple keeps Emma after school so I can go back to get her boots. In the hallway outside Mrs. Slaughter's room, a man wearing a hooded black parka over a thin dress shirt and tan corduroys is drinking a Starbucks and studying the hallway art. Kismet I think, for this is the very person with whom I've rehearsed many a conversation in my head. It's Mr. Klein the school social worker. I know him from his picture on the school website. My rehearsal of this encounter goes something like this;

"Hello?" I say with a little dip to one side to catch his eye.

"You must be Emma's mom," he says, cracking open into a wide grin like he too had been anticipating our meeting.

"Why, yes. I am."

"She is a lovely girl. So well behaved in class. So sensitive and thoughtful. A tad quiet, but very, very well adjusted, I'd say."

"Yes." Humility drops my chin and I look up at him through my lashes, which in this fantasy are thick and lustrous without even a lick of mascara.

In the hallway now, I see that his hairline recedes up off his head in two bald arcs but the thin, mousy growth off the back is gathered in a long pony-tail captured with a dark piece of leather wound around several times. That bit you can't tell from the picture that I used to cast him. The leather in his hair matches the scuffed briefcase that dangles from his other hand. He stands directly in front of Emma's cubby blocking me from her boots. I suck in a deep breath. Here we go.

"Excuse me. I just have to get these boots." Shrinking, I try to fit in front of Mr. Klein without actually touching him. His tan loafers are Bass Weeguns in urgent need of polish. Mr. Klein blows on his coffee. I contort down towards the boots and look up helplessly. Finally he steps back so I can gather the things from the bottom of her cubby, but I can feel his bulbous eyes reigning down on me from above. The hair on my neck goes prickly with the realization. When I stand, he extends his elbow in greeting. "Happy Holidays. Larry Klein M.A."

His fists are occupied, what with the coffee and the thick brief-case, and I'm not sure what to do, so I fold my fingers around his elbow. Humorlessly he lifts and lowers his wing in a mockery of a handshake. It's how a handshake would go with a truncated person. Someone who's had their arm lopped off at the elbow after some freak accident adjusting the blades of a wood chipper, and with time and therapy has learned to extend it freely as evidence that he'd moved past it and so should you.

"Hi, I'm Emma's mom, Jennifer. She's in Mrs. Slaughter's class." He's taking me in with these eyes that refuse to hold a position. The way they move over me is lascivious and unsettling. "Which one of these — is your daughter's?" he asks, turning his attentions to the classroom art before us. In my forward vision I'd have identified my girl's work on approach from clear across the hall. But in reality, this is the first time I've noticed the tacked up sheets. There's a period here of frantic searching, because the assignment was to write a wish for the holidays and draw with marker an accompanying picture. "Peace," spelled inventively, four or five different ways is the common answer. But then one paper with a downward-sloping train of words in the lower right corner catches my eye. It's Emma's person. That's clear from the huge circle of nose on the boy in her drawing. Below the person she's written, "A job for mi daddy."

All is disintegrating within and before me. Rather than direct Mr. Klein to her work, I hear myself muttering some vague lie about my inability to find it. The truth is we've covered with Emma the concept of self-employment many times. But still, on school holidays, she's seen her dad watching The View in his bathrobe at 10:30 with his first cup of coffee. And she knows that neither one of us have a real office or a boss (or a 401K for that matter.) And she knows that we cannot buy her a Shetland pony or her own nail salon because they're too expensive. So add up those illustrious facts and it's not a pretty financial portrait.

"Actually, at our conference, Mrs. Slaughter suggested I might talk to you. My daughter is really shy. Not at home. She's fine at home. Talks a blue streak. We have to shut her up. I mean, not physically or anything, we don't tape her mouth or restrain her in any way. We never even use the words 'shut up,' but here at school she doesn't say so much . . ."

"Shy, eh? That's Selective Mutism." His face is alight in a reverie of diagnosis. If he were a cartoon his eyes would spin. Then as a bell dings each pupil would settle on duplicate images of, say, apples. Jackpot. Stream of coins cascades from his mouth-spout. "Yes. Selective Mutisim: where the child won't speak at all in certain settings like school." He barrels through this tidbit. Then he swings his briefcase up and over his head. It's a gesture that solidifies the strangeness of the encounter. With the hasty diagnosis I feel the sturdy flooring shift beneath my feet. Suddenly it's imperative that I press my case. Participate actively in this conversation.

"Well she does speak, just not a lot. And at home she's fine, she has good friends and talks to them and us. Like Maxi, in her class. She talks to her. They're silly little girls! Laughing like hyenas over the word 'poop.' They pop heads off her Barbies together . . ."

The hallway is hot. Or maybe it's my heavy coat or fleecy hat. From the center stairs the janitor, Al, appears with a push broom half the width of the hall.

"Evening," he says with dip of his head. I realize how late it must be. After a smile in Al's direction and a few whistling blows on his beverage, Klein speaks more to himself than to me. His eyes dart like billiard balls loose on the table. "I'll make a note in her file. Then after break we'll test her." He rocks up on his toes on the word 'test' as if the word produces a pleasurable welling somewhere within. It makes him briefly taller and in a purely visceral response I step back as he plows on.

"We'll pull her out of the class room setting. Remove the other distractions of the Kindergarten surroundings. Put her in the office with just my puppet and me. Have her talk to him. Theodore's his name. Theo if you prefer. The kids adore him. You know a friendly face. Get her going with Theodore. Then we'll bring in some of the less intimidating kids from her class one by one. Sit them across the table. See how she does with them. After the break we'll formulate a plan. Then, come spring, we'll test her again."

Having mapped out a course, he settles back on his heels and says to the dropped fluorescent ceiling fixture illuminating the hallway, "Don't worry, with the help of their team these cases usually move up to first grade with the rest of the class."

It's not at all in my nature to question the authorities that be, but the string of words that have flowed out of the mouth of this weasely man with the akimbo briefcase, amounts to holding Emma back. Flunking her. Who flunks Kindergarten?

"But I don't want her to be labeled. Do we really have to do all that?"

A smile spreads on his face like an oily spill. And for the first time his eyes settle on me.

"Labels aren't bad. They can be quite . . . useful."

"I'm going to have to talk to my husband."

I am working here without a script or a director. An undertow of panic hauls me fast away from terra firma. Boots in hand, I back down the hall in the direction of the front entrance, piling space in between us. Just wait, when I get home the right lines will come to me, two hours too late.

"Well, I'll just make some notes in her file for now then. And we'll get started on a plan in January." I'm almost to the door and he has to call after me, but I'm glad I gave clearance because he employs considerable strength to swing his briefcase back up and over his head, accompanied by a grunt like the thing is a free weight.

"Her name is Ella?"

Without hesitation I pipe, "Yes, Ella with an 'L.' Happy Holidays."

And then I turn and run away. I hug Emma's boots to my chest and haul ass out into the fading December light, my head swimming and my coat unzipped. On the sidewalk the accumulation of snow softens my step. I can't hear my feet land. It's fitting because the whole of me reels with fresh snippets of our conversation that just won't reconcile at all with my rehearsed version. The one I'd gone over so many times it's hard to supplant like that; to substitute it with the gathering alarm I feel at Mr. Klein's pronouncements. Before I even get to the corner, I see Margaret's Santa aglow with his weird inner light lording over the crèche, Santa's fat inflated arm raised in greeting. The Wisemen have little caps of snow on their heads. And baby Jesus who shouldn't even be here yet is covered with the stuff. I am suddenly filled with competing inclinations. With urgent resolve I think over my person seeking something sharp: like a switchblade, or a Swiss Army pocketknife. I want so much to do harm. And the soft vinyl of the grinning Santa would give so swiftly and irreparably under even the slightest pressure of a blade. But also I want to continue my coat-flapping scurry homeward to take Emma in my arms and cradle her to my bosom even if she squirms and announces, as has lately been her wont, "Now is not the time for babying." For I am no more able to explain to her how Santa and Jesus can coexist in Margaret's lawn than I am why she might have to repeat her Kindergarten year.

Over the break the encounter with Mr. Klein rolls around inside my head. I entertain it like a malleable thing. Sitting on it. Pummeling it with my fists, shifting his emphasis, casting light on different phrases. I can't bring myself to speak to anyone except Ted about the encounter because I feel unable to process it for myself. As if it was all just a hazy nightmare and if I don't focus on it, it might all go away (poof) with the fresh calendar and two weeks off school. I do, though, scrutinize Emma who is as chatty and outgoing as ever. Particularly because her impersonations of Mrs. Slaughter have become omnipresent and more robust. She's never without a clipboard. With a sassy sideways thrust of her hip she extends her pink-plastic sunglasses on the beaded necklace around her neck. Her voice is loud, supported through her diaphragm, raised for many small ears to hear. "Young lady," replaces "Mommy." As in, "Young lady, you should be finished in there." This from the hall side of the closed bathroom door. We should have converted Ted's office into a guest room. Put up a white board and a word wall and invited Mrs. Slaughter to stay, rather than endure Emma as her 24/7.

I'm still half asleep when from behind me I hear, "Jennifer. Is Jennifer here today?" I raise the hand that's not pouring from the coffee pot. Caffeine has yet to curse through my body. Social skills dormant, I smile and bring Emma to me in a wordless hug. She pushes off from my shoulder.

"There you are, Jennifer." She makes a check.

"People should be finished with their snack by now," Emma barks at me at breakfast. A spiral notebook is resting on her hip,

"Good morning, Em. It's not a snack, it's Shredded Wheat. Breakfast." I am, and will forever be her buzz kill.

"Um-hmm," she says like she's caught me. Then she squiggles a line across the page on her clipboard and taps out some concluding dots with a flourish. The scrutiny ruins my three minutes with the newspaper and I ditch my bowl in the sink.

"I'm expressed with the way you cleaned up your snack, Jennifer," she pipes, tailing me.

"Impressed. The word is impressed."

"Ah!" She jumps on my outburst, pulls down her mouth and points her pencil up at my nose. "Did I ask you a question?"

That night she finishes her mac-and-cheese, and leaves the table only to return with the clipboard and glasses. She paces in front of Ted and me.

"Boys and girls stop fooling around."

Ted shoots me a look, chewing.

"Did you hear me?" Emma's palm lands on the table between us. "I said, I see you when you fool around!"

The break is frigid and long. A crawling collusion of days. Among the Christmas cards from Cornwell is one from the Lamaze gang. Each of the moms signed it and wrote a little update. All of their children are enjoying Kindergarten with Miss Ginger. From the card I learn they sleep there on little rest rugs with their stuffed animals. Some of the kids can already write their names and, come January they're all going to start work on writing upper case letters.

The next day I run into the Talbots end of the PTA triumvirate at *Creative Learning Toys* while trying to find the lower-case magnetic letters Mrs. Slaughter has warned we must provide our child by the end of break. The Talbots is the one whose name I don't recall and she's forlorn over the impending return to school.

"We've just had too much fun!" she says. Her eyebrows contract in grief. In her hands are the last two boxes of lower case letters. Upper case is all that's left on the wooden shelf. She follows my eyes. "One for home and one for school," she explains. "My two girls took a sewing class over break and came home with most darling fleece pajama pants. They loved it. And the library and Barnes and Noble, we lived there." Here she gestures with one of the boxes. Its letter contents rattle like maracas. "And we baked and baked what with all the family around. My floors are still crunchy with those red and green sugars! I just love it! My Katie. Do you know her? She's in first. She was so exited to use the spring-form pan. And, what else . . ." She's stumped only briefly before she returns to her recitation with another shake of her box. "We had no TV."

I assume the thing broke but there is quick need here to revise my pitying, "aw," because she's proud, if not braggadocios. "At night we just played board games, Clue Junior, Scrabble, Connect Four in front of the fire."

Through the last part I watch her bright smile and her moving mouth. It's coming. I foresee the rotation of focus. And then she says the words. "How 'bout you?"

There must be something to present other than the interchange of bowl games and children's programming on our TV, and the arguments over who gets to watch what when. I've left one of those tiffs to come to the refuge of the store. In the end I stammer about visiting my parents for the weekend and at the same time I can't believe I'm packaging the trip as a highlight.

My mom used to teach and she when we arrived she adjusted Emma on her lap, "Oops off, not that way, yes, there." Then she pumped her with questions about school. They were the very same questions she asked me when I was Emma's age. "What is your favorite time of day?"

"Recess."

"But of course," she smiled.

"And choice."

"And what is *choice*?" My mother frowned at me as if I'd suggested the word to the district.

"Free time. Right Em?"

"So you mean *play*."

"No, *choice*," Emma protested hotly. "We get to choosed."

"Yes, Em. *Play* is what we used to call it."

"Why the word 'choice?'" My mother asked again. And from her expression I saw that she had chosen to take the conversational path through the thorny bramble that only she could find.

"Because the *kids* get to decide what to do. Not an adult. Not the teacher."

"I don't like it. It's conditioning them to be pro-abortion, don't you think?"

I knew better than to chomp on her lure but I did. An hour went by with her arms and legs crossed in her wing back chair deconstructing my arguments and sending them back to me as a ghoulish distortion of where I began. But the segue did accomplish one thing, it kept me from having to talk about the encounter with Mr. Klein before break. Because, despite my better judgment, I had the urge to seek her advice, even though I can predict my mother's response.

"Pish," she'd say. That single exhalation is how the woman expresses her response to anything that she perceives I over-think. It was that response when I was in high school that silenced my agony over which dress to wear on my first date with Kyle Oakley. Her selection sailed onto my aqua flower pop bedspread next to me. "Pish," she said as it landed. "Wear this one."

I expected the single word when I hastily decided to drop out of college to be an actress. Instead I got silence: two years worth. I get how she felt now, but it took my relationship with Ted to help cobble my mother and I back together.

"Wonderful. Family at the holidays is so wonderful," Talbots says. Her eyes drift here and she takes in the empty space on the shelf. Then she looks down, and carefully considers the two identical boxes in each of her hands. After a fraught moment, deciding, she extends one with a demure smile as if she was bestowing upon me the birthday necklace she found tucked into the corner shelf of a specialty store after two hours of shopping.

On the last Sunday before school starts again I plow through the towering pile of construction paper projects, sequencing worksheets, newsletters, district information and early math worksheets that have accumulated since September. Ultimately, one pile becomes two: the keep and the go. Each is the height of a plush footstool. While I tackle the papers, Ted unpacks hard cover books from the box in the entry. Even though we've procrastinated a full five months, the task irritates him. I'm going to miss it, that box. In the intervening months since we moved in, I've accumulated a fair number of fond and fraught memories in the entry; Margaret's box of candy bars, and how, in September, it didn't even occur to me to just say "no" to her. And before that, collapsing on the corner as I read the name of Emma's teacher for the first time. I think back to how promising Slaughter seemed at the beginning of the year. How she attended to Emma, to all those kids the first weeks. Stooping in that posture that must have killed her back to make her face level with theirs. How she seemed so capable of shouldering my expectations for Emma. Sliding a "Join the Chess Club" paper into the "toss" pile I reflect on how naïve I was, to think that shiny esteem could survive the test of time without tarnish.

"Do I have to give you a referral, Duncan? Because I will. I'll give you a referral and YOU can explain what you were doing to PRINCIPAL OTIS." From the family room comes the sound of Emma/Slaughter berating her Pooh bear. It's all gone to hell in a handbag.

"PEOPLE SIT DOWN. Duncan, that is it, young man. You go to the office now. MARCH!"

An hour later Emma is poking around by the back door. There's a useless little porch out there off the kitchen where we stack our garbage until pick-up. She's got her nose stuck into the old book box which is crammed in next to two giant Heftys stuffed with the colorful detritus of Christmas wrap. "Mom, what's this?"

"That's all garbage, kiddo."

"What?" she says. Then out she scoots with a fist full of her old projects in her hand. On top is a cardboard pumpkin that rains glitter when she holds it up. "I *maded* this."

"Oh that? *That's* not garbage." I turn to Ted who's washing plates and handing them off for to me to dry. "What's *that* doing in there? That's your pumpkin project."

"Jen, you told me to throw that pile away." He sets a dripping plate in the rack.

My eyes are wide and pointed. I lean over the sudsy water fishing for his attention. "That pile? No, hon. They were *both* keep piles."

"Okay, but that's not what you said before."

He doesn't get it on purpose. He's still mad from having to cart all those books upstairs. And his hands are sunk in suds.

Emma's back in the box. She emerges clutching more things. An egg crate caterpillar, three line-drawings of rainbows, a stick person holding a stick animal aloft on the end of a line like an inflatable. "Mommy I worked very hard on this." Her voice is thin and high. She's disappointed in me. I can swallow anything except this particular flavor of guilt.

"I know honey. I love those things. We're saving all of them. In that box. Right Ted? Didn't we decide that *that* box would be perfect for saving all Emma's things?" And we do. We save every last damn scrap of paper in the cardboard U-Haul box. At least we'll keep it in the basement until she's old enough to go away to summer camp and we can cull through it again.

January 4th

"Emma, you can't wear your coat like that, you have to zip it up. It's January, honey, and it's only going to be in the teens today." The thought of Emma as a helpless adult tottering up to her boyfriend with an open blouse, so he can fasten each tiny pearlized button before she heads off to work, stops me before I lay a hand on her coat.

"Try to do your zipper by yourself."

She grasps both halves.

"Good, sweetie! Now, put that thing in there. In the slot."

After several thick-fingered attempts, she gets the thin bit in the slot.

"Right. Now pull up on that thing."

Her hands pause. She stands there reverently holding the bottom of her coat. Precious seconds evaporate in the lull.

"Pull up, Emma!"

She does, and the whole front of the parka buckles up to her chin.

"Pull down too. No, pull up and down at the same time."

I am a ball-strung bull. My cage door opens. "Let me do it. Let me do it." I throw myself at the bottom of her jacket, complete the zip, and steady my voice. "Now, if you go outside for recess you have to zip your coat and wear your hat today okay?"

In front, Temple waits on the front walk with Maxi who wears no hat or gloves. Her hands are jammed in her pockets.

At 11:10 I slink down in my overheated minivan and turn the corner onto the street that passes playground. Sure enough there's

Emma running full gait across the mulch, jacket open and flapping behind her as useless as penguins' wings. Tomorrow she gets long underwear under her dress.

In the backpack today:

A note from Mr. Klein asking me to stop by his office at my convenience

A reminder that Tuesday is our day for snack

A flyer announcing that registration for any citywide summer camps and T-ball leagues should be postmarked no later than February 1st

Someone's paper lunch sack containing an apple and a used napkin that has writing on it; a round lettered script in fuchsia ink that reads, "I love you, Ahmed, You're better than that boy. Don't let him bother you," first the words in English and then what looks to be the same words in French

A letter from the nurse that begins, "Dear Parent/Guardian. Someone in your child's class has developed hoof and mouth disease . . ."

A reminder that Wednesday is field trip day and I've signed on to be a volunteer

I catch up to Temple and another mom before school. The second mother is standing with her back to the open rear door of her mini van clutching a manila folder. I've narrowly missed a transaction where Temple received an orange notice. She's folding it in two as I approach while two preschool boys chase each other on the parkway beside. I hear the word "camp" distinctly emerge from their conversation that is otherwise hushed and secretive. There's a definite tone change as I approach the moms. They close their conversation in cryptic vagaries, "Okay I'll give her a call."

"It'll be good!"

"Get in the car, boys. We're going now."

"What?" I say, sneaking a peak at the paper in Temple's hand before she folds it in half again. I see the word "Discovery." That's as far as I get. "What's that?"

"Oh," she says, weary and detached. "Some summer camp thing." Then she thrusts her mitten out in front of her, looks up at the sky and says, "Shit. Is it snowing? It's not supposed to snow today is it?"

"Summer camp?"

She looks at the paper in her hand as if just remembering it was there. When she speaks it is into her scarf. "Yeah. Total word of mouth. It's supposedly amazing."

"What? No one's mouth has shared any word with me," I say joking in the vernacular of Junie B. Jones. Silence. "Word of mouth, like invitation only?"

"Yeah, I think." She considers her words, allowing them to trail off. "Must be. Crap. I was gonna try and make it to Ikea and back today, but if it's gonna snow, there's no way."

I've already decided to spend the morning finding out more about the camp because suddenly I feel that Emma must do it.

"Can I copy that flyer thing? The camp doohickey?" I ask gingerly because Temple's closed up. She stomps a couple of times like a foal who's ready to bolt.

"Well, I don't think you're supposed to copy it. But, yeah." It's a reluctant ascension, and as she gives it, she stuffs the folded sheets into her bag.

I resist the overwhelming urge to tease the bag from over her shoulder, hug it to my tummy and charge across the street to the sepia pile of old snow banked over the curb while screaming, "Nah, nah, nah, nah, nah. You can't catch me."

From my cell I make seven phone calls on the way downtown, finally locating the director of the Discovery Camp System. It seems that over the two weeks of morning camp, they'll learn all about running, catching and pitching sports, as well as creative drama and story telling. The woman gives me her pitch on the phone like I'm weighing this summer option against many others, and I realize that what they'll do is secondary to the fact that it's so desirable. Like securing the table in the kitchen for the twelve-course degustation at Charlie Trotter's. Yes, yes the meal is a memory, but securing the reservation! Now that's the real feat.

As if she senses my simmering, Temple calls after the kids are in bed and we meet at her house to finish the bottle of wine she opened while she and the kids did homework. The stacks of papers for each child to return to school are in neat piles on her dining room table. She pushes them aside to give us some room before presenting me with my very own orange piece of paper; the application for Discovery Summer Camp.

"That other mom said not to copy it. I was gonna give it to ya all along, darlin'."

In minutes we've both sucked down a glass and are opening a second bottle. I've already recreated our whole parent-teacher conference for Temple and end my rant by asking her to tell me what she thinks about Mr. Klein.

"Don't know him. But, hey, at least she didn't recommend a real shrink like she did for Maxi."

"But Maxi's doing so well. She reads even."

"True but apparently she keeps pulling all the heads off the dolls and throwing them away in the classroom trash."

Yes. I know this behavior from the girl's playdates at our house.
"No," I say. "I can't believe she'd do that at school."

"Yeah. With every freakin' doll. Course I denied it to Slaughter, told her she was crazy."

"You did not."

"Did too. Hell, I know Maxi does it. Sometimes she even uses Sharpie to black out the doll's eyes before she decapitates them. So we found this woman: a child psychologist, but we've only been twice 'cause she doesn't take insurance. And we had issues with the waiting room. Maxi was playing with my phone, while I'm readin' some article about how to stop yourself from smackin' your kids when you feel rage at 'em."

I avert my eyes.

Temple flicks me with the back of her hand. "Kidding! So Maxi's off snappin' pictures of everyone there. Stickin' the phone right into their faces. Turns out people don't like to have their pictures taken when they're about to go in to see their shrink. And this woman who is supposed to be so fuckin' great with kids didn't get the humor in it at all."

Later that night Ted says, "Emma doesn't need a speech therapist.

"You know that. I know that. But Mr. Klein thinks she does."

"Tell me again. This Klein. He's the Principal?"

"No, he's the school social worker or whatever. He wants to pull her out of class and do some tests. He's even got Slaughter on board. They drew up a plan."

"What kind of a plan?"

"Interventions to help her talk more in school."

"They won't hold her back, Jen. You know that."

"He didn't exactly say, 'Hold her back.' Temple said the school doesn't use those words anymore. It ruins their funding or something."

After a silence Ted asks quietly, "What do you think?"

"I don't know. I'm gonna talk to Nicole."

"A plan. Sounds like a blueprint for a house. Hey, did you know Temple and Denny are getting a new kitchen?"

Nicole is doing her Wii Fit program when I call her again for advice. She's breathless and tells me to hang on. When she comes back she's all business. "So what sort of specialist do you think Emma needs?" Before I can answer she plows on, "I mean if they're talking SID, DSI or even SPD I've got the best OT, which is like PT? But, on the other hand, my PhD guy is great for ADHD, ADD, ODD anything behavioral. Does that help?"

The phone blurs as my eyes fill with tears. "Nicole, Emma is just shy, I think."

"Really? She doesn't seem shy to me."

"She's not, to you. But in school she is."

"Well, if they're seeing issues, you're best nipping them now, in the bud, with some sort of plan."

"Yes, they've talked about a plan."

"Good. Plans are good. So did they say whether it's articulation or processing? Actually, It doesn't really matter. I've got someone in Speech Path who's great working with your child's IEP." There's a long pause here.

"Hello? Jennifer, you do at least have an IEP right?"

I don't remember when it started, the mothers of older children phoning Ted for math help. I often regretted telling Temple that he was good with numbers. That word spread through the parent culture like strep throat. Now the phone will ring between seven and eight o'clock at night and it'll be Temple or one of the middle school mothers she pals around with. In place of normal conversation I'll get, "So if you have two containers and one holds seven cups of water and the other four. How could you fill them and pour to arrive at exactly five cups?"

It's a courtesy, tonight, Temple asking me. Those sorts of questions were called brain-teasers when I was growing up. Now it's called pre-algebra and it makes me feel like I'm the kind of doughy-brained person who could be perfectly content for an hour or so contemplating the slim web of flesh between my toes.

"Hold on," I say, for the third time this week. I call for Ted and he spends a professorial minute on the phone and then, buoyed, wants me to sit still while he explains the answer to me as well. These moments are excruciating. When he pulls out the scrap paper to penetrate my lack of understanding with a diagram, I know I'm in for it. I'm a horrible wife for my impatience. I force myself to sit there in a bitter stew of stupidity, impatience and guilt. Once I lost it and screamed, "I don't care. I don't want to know." And I ran from the room, my face hot.

Tonight after some appropriate, if not half-hearted, "Oh's," "I sees," and "so you pour off that one, okay," I wait on the side of Emma's bed with two books on my lap while Emma brushes her teeth. The books are Level One readers. 'Preschool to First Grade' is listed on the back as the target age range. It goes well for the first page of "All Tutu's Should Be Pink." Listing against my side, Emma looks at the words as my finger follows them underneath. But by page three she's gone headfirst over the side of the bed. Upside down grunting follows, and before I can haul her back up by her ankles, she kicks up her legs so they fly over her head and the whole of her lands hard on the floor.

At this rate she'll learn to read when she's twelve. She'll be seated at the same table she's occupied for six years in the back of the Kindergarten room. Only then she'll need a training bra and a just-in-case panty liner and her only friends will be all the red-shirted girls whose parents envision basketball scholarships.

"Is that gymnastics?" Emma pops up from the side of the bed. "Yes, it is!" I say with cheap, plastic enthusiasm. ("My mom," she'll intone to her therapist, "wasn't ever genuine in her praise.") My finger rests under the word, "THE," in the Pink Tutu book. "What's this word, Emma?" I flash the page towards her. Quid pro quo. I answered her question. The least she can do is answer mine.

"I don't know," she says without looking at it.

"Come on," I say, my voice as level and slick as a leering man hocking knock-off Louis Vuitton's out of the back of his truck.

"Bat," she says, already in position to do her little flippy thing off the side of the bed. It's eight o'clock. Her lights go off any later she'll be a whiney heap by three o'clock tomorrow.

"Okay, it's time." I announce as Emma's bare legs fly overhead. She lands hard this time on her back and immediately starts wailing. I'm to her in a second.

"Are you okay, Em?" She glares at me and rolls away from my offer of comfort.

"What do you care?" The words are separated, robotic, not unlike how they'll sound when she eventually reads them from a book.

The next morning picks up where we left off. "Emma, come on! You're going to be late for school. You're bringing snack today, honey. You've got organic animal crackers, clementines and Oreos. I'm putting the bag by the front door." I haven't showered yet and I have to be downtown in exactly one hour to audition to be a Toyota salesperson.

Ted is puckered for a kiss, an apple in one hand. Flying past him I graze his lips with my own. Emma hops to the top of the stairs. Her legs are fused together by the waist of her red tights. I take the stairs two at a time and hand her the gummy-bear vitamin I plucked from under her cereal bowl when I cleared the breakfast dishes.

"Mommy, these tights are broken," she whines, stomping a foot for emphasis.

"They're not broken, honey." Gripping the tights on either side I yank them up over her tiny rear! "Jump!" I command. The force of me pulling lifts the whole of her off the ground. "The school bell rings in seven minutes." Is there a recipe for sense of urgency? I cannot be the only mother whose child goes wet noodle when faced with the concept of hurrying.

"Turn around. Look at my face, sweetie." I'm still on my knees. "You've got to eat the Gummy-Vite, brush your teeth and go potty now. You're walking to school with Maxi and Temple today. And they'll be here in two minutes." It's really more like five, but two sounds more compelling. Even for a child years away from being able to tell time. I race to the front door, fling it open and am assailed by a blast of arctic air.

"Ted! Love you, hon. Don't forget to mail the bills!" The checks I wrote last night plundered all but $62.45 from our checking account. It's not a pretty picture in that tiny vault. It's become a constant source of underlying friction in our home: like the clang of the commuter trains we can hear all night from the station a half-mile to the east. Ted gives me a hale salute from beside his car as the phone rings from somewhere in the living room. I hunt for it in the space between the rings and stop to divine its whereabouts when it rings again. Finally the machine kicks on with the sound of my own breezy voice announcing the fact that we're not home, I find Emma on the fuzzy white rug in the bathroom in front of the sink studying the seam in her tights. The caller hangs up and a loud dial tone fills our downstairs. Then I see it: the red-bear Gummy-Vite catching a wave at the bottom of the potty. I pull my girl up to standing by the wrists. "Come on, Emma. Get your teeth brushed, now!"

The doorbell rings.

"Shit!"

This is what my mouth says: an unmistakable, clarion cuss. Everything stops for a second so that Emma can be sure to absorb the bad word mommy's mouth has just said. And so she can give me *my* mother's look of disappointment and say, "I hope Santa didn't hear you, mommy." From the living room the phone starts ringing again.

There are some days when the choices are few. I can stay in the tiny, shrinking-like-a-Bat-Man-torture room and be mommy dearest with the toothbrush, or I can leave. I chose leaving. Out of the front picture window I see Temple and Maxi gathered on the sidewalk like lost carolers, waiting for some sign that we're coming. The phone still rings.

Through the glass I mime what I imagine are frantic, yet clear, gestures for, "Wait! She'll be out in one minute!"

After the pleasant me announces for the second time that we're not home, the voice of my agent says, "Gooood morning, Jen. It's me, Blane. Babe, I've got an audition for you next Wednesday at 10:00. It's for Spring Morning? Have you heard of that? It's a douche. Some of you ladies have turned it down, but it's a national spot. And it doesn't shoot until March or April. So we've got time. Let me know what you think." A national could pay thousands, tens of thousands depending on how often it airs. God, could we use that now.

"Mommy what's a douche?" Emma asks. She's standing over the toilet her Dora the Explorer toothbrush in her hand.

I squeal when I see her. I'm equipped to do little else than ready her out the door. Explaining what a douche is, doesn't come within spitting distance of my priorities right now. I ignore her question while taking in the suspicious positioning of her brush.

"Emma what are you doing?"

"I am cleaning the potty, mommy!"

"Not with your toothbrush! Come on! Move it. Coat. Now!"

Halfway to the door, she stops. Immutable, her face twists into a pre-cry. Her lips curl back and her eyes squeeze shut. "You are being angry with me," she wails, as a sob makes it's way to the fore and tears squeeze one after the other from between her lids.

"No, I'm not, sweetie."

For some reason, I can't cop to being angry. Never do. "I'm just frustrated, Em." Frustration is marginally superior to anger. It's a perfectly acceptable response to a challenging situation. I sink to my knees, hug my kid and wipe her tears with my thumbs.

"Okay, Emma. You okay?" She gives me her wonky smile. That she's game and wanting to win me over in the middle of this chaos splits me right open.

"Okay. Coat on. Boots on." I narrate as we go, in a transformed syrupy voice that pours forth from the gash guilt made in my irritation.

Every fiber in my body is screaming, "GO!" to the neighbors, to Emma, so that I can have a tiny vodka and a foot massage. Okay I'd settle for a shower.

The neighbors have started their migration down the block. Emma runs on her toes, Strawberry Shortcake flopping on her back, to meet them, "Emma?! Have a really good day, sweetie!" I call in my most saccharine voice. And I smile and wave like the dickens. When I close the door there they are: the bags of snack mocking me from their listing pile by the front door.

January 17th

"Good! Now another bunny ear, sweetie. Where does the bunny go?"

"Into the hole?"

"Right!" We're both, mother and child, crouched in the school hallway. The floor is grimy and slick. Emma's working on her shoe tying. I'm working on keeping my hands to myself. The slamming of metal lockers up and down the hallway forms a constant unnerving din and, unaware he's leaning against me, Rico takes in a robust pull from his inhaler. He clutches a fistful of my coat as he counts to four and then doubles over in a dramatic fit of exhalation. Today is the field trip to the aquarium I signed on for some weeks ago, and the fact that I'm a chaperone also entitles me to linger after the bell. It rings here igniting a more urgent round of locker slams.

"Good job. Try the other shoe sweetie." Emma's worked a knot in the first shoe that I'm fairly confident will hold.

"Hello, *Emma*. Happy New Year." A man's voice: a recognizable voice that pierces me through. To my left are the Weeguns of my avoidance. Sunk into them is Mr. Klein, a coffee mug emblazoned with the words Fairfield Feelings Forum, is in his hand. He blows on the steaming liquid inside. I stand and he speaks in my direction, though his attention fails to land anywhere specific. "I've got a plan outlined for *Emma*."

"Yes, well, can we talk about that later? It's field trip day and I'm a chaperone." It's a bright light of a response. Filled to the brim with promise and avoidance. As if this field trip could, in itself, be the key that unlocks the door of Emma's shyness.

"Of course, Mrs. Lansing," he says in his wet voice. "And it is *Emma*, right? I had the name wrong somehow." He shuffles off backwards down the hallway, holding us in his divergent vision for some time before turning around. It's a somewhat threatening leave-taking, and it makes me more resolved in my effort to elude him. Besides, in the month since school started again, Emma's bragged about bringing of a box of dominoes for show and tell. When we pressed, we got a robust tale of the sharing, including what she told the class, who farted when she was almost done, and who wanted to keep the blank ones. The whole scenario confirmed my suspicion that Mr. Klein may have been overzealous. Perhaps he's compensated based on the number of children on his roster.

Outside now, we wait in line to board the school bus. Emma hugs my leg and coos, "This is my Mom," to any other child who glances our way. I wonder how it would play if you added, "holding the douche bag." I still haven't told Blane whether or not I'll audition for the douche spot. I should have called him back yesterday. Instead, I'm stewing over whether or not to go without actually acknowledging that the only thing in the "Reasons For Doing It" column is the money.

We are in line between swaggering, hands-down-his-pants Duncan, and Maxi who wears an inadequate fleece hoodie and has nipped holes into her pink leggings with her Fiscars. Little flashes of skin show through down both legs. When it's our turn, I climb up onto the steps to take in the gentleman driving the bus. He is chipmunk cheeked and heavy lidded, with skin so dark it's purple. I'd put him at sixty-five or so. Everything he wears, from his jacket to his shoes, is navy like a uniform except for the jaunty tweed cap canted back on his head.

"Hi, are you the driver?"

"Yes ma'am." He has a voice filled with gravel and he grins and touches his cap like I amuse him. "Name's Buddy."

"Hi Buddy. I'm Emma's mom and this is Emma. We'll both be riding with you to the aquarium today."

"Well, watch your step then, Emma's mom. That first one's a doosey."

I know he's said this many times. Probably twice before I even stepped aboard, but I'm touched and cleansed with relief that he . . . cares.

"Let me tell you, I've had many a child not lift their foot up high enough and catch a toe on that nasty step. Especially the bitty Kinderpeople. Right there. They bang their shins and down they go. Writhin' and cryin' like they dyin'. You git what I'm sayin'?"

It's been years apparently since anyone gave the poor man the opportunity to speak. I take the step successfully.

"Thank you. Good. I watched my step. And here I am. All aboard. Thank you, Buddy. You've been driving the bus for awhile then? And your eyes and ears are still good? And you like driving the bus? Obviously, because here you are . . ."

Emma shoulders me from behind. "Mommy, get on!"

My previous concerns about the driver feel a little silly now. Although, picking my way down the aisle I realize that this is the very same bus that we used for our field trips thirty years ago. Muddy water pools in the ridges of the rubber floor mat and the windows are obscured with steam. Emma and I slide into a row at the back. Rico and another boy, Saleem, are across the aisle having a friendly morning shove and spit at each other. I think they will be bond traders. The bus is filling with children. With the arrival of each one the decibel level on board rises exponentially.

Emma is petting my arm as if we've only just been reunited after a protracted and dangerous separation. Between the cacophonous hoots that surround us, I think I hear a boy soprano sounding out. "Ffff-u-k,k,k yu – yu - you." I question what I just heard. It's definitely sounding out. Phonemic awareness. But the combination of sounds couldn't be right. "Fuck you." Saleem's soprano voice reads confidently. This is followed by, "Bish." The word sails across the aisle from the mouths of the previously dueling boys. They are giggly and secretive, and being the sole adult presence in the rear, I climb over Emma and see the graffiti scrawl on the seat back that faces the boys. "Fuck You, Bish." Is swiped onto the vinyl in thick point marker and further down near the floor in tiny letters is the name "Leslie." Not wanting to usurp authority, I beeline up to the front to where Mrs. Slaughter confers with the bus driver.

In seconds she is hauling Rico and Saleem back up the aisle and hollering for non-reading volunteers. "People. Listen up," she shouts. Then she claps her hands with such vigor, they sound like two wooden blocks banged together. "Who's in my Baby Bunny group? Where are my one's and two's? Come on, people! You know your DRA's," she says, raising her own hand by way of example.

It's the first time I've seen her in a coat; a pilling, cowl-necked sweater coat that falls to her knees. It's belted at the waist with a leather piece studded with tiny turquoise beads. Now, she pulls the English-as-a-Second-Language Taiwanese girl from her spot towards the front and shoves her down the aisle towards me. "Emma's mom, you sit in that seat with Emma and Xi," She presents her solution brightly. "They're baby bunnies. They won't be able to read it."

She's delighted with the solution and the fact that I have to ride in the steamy, overheated bus facing the slander makes me realize I should do the douche audition. It couldn't be more humbling than this journey. The bus engine rumbles. A cheer goes up from the kids – none of whom I can see because they're all shorter than the seats. From my vantage in the back, the bus looks empty. The driver maneuvers us away from the curb: or from the pitch and bounce, maybe over a body. It's like driving on the moon. With each lurch and dip the kids scream and hoot at a timbre just below a dog whistle.

Emma and Xi grin shyly at each other as we're all sent skyward by the bump and jolt of the ride.

At the aquarium it's clear that seventy-five other grade schools have coincidentally chosen this day to visit. The group entrance is already clogged with tiny bodies encased in grimy down coats and the occasional frantic adult trying to corral their troops. I am in charge of Emma, Maxi and Rico.

"It's a clusterfuck." At barely a whisper I hear this in my ear.

Henry's mom stands beside me. She has a small boy attached to each hand.

"Isn't it?" she asks, her eyes twinkling.

I'm not sure what a clusterfuck is. But it sounds like the perfect description here. And I'm infinitely relieved to have Henry's mom to share the day. We agree to stay together and deliver simultaneous instructions in the echoing holding area outside the first exhibit.

"Okay, Maxi, Emma, Rico. I need you to stay close together, guys. Maybe we should all hold hands. And . . ." I'm here in my commands when they all turn and bolt in different directions, as if that had been my instruction. They are immediately lost in a mangy throng of middle schoolers in plaid uniforms. I scramble to recall that Maxi is wearing a purple velour dress and Rico a red tee shirt.

"Wait for me! Maxi, Emma, Rico!" Down an angled hallway, I see the backside of Henry's mom already hot in pursuit of her boys. And ahead of me I see a flash of purple round the corner past the exhibit marked, 'Seahorses.'

"Emma, Maxi, Rico. Wait." The end of the hall opens out into a dim room filled with dark caves. Whatever light there is leaks wanly from large aquarium tanks set into curving black walls made to look like stone.

I immediately plow into two dark-skinned adults dressed in black. Five minutes later, smack in the middle of a second curling cave with lighted aquaria on either side, I see two small girls standing on tiptoes to see into a shellfish's watery environs. It's small consolation when I recognize them as Aubrey and Xi, and realize they're equally chaperoneless. I've crossed half the place at a sprint when I see Maxi's purple dress round a corner into a chamber marked, 'Eels.' Panting I catch up with her. In their world, all is right. She laughs at Rico who has his tongue pressed to the dirty glass.

"Maxi, Rico. Where's Emma? Guys, where's Emma?" It is as if I weren't there at all. "Kids, look!" I exclaim. "Look at this Moray eel! Why it says, 'Moray eels live in shallow depths of tropical seas.' Isn't that amazing! Look he blinked! He's gonna do it again." Obliging, they stare at the lifeless plank of silver fish as I back carefully away.

"Watch him! Now stay right here. Do not move."

"Emma!" Panic rises in me like bile. Putting more distance between myself and the other two doesn't seem like a great idea, but right now I'm doing battle with the image of my little girl being hauled off by one of the other schools' bus drivers. In the right pinch any sitter will do. I think I hear my name. I do hear my name. I spin and run smack into Mrs. Slaughter. She has gallantly taken charge of Duncan, Eric and Saleem who has clearly been crying.

"Hello. How are you doing?" she asks.

"Fine. Good. Yes we're having a wonderful time. No one told me it was a race." It was a joke. I'm convinced that it's obvious my opinion of her has soured, so I over compensate with warmth.

Mrs. Slaughter frowns in reference to my solitude. Then she says, "So have you won, or lost?"

From behind her Duncan's face is stewing. "Mrs. Lansing. Whewe is Emma?"

Over his shoulder I see her. Smiling from ear to ear, she's splashing about in the drinking fountain. She's managed to soak her shirt through and spends the remainder of the trip whining about her wet shirt, stretching it away from her body and demanding in a loud, wheedling wail that I produce another dry, pink shirt from the cavity on my person where she's convinced I have secreted away not only her entire wardrobe but a whole cache of change. Because, unlike two of the other chaperones, who thumb coins into the junk-food vending-machine slot like they're at Harrah's Casino, I have brought no money for the machines or the gift shop. As a result, my charges and I part ways equally disenchanted with each other. On the way home Emma, Xi and I get the same, profane seat and I get a call from Blane.

I can hardly hear him. Aubrey and Maxi hang over the seat in front of us screaming at the girls on either side of me.

"The dryer blowed my skin. On my hands. It blowed my skin over."

"Can I see your phone?"

Small, dirty hands in my face.

"Where are you?" Blane says.

"I'm on a field trip," I holler into my phone.

"Are you serious?"

"I would never joke about something like that," I holler.

Draped over the seat, I wonder briefly if Maxi and Aubrey can read upside down. If they will arrive home from school bragging about the new words they learned. I toy with asking them their DRA's. And then I realize that, in this moment, I don't care.

Blane says something I can't hear.

"I can't hear you, I'm on a school bus."

He's charmed by the notion. "Oh my god. I could die," he sings. "That's so cute. Is it yellow?"

I tell him I'll call him back. The rest of the day the phrase, "Fuck you, bish," bangs around in my head.

Temple hoots at my story then wags a finger at me. "That's why you gotta wait 'til the third grade to be a chaperone," she says. "Plays. Symphonies. Plush seating."

"I don't have to use it in the spot. Just hold the box it comes in and talk about it."

"And it's a national?" The potential money is what it comes down to for Ted. Never mind about my sense of dignity. He's going to tell me to hock the douche if there's some solid coin in it.

"Yeah. I think so."

"Huh." He thinks for a moment. "Do you believe in it?"

"Do I believe in douching? No. I've never done it."

"Do you want to do it?"

"What, douche?"

"No. The spot."

"I don't know. I'm torn. What if I book it, and it runs nationally. So far so good. But they air it every weekday during Good Morning America and all our new friends see it?"

"Then they'll just think of you as clean. As cleaner. Right?"

"I don't think so. It's not a Q-tip."

"Well, then think of the dough. Ca-ching," he says. "What'd that be, like twenty-grand right?"

At six thirty in the morning, in a pre-coffee moment, I stand in front of my closet wondering what a douching woman likes to wear to, say, a nice-casual luncheon at Bennigan's. I'm pulling on my khakis when Emma comes in, flushed and whining. It's unusual for her to be up this early on her own and then she bark-coughs and I'm seized with a sort of panic. There was a birthday party on Saturday to celebrate the turning six of Haley. All the girls made Shrinkydinks, freeze danced and exchanged this nasty virus. For a moment, holding my ember of a girl on the edge of the bed in the dark, I agonize over whether to keep her home if her fever can be hidden, I mean – abated with Children's Motrin. Ted comes in to shower, puts his hand on her head and shrugs, "She feels fine. I'd send her."

In the end I can't. I can't send her. I dial the "safe phone" as instructed in the school manual to leave a message that Emma won't be in school. I hang up resentful that no one is congratulating me for following school rules to the letter. Someone should call back and say, 'Good For You' for keeping her home when she's marginally ill. 'Good For You' for remembering to call the attendance number and not the main office.

Now I'm stuck. Ted has a third meeting with the Mullen's Hardware people. It's an account he's sought since we moved here and he says they're on the verge of committing. Because her fever disappears within moments of sipping Motrin, and because she's jumping on a makeshift trampoline of piled couch cushions by the time they'd be discussing the day's weather in her class, I decide to bring her to work with me. I've brought her before in a pinch. But never when she's sick, and never to this particular casting director's office and, as I'm waiting for her to buckle her seat belt, it dawns on me, never to a douche audition.

Of course there's an accident on the expressway and traffic is eking along at a time of day when we should fly downtown. In fact I'd counted on flying downtown and now it's clear I'm going to be late. Emma's in the backseat humming the same tune over and over. I can't name what it is until I squish into the next lane and find us suddenly sandwiched between two semis. From the backseat I hear, "Wake up in the morning feelin' like P. Diddy. Before I leave brush my teeth with a bottle of Jack. La-la-la-la-la-la, I ain't comin' back."

"Where'd you here that song?"

"Maxi teached it. Karla hased it on her pod." She coughs. Then asks, "What's Jack?"

"Well . . ."

Four seconds of silence pass in our hemmed in automobile. And then, as I'd hoped, Emma returns to humming."

In the octagonal waiting room a large framed movie poster from the Charlie's Angels remake hangs over the exposed brick. Three actresses are already seated, waiting. The room is tiny. Large enough only to hold a small table containing the sign-in sheet and a pencil nub, and the eight chairs that line the perimeter. Douching women must feel confident in khakis because all of us have them on. Emma gets a robust burst of attention from the actresses when we enter. They all are clearly unaccustomed to children, and they shoot us mugging, gleaming-white smiles. A woman caked with makeup a shade too dark for her own skin says to me, "She's adorable."

And then Emma lets loose with her magnificent barking cough, spewing it out into the middle of the tiny room. The germy droplets are visible in a fine conical mist in front of her mouth. The woman who's just spoken, recoils in a literal knee jerk response, and then goes back to studying the paper on her lap.

"Cover your mouth, Em," I say quietly patting her leg. And she does in a gesture so belated, it's meaningless. After mouthing some words down into her lap, the made-up woman lifts her head. Her eyes have the fuzzy gaze of the daydreamer but her brow is crunched in empathy. When she speaks it is as if she is alone, or crazy or both. In an emotional whisper she brings her hand to her heart and says, "Vaginal itching got you down?"

Emma falls asleep in the car on the way home. My cell rings. It's Ted fresh from his meeting.

"How'd it go?" I ask.

"Great. They asked for a contract. They didn't sign yet. But they've got it. Mullen himself took it. Slid it into the side pocket of his briefcase. Looked me right in the eye when he shook my hand. Said he'd be in touch. Can't do any better than that."

"Excellent."

"How 'bout your thing."

"Great." Laced with sarcasm. "All these women in the waiting room talking about this Spring Morning Douche. I kept trying to correct them while shooting little glances at Emma. 'You mean poofs, right?' It was fine. Most of them caught on. They thought it was very funny. Coming out of the audition room this one leggy model squealed, 'The *poof* people liked me, they really did. They liked me!'"

"Hey Jen, what's the name of Emma's Kindergarten teacher?"

"Mrs. Slaughter. You know that."

"Right. I knew it was something like that. I saw her today. And I'm racking my brain. Slay. Butcher. Murder. I know it's none of those. So I end up doing a, 'Hey! Hi. How are you?' With far more enthusiasm than if I'd remembered her name in the first place."

"Where'd you see her?"

"She was parked behind Mullen's. Her passenger door lock was frozen and I helped her with it. Little WD40. No problem."

"What was she doing behind Mullen's?"

"Don't know. Trying to fix her door, I guess. I got so lucky, Jen. I was just seeing if there was anything on top in their trash for my meeting. And they had a guy, an employee that dumped his own Master Card receipts from his wallet into their garbage. They were on top. I mean it wasn't even a customer's data. Can you believe it?" I could see him raking his hair in amazement.

"Ted, you were rummaging in their trash when you saw Mrs. Slaughter?"

"No. Just going through what was on top."

"Did she *see* you going through the trash?"

"Yeah. I just said that."

That afternoon I play fourteen games of Candyland with Emma. Every fiber of my being longs to be doing something else; Swiffering the floor, cleaning behind the toilet. Anything. Temple, on the other hand, is appalled that I gave Emma Motrin and kept her home.

"If you're *sending* them to school you give the Motrin, darlin'. If you're keeping them home, withhold it, that way they just loll around all day and you can get shit done. Then again I haven't been able to even look at the school nurse in years. Not since I nearly killed a child in her office."

"You didn't."

"I did. Back when Karla was in fifth I sent her to school even though I knew she was comin' down with somethin'. You never can tell the speed of onset. Thought I still had at least a whole school day. Anyway. I get a call from the nurse to come get her, and I go in and this other little girl was bawlin' her eyes out with her mouth hangin' open. All I did was tell her to take a deep breath. She did, through her nose. Now how was I supposed to know she'd stuck a pencil eraser up there. That inhale launched it all the way up to her brain. I think the nurse broke somethin' screamin' at me."

February 6th

Large, laminated, cartoon drawings of past presidents line the
school hallway: jolly, jovial guys with multiple chins and pater-
nal wrinkles. *Hello . . .*I cover the name at the bottom to test my
memory. Seconds tick past. It's hopeless. I can't name him. I take
my hand away to reveal the name: James Polk! *Hello, James Polk.*
The next grizzled dude turns out to be Zachary Taylor. Who the
heck are these guys? Sometimes grade school seems to illuminate
all that I've forgotten. It's just the beginning, I know. Soon my
daughter will come home with complicated questions about this
historical battle or that dangling participle and I will be revealed
for what I am: a fraud. A fraud who has, in a box, a college diploma
I must've stolen. Or perhaps I sent off all these historical facts in
a weedy haze of bong emission, ironically, in college. How does a
parent handle this when the real homework starts? Like next year.
Maybe I should enroll in grade school as well, in the grade just
ahead, so I'm prepared. I'll drop off Emma and instead of leaving,
I'll catch the rear stairs up to my homeroom where I'll squeeze into
a little desk in the back and learn all the stuff that I've forgotten.
That way when she says, "Mom, can you help with this page of
fractions?" I'll say, "Why certainly love, let me see them." As if
it was a shoe to tie. A water glass to fill. Something that renews
my sense of competence not tears it to shreds, which is the future

I face now if I don't learn some things. And fast. Then another thing about college comes back to me: I wonder if there are Cliffs Notes for grades one through five?

In the backpack today:

A red heart cut out of construction paper

Emma's lunch box containing a snack-sized bag of miniature carrots and an unopened single serve applesauce with plastic spoon

A math sheet with drawings of a penny, a nickel and a dime

A snowman painting

The 100th day project, homework assignment:

It reads, "February 12th is the hundredth day of school. Please help your child make a poster-board project using 100 items. Please group the items in tens."

"Emma, honey. Come on. We've got a project to do!"

"You're gonna let Emma help you?" Ted asks.

"What do you mean?"

"I mean you do tend to take over."

"That was just the Valentines. There were twenty-two of them."

"And twenty-two pink ribbons to tie around the accompanying heart pencils."

"It was either ribbon or a rubber band. I wanted them to look nice."

"Exactly," Ted says.

I turn to Emma, "Sweetie, what would *you* like to use for your 100 things? We could use, coins or paper clips or . . ."

"Candy."

So I buy two jumbo bags of M&Ms and two sheets of poster board. At home I present her with the choice of the pink poster board or the white poster board. She looks from one to the other and she leaves. When she returns, she's carrying an eight-by-ten piece of grey shirt cardboard from the dry cleaner.

"Are you sure you want to use that for your project, sweetie?"
Ted is in the next room so I raise my voice to announce, "It's *your*
project so, okay, that looks good!" Process, not product, right?

I set her up in the family room as Pinky Dinky Doo fills the TV
and the announcer says, "The following program builds kinesthetic
awareness and exposure to spatial relationships." Partly because I'm
unable to define what that means, it gives me great pleasure to turn
her off. My gusto for the project is inflated to make up for Emma's
lack of it. "Now, would you like to do a design? You could do a face?
Or, we could make words or numbers!"

She picks up the Elmer's and squeezes a silky white puddle onto
the middle of the cardboard.

"Or, good! You could just put that great big glob of Elmer's
right there in the middle." I am careful to keep my composure here.
"Okay now, Emma, how many M&Ms do you need for that first pile?"

"Ten," she says confidently.

"Ten. Good! Oooonnnne. Twoooooooo."

It's important to note here, that hovering over her work, I've as-
sembled my entire body to be passively supportive and encouraging:
A slight smile plays about my lips, my chin is at rest in my fingers.
And here comes my perky inner cheerleader with the cute upturned
nose, and slashing arm movements. "Good job Emma! Niiiiiiiine,
Teeeeen, Elev . . ."

Her pudgy finger nudges an eleventh M&M into the first pile.
Then she pops an orange one into her mouth. Patiently, sweetly, I ask
in my most melodic of voices, "Emma? Are you sure you want to put
that M&M in that pile? Don't you maybe want to start another pile?"

She chews and turns to stare at the dark TV as if any moment Pinky
will reappear. "What do you think, Emma?" This is what I say to her,
but what I think is, *You can't put that one in that pile! You've got to start
another pile!* Here, in my fantasy, I shove her off the stool, and the voice
in my head screams, *Move over! Let me do it. Let me do it. Let me do it!*

Quickly I redraw the blind of my own composure, declare the counted pile off limits for eating, tease her away from the dark TV, and get her turned towards her project, though her interest in it has suddenly circled the drain. I am left counting with an increased vehemence as if I could with my manic words reignite some fervor here.

"Thirty eiiiiight. Thirty Niiiiiiine."

After twenty minutes another part of me realizes, this is really boring. I am suddenly bone tired, numb with lethargy, and I can't help checking out. In super-slow-motion Emma is coaxing a green M&M from our main pile into the third puddle on her page. As I cast about the paneled room that is our 1970's family room I stifle my fifty-third yawn and think that maybe I should paint this room sage. Emma is passing the time waiting for my response by tunneling up her nostril with her pinky.

"Forty. Good girl!"

On the fifth pile the Elmer's bottle will only cough up weezy farts. I call Temple to see if I can borrow some glue. She's silent for awhile, considering.

"We're usin' it for that freakin' project, darlin'. I'd love to share, but I don't think there's even enough for ours."

The declaration miffs me. If the need were reversed I'd cough up some glue for her. In the car moving rapidly towards the drugstore not six blocks away, I have the urge to keep going. To put miles in between myself and the project. My rational mind watches me driving, all knotted up, knuckles white on the wheel and tsks. It's silly I know, but I've been imprisoned by this assignment. And I cannot or will not relax until the homework is done. When I arrive back at home, Emma and Ted are playing Uno. The game has taken the place of the project on the table.

"Project time!" I sing holding up my enticing fresh bottle of white Elmer's school glue.

"Hang on," Ted says. "Someone's about to beat me here." He winks at Emma.

Em holds three cards in her hands compared to Ted's six. She discards and giggles.

"What? No fair." Ted puts on a pout.

On the next turn Emma calls, "Uno," and Ted has a fit. A mock fit. Much to Emma's delight he puffs and blusters and grabs her, pulling her onto the floor. Then he tickles her relentlessly above both hips. She erupts into breathless giggles. I pull out onions and garlic to start the chili for dinner. And after three, "Daddy stops," I interrupt with, "Ted, when she says, 'Stop,' you've got to stop." And I can't help adding, "Em. Let's finish your homework."

From the floor Ted says, "Homework. Boo!" And gives me a double thumbs down.

"Homework Boo!" copies Emma. They have in their little devil-may-care, fun-loving conspiracy made me the evil taskmaster. It's deeply unfair, this assignment.

"Why don't you finish it with her, Ted?"

"Me? No. You're doing a hell of a – heck of a job."

"I'm not doing it, Emma is."

"Yeah, that's what I meant." He hops up, grabs his elbow and brings it across his chest, stretching. I'm going for a run."

"Da-ddy. Da-ddy. Da-ddy." Emma bounces on the couch in time to her chant. I slice and slash the onions into teeny tiny bits. When I finish, the two of them are standing over the already counted pile, picking out brown M&Ms and popping them into their mouths.

It's too late when we try again. We ate dinner so long ago we're already farting from the chili beans, and I'm waiting for Ted to finish his shower before I start hand-washing the dishes because only one faucet at a time gets hot water. We should've started this project days before. Now I know. It's past Emma's bedtime and we've been at it again for twenty minutes. Ted comes in wearing flannel pants and stands in front of the open refrigerator door. Then he opens the freezer as well. From where I'm sitting I can feel the room temperature decline by several degrees. The effort of withholding comment makes me want to weep. Instead I say, "What comes after 89?"

Emma yawns: a long, indulgent, open-mouthed breathing in.

"What comes after 89?" I am a broken record. "What comes after 89?" She stares at the candy. Her eyes are watery. The propulsion of words gathers steam. It cannot be stopped. Suddenly I'm screeching, "NINETY! Emma. Ninety, ninety, ninety!"

The second the project is done, the weight of the world is lifted from my shoulders. And we set the soggy cardboard on the kitchen counter to dry. After a few minutes it's clear that candy coatings and Elmer's are completely, chemically, at odds with each other. The candy coating that's touching the glue gives way and runs in muddy rivulets into other islands or off the cardboard entirely. And the whole thing refuses to dry, as if the candy coatings have altered the fixative property of the Elmer's multi-purpose school glue. At nine-thirty that night there's a tap on the front door. Temple waves a bottle of Elmer's at me through the peephole. I am filled with guilt-propelled affection.

"Sorry. Maxi just finished."

"Just now?"

"Yeah. She had to use freakin' hair. One hundred human hairs of all things. It worked out cause after an hour I was pulling mine out. Literally." She scratches her head.

"Yeah. Glad it's over."

"It's not over. It's just beginning. You think this one's tough, just wait until fifth grade. They have to make an entire freakin' bridge out of popsicle sticks. Turns out half the parents in Karla's class are engineers. Like that is fair. We had to hire that firm White, Ellis, Carlson and Pope to help with hers."

I laugh and she screws her mouth up in such a way that I am left unsure if she's kidding.

Overnight I root for Emma's little project like it's the Charlie Brown Christmas tree. And in the morning we walk to school. Emma holds her project out in front like she's delivering the host in a gallon Ziploc. I am her bodyguard, tensed and agile as a cat – ready to strike out at anyone who comes within a six-foot radius of us. We cross at the crossing guard giving his swinging STOP sign wide berth.

Duncan, hand on his little package inside his snowpants, swaggers up close to Emma craning at her project through the Ziploc and I slip between them.

"Hi, Duncan. Good morning!" I chose these words instead of *get the fuck away from us*, as is my silent wont.

His face screws up into his question, "Is that her pwoject?"

No it's her project is what I think, but what I say is, "Why, yes kiddo it is. Where is yours Duncan?"

"My mom has it," he says, as his hand shoots out towards Emma's soggy board. But I intercept with a quick clap on his tiny wrist. "No honey, don't touch it. It's not quite dry yet."

He screws up his face at me as if he's staring directly into the sun and he says, "Then how is the teachew going to hang it up?"

I look down at Emma, "Sweetie, this is the first I've heard anything about hanging it up." My stomach sinks. A capital 'D' dances in my head. All that effort down the tubes. Once inside the school, I march Emma down the warm hallway. We're the very first ones into the classroom. There's a little space on the radiator and we set her project down on it.

"Excuuuse me!" It's the clarion call of Duncan's mom who wields a huge project over head with both hands like she's delivering an extra-large, meat-lovers pizza. "Hi, Emma's mom," she sings. "Excuse me. If you could just clear a little . . .100th day of School Project coming through." She's wearing a tight skirt with a flounced hem. It swishes back and forth when her ass moves from side to as she guides Duncan's project in for a landing next to ours.

I look back and forth between the two projects. On her huge, pristine piece of white poster board are ten glorious balloons formed of multicolored beads, perfectly affixed and eager to hang vertically. Proud to do it. Mighty proud to do it. In a Coach shopping bag dangling from her wrist are twenty-two pairs of 3-D glasses for better viewing of the project. She's looking at Emma's runny glob. "That one is cute!" she says showing her wilted smile. "But did someone spill something on it?" She turns on a heel. "Mrs. Slaughter, someone has spilled something over here!"

And off she taps to speak to Mrs. Slaughter who is kneeling on the floor helping Duncan put the contents back in his spilled lunch box and fending off children who are grappling over a small, metallic bag of Sponge Bob fruit gushers. Three other children play tug of war with a six-foot and growing, pink-knit scarf.

As I make my way to the door I take in the other projects as they're delivered. One has 100 pennies taped to a huge green poster board. Together they shape of the words 100th Day of School! Another is a little flower garden made of multicolored buttons.

"Hey Jen." Temple is before me, an actual pizza box thrust over her head. Maxi is beside her, her head tilted back on her neck.

"Mob, mob, mob," Maxi bleats. Temple ignores her and speaks to me out of the corner of her mouth.

"How'd yours turn out?"

"Fine." I lie.

"Really? This was a total pain in the ass."

"Moooob." Maxi revs the word in an annoying wheedle.

"What. Jesus." Temple snaps at her.

"You said I could see it when you were done," Maxi whines.

"Oh, all right but don't touch it."

Temple pops out the cardboard tabs and lifts the top revealing dark hairs whirled around each other in looping cursive to form the letters ONE HUNDRED. Ten. Ten perfectly scripted letters crafted out of mousey dark, human hairs. Now who did this I wonder? Your snuffling six-year-old squatting over the banquette? I think not.

At least I'm spared having to respond. Temple's off hunting for a special place to park her art.

Duncan's mom sidesteps the scarf tug-of-war and talks to the top of Mrs. Slaughter's head. "Did I tell you about Duncan and his 'Flash Skills' books?" When she says, "Flash Skills," she lights up. Her hand opens and she seems to paint a magical picture in the air. "He's nearly done with the series." She stops here as if expecting an impressed response to fall into the pause she's made. Then she continues, "With all seven of them. And our plan is to donate them to the classroom when we're finished."

Mrs. Slaughter rises on the word 'donate' and composes herself. I give Emma a hard, compensatory kiss on the top of her head. In full possession now of his Spiderman Lunch box and all its contents, Duncan throws his hand in the air and pipes, "Raise your hand if you've ever bawfed on your front steps on the way to school."

Duncan's mom falls fast to her son's side and clamps her hand over his mouth. Then she throws her head back in hooting laughter. "What? What you did this morning? That! That bit of spit up? I wouldn't call that throwing up, Duncan. I'd call that an allergy to cinnamon. Yessirree."

She has a vice grip on his shoulder and she smoothes his hair with her other hand. "Besides, you were just excited. Excited to turn in your project. Excited for school!"

Holding his chin then she looks into his face – her eyes wide. "Now remember," she says, "Mommy has a meeting with a client who's coming all the way from San Francisco this morning, so if for any reason you have to visit the nurse," she loads her eyes and cocks them at the boy, "try to wait until this afternoon, 'kay?"

At the door Mrs. Slaughter clutches my elbow and says, "Emma's Mom, you do know that candy in the school is against our wellness policy." My first thought is Margaret's box. My face burns. That was so long ago. The beginning of the school year. Has Margaret been talking? Have I been implicated somehow? Might it affect Emma's career here? I am shot through with determination suddenly to right my wrong. And then I breathe and realize that Mrs. Slaughter is staring at the gloppy puddle that is Emma's project.

All day I pray for the staying power of Emma's hundred things. I fend off images of the M&M's hard-shell coating dissolving in Elmer's. One by one they plummet to the floor falling on their still colorful backs, clicking as they land, belly-up, like shirtless suicides. After school I pour Emma a snack of leftover M&Ms. And I brace myself. "So, Em, did Mrs. Slaughter hang up your project today?" I ask.

And she looks up, completely unaware that her project is the Hyundai in the Lexus lot. She shakes her head from side to side. "No," she says, an astonished smile lay across her face, like I'd asked if she wanted to wait until later to open her birthday presents.

"Well, maybe she'll do it tomorrow."

This is what I say to her, but what I think is . . . *You just wait kiddo! In a few years we'll be in fifth grade and, I, am going to build you the best-damned bridge Jefferson School has ever seen!*

March 3rd

The following week a pall settles over the school. Usually children's voices drift from the classrooms and an errant child or two bounds down the first floor hallway going to or from the restroom. Not today. Today there's an unsettling quiet as in an over-shushed library. A large sign inside the main door reads, "Quiet please. Testing in process." In the lobby the fountain brigade SIC committee directs two men with low-slung tool belts and extended tape measures in a furious pantomime. Together they study a patch of terrazzo in the lobby center. In the office I sign in and peel off a Visitor nametag from a roll of them. Mrs. Gravely, the secretary, turns her back to me. She's on the phone sharing some complaint in an indignant series of "Umm Hmmms." "You know what I'm sayin'?" "Ummm Hmmm." A finger holds closed the ear that isn't listening to the caller. On a wall above the teacher mailboxes, a list of classrooms and their corresponding parent volunteers is posted. I'm assigned to a third grade room on the second floor.

In room 207 the dark circled eyes of weary, large children flick up to my face in solemn greeting. Although it's only March, several of the boys wear long shorts. Pippa, the PTA lady, is here at the front of the room, and I immediately steel myself for a shit job. I identify the teacher by her lanyard and the stack of test packets clamped to her chest. Awaiting further instruction, I stand pressed against a back wall between a chart of the periodic table of elements and a cartooned pepperoni pizza divided into sixths, as a line of eight-year-olds clutching number two pencils forms at the pencil sharpener in the corner.

"Thank god I'm not late." A squat mother in a jean skirt and thick hose breezes into the classroom. A Trader Joe's reusable bag is draped over her shoulder. Her rubbing legs make a zipping sound and with her wafts a fresh orange blossom scent. Briefly, I wonder if she's a doucher. She's relieved to see me in all my waiting purposelessness.

"No. They haven't started." I smile, but her attentions land on an equally doughy girl across the room. At the girl's desk, the mother retrieves a bottle of vitamin infused water from her bag. Then she sinks beside the girl and produces a box of raisins and a snack-sized Ziploc full of almonds. The girl seizes them, shoveling handfuls of both into her mouth at once. At the front Pippa says a few words to the teacher, then straps on her broad smile, claps her hands and tells the class to stand. Kids slide, smooth as snakes, from their seats.

"Raise your hands to the sky," Pippa says with evangelical brightness, stretching her arms over her head so high her layered tanks creep up over the top of her yoga pants. "Go ahead. Touch that sun." The other adults participate but it makes me feel silly. Especially when she folds at the waist, places her palms flat on the floor and instructs us to do the same. I see the floor. I aim for the floor. I wave at the floor.

"Now touch that floor. Go ahead. Now bounce and sway. Release all that anxiety. Let it just shoot out of your fingertips. There you go." Some of the boys seek each other's upside down faces, shoot at each other with their fingers, and laugh. One, who has come to school with a cold, begins to cough. The calisthenics last until the moment the test is to begin. The teacher glides past desks planting test packets face down in front of the students. Officiousness suddenly rules, and the kids slide back into their chairs and twiddle their pencils in anticipation. One by one they fall as silent and wide-eyed as cattle before the brand.

"Last chance to sharpen pencils," the teacher announces, and who pops up but the snack bringing mom with two blunted number twos in her fist. Without looking at us she makes for the sharpener, nose first, zipping between desks. The teacher finishes distributing over the whining grind of the woman's efforts at the sharpener. As if reading my mind, Pippa is beside me to explain. After watching the woman's legs zipper back to her seat, Pippa looks at me and draws an air circle next to her ear while crossing her eyes. When she speaks it's from the side of her mouth. "Her name is Arial so she thought it'd be cute to name all her kids after other fonts. She's got Georgia in first and Verdana in preschool. That's Lucinda. Apparently Arial lobbied the school board for the right to take the ISATs so she'd know better how to prepare the younger kids for it over the summer months."

"Really? Why? I thought they only used the test scores to evaluate the teachers."

"That's the rumor, or the pitch anyway. Come fourth they use the results to track and place your kid."

An hour into the test I see a hand in the air.

"Yes."

"I need to go to the bathroom."

I grant permission and Arial squeezes out from her desk, rubs her eyes and zippers out of the classroom.

All in all, it's an easy day. As boring as Candyland until, with twenty minutes left in the session, the whole school awakens with the sound of a jackhammer. Pippa bolts from the room and returns in silence, rolling her eyes at the audacity of the SIC committee. I should've brought a book. And given that so far I have nothing going on downtown the rest of the week, I stop into the Principal's office on my way out to see if I can do another shift. It's a strategic bit of volunteerism. The kind that may put me in good standing with Otis, but avoid the scorn of other mothers. I've heard snatches about the first grade teachers and want (and want Emma) to remain visible for the best placement.

A crater the size of a basketball has been blasted into the lobby floor. And a makeshift fence of caution tape surrounds it. In her office Principal Otis is on the phone but waves me into the seat in front of her desk. She looks tired. As she listens, she pulls a small bottle of Zicam nasal spray from her drawer, sticks it up her nose and inhales deeply. The moment so vividly recalls to me my second boyfriend. He possessed a keen interest in anything that could go into his nose. Cocaine. Afrin. A series of piercings. The bit with the Zicam is somehow too intimate to watch, so I busy myself staring outside. Hand in hand a mother and listless girl I recognize as Xi head away from the school. At the sidewalk intersection Xi stops and throws up.

"Just the fifth grade. Okay." I'd forgotten Otis was on the phone. "And boys and girls? Or just the boys? Both? Okay. Are girl gangs that much of a problem? . . . Really. Okay then you can have the whole grade."

She hangs up and smiles at me. "Sorry."

"It's fine. I was just upstairs, with the third grade, helping with ISATs. And if you want, I can do Thursday too."

"You'll have to check with Pippa. She does the schedule." She sniffs deeply and grows reverent. Don't know what we'd do without that woman.

March 16th

Our second parent teacher conference falls mid-March at the end of a week when I'm auditioning every day. My immersion in my own work has the added benefit of making me more objective about Emma's school year. Even though the participation section of her spring report card comes home as blank as it was in the fall, I'm confident in my new, professional resolve. Also, I'm steeled for this conference, armed with a fist full of internet research on Selective Mutism to disprove Emma's candidacy. I have a whole speech that I crafted from earlier notes and I'm determined to be brisk and unsentimental.

Ted stops at the classroom door to great the class guinea pig. He talks to the rodent like he's the friend on the bar stool opposite. "Hey, Snowball. How you doin', man? Furry-paw high-five?" His cage directed chatter siphons off my drive as I sink into the tiny chair. I should have brought my own full-sized foldable chair like to a soccer game. Mrs. Slaughter is amused, studying Ted from behind. He realizes we're ready to begin and plops himself down beside us. What opens up is a sinkhole of small talk. *Thanks so much again for unfreezing her car door. How windy is it? Can hear the rope clanging against the flagpole in front of the school from her classroom.* Hand cupped to her ear. *Blah, blah, blah. Do you have conferences all evening? Oh, too bad. What? Missing a huge sale at Pier One. That's unfortunate.* Chatty, finger-cookies-and-English-Breakfast-Tea small talk. I hold myself apart, staying quiet. In my head I'm rehearsing my spiel. Fanning my resolve like damp kindling. Assessing the moments for the proper opportunity to jump in and engineer a turn in the conversation towards the productive. Suddenly Mr. Klein looms in the doorway wielding his scuffed attaché.

"Hey gang. Sorry for the delay." He blusters into the room as another woman appears in the door. She is harried and demurring with wispy, flyaway hair held in place by several inadequate bobby pins. Her face is ruddy and her nose sports a spidery collection of broken blood vessels. In her arms a messy pile of papers threatens to dump. Mrs. Slaughter stands at the woman's entrance. "Mrs. Willis. So glad you could join us. Mrs. Willis is our wonderful speech therapist." Ted rises off his tiny chair in greeting.

"I think we're all here, now." This arrival was what Slaughter was stalling for, the massing of her supporting troops. I sense an ambush and wish we'd brought more people along. Suddenly my own paltry pile of research on recycled printer paper is no match for the warm-bodied accumulation before me. Mrs. Slaughter jumps right in. "We think would be useful to contemplate the idea of a second year of Kindergarten for Emma."

"Okay," Ted says carefully. "Why?"

"Well," Mrs. Slaughter begins then hands off the conversational football to Mr. Klein with a gesture. "The team agrees." Here there are vigorous nods from the other side of the table.

"Whose team?"

"The team that drew up Emma's plan."

"She has a team?" Ted says to me.

"This is her team," Mrs. Slaughter says. "Principal Otis also wanted badly to be here but she's ill."

"Let me thay thomething here." When she speaks, Mrs. Willis's voice proves to be a nasal whine that works its way around the chambers of her sinuses before coming forth from her mouth. She is also unable to produce a proper 'S'. It's a worked-on lisp, one that could almost pass for corrected speech, unless you're looking directly at her, as we are now. "We should examine hearing loth. Have her evaluated for that. Early ear infectionth can contribute mightily to thith thort of inability to form letterth and complete thententheth." She clears her throat and looks down at the paper on top. "Kidth teathe too. Itth horrible. Becauthe Caroline ith difficult to underthtand, her confidence hath taken a beating. Covering her armth and legth with the glue ith a diverthion."

Despite the interrupting gape of Slaughter's mouth, Willis plows on. "We don't want her to thtop thpeaking because she'th afraid to. That would be bad. But we can prevent that through interventhion." Happy to have the floor: to have five heads in the room turned towards her, she seems primed and delighted to continue with her contribution.

"Emma Lansing. These are *Emma's* parents," Mrs. Slaughter interjects. Confused, and flushed, Mrs. Willis scrabbles among her papers.

"Ith that the Mutithm kid?"

"Right," booms Klein, shifting in his seat. "Selective Mutism. Unwillingness to talk in certain settings like school." He makes a slurping noise here. A sip without a beverage.

Slaughter continues, "We agree that her silence at this point might mean she's simply not ready to move up. That would obviously be *your* decision to make with the aid of a speech therapist and perhaps some additional testing. But Emma's a dear. I'd love to have her next year as my special helper. You know, she loves Snowball. I could tell her that I need to keep her in my class to take care of him next year."

"So her punishment for being shy is that she has to attend to the needs of a rodent for nine months while the rest of her class goes on to math facts and trendier clothes?" My voice quavers here. "I really don't think she has Selective Mutism. I've done some online research and . . ."

"Online?" Klein repeats with a pejorative sneer.

"Yes, and . . ."

"I think," Ted interrupts seeking the bottom of this. "What I hear you saying is that she's beyond shy. Am I right?"

Again the vigorous nodding of heads. When she speaks, Mrs. Slaughter directs her comments to Ted, and Ted alone. My dissention has rendered me superfluous. "Selective Mutism per se, is not a diagnosis the school is equipped to make. For that you'll have to seek some outside support. Get her evaluated by an SLP. That's your next step."

"I got a name if you need one." Klein reclines in his chair and rubs his man boobs with his palms. "He's only got one foot. Lost the other in a tussle with an ATV. Don't think I need to tell you who won. He keeps his pants pinned below the ankle on that leg. Sometimes that's distracting for the younger kids, but if you're game, I'm sure he'll give Emma a hand."

Ted's is the sole laugh.

Slaughter leans forward, pointing towards the blank section of Emma's report card. "She needs to ask and answer questions in class. I need to *hear* from her to determine what she knows."

"What about the dominoes at show and tell? She talked in front of the class. She did. She told us the entire story of the dominoes. Passing them around. Saleem farting. We're missing the blank ones because she gave them away."

The phalanx of them; teacher, speech therapist and social worker let me run out of steam, each blinking in a deliberate and patient way, sharing the same bland smile. At the end they link eyes and Slaughter cedes to Mr. Klein whom, with his billiard ball focus, tips his chair back and explains that these fantasies on the part of child are to be expected. "It's their wish – to be verbal."

"So you're saying she made it up?"

"Yeth . . . Afraid tho." Mrs. Willis touches her hair and nods, in a vigorous way she's not entitled to, and that, more than anything launches me.

"She didn't show the dominos?"

"She showed," Slaughter allows, "but said nothing. When it was her turn to share, she held the box aloft from her desk and then set them back down without saying a word."

Tears nip painfully behind my eyes. I stand from my chair with clumsy difficulty and escape the table, dropping words as I go. "Well . . . that is not how Emma recounted it to us. She told us both that . . ."

"What do you do for work, Mrs. . . . ." Here Mr. Klein has his own desperate turning of papers. I fight for composure watching him.

"It's Lansing."

"Right. Lansing."

"I am an actress." Facing them all I straighten my back, gathering my spilled pride. "But I don't see what . . ."

"So you do know what it's like to make things up? And you, sir, what's the ole line of labor?" Mr. Klein smiles and turns his face to Ted, while his eyes travel the four-leaf clover cutouts suspended from the clothesline that bisects the room.

"You don't have to answer." Mrs. Slaughter jumps on Ted's response.

"It's been a tough year, for the family," she says for us.

"He has a job. We both do. We're self-employed." My voice is shrill.

"Yes," they all coo at once, in a way that says they understand the oxymoron that is this concept and, as a result, feel inordinately sorry for us. Behind this too, is the unspoken accusation; that our 'tough year' is to blame for Emma's silence.

"All the more reason," Mr. Klein says with the lilt of a punch line. Inside his briefcase he lays Emma's file on top. Then he fastens both snaps closed. It's some sort of signal. A concluding flourish. At his gesture Mrs. Willis picks up the top sheets of her messy pile and, without real effect, attempts to square them by jumping the edges on the tabletop.

"Really. We have jobs. Ted's in identity theft."

"I'm a consultant. I educate small businesses on how to properly dispose of sensitive documents, credit card slips. Employee files. Etcetera." He's fine-tuned his pitch. It fits him well now.

"Do you shred?" Mrs. Slaughter asks over her lenses. As with all her questions, it's unclear whether she's for, or against.

"I do. We shred everything that comes into our home that has our name and address on it."

"My huthband bought one at Walmart. It jamth. All the time."

"It can – if you feed in too many sheets at once."

"Thix. It thays thix, but it doethn't take thix. You have to do one at a time."

"I've been meaning to get one of those shredder things ever since James Dickerson-Hale brought one in for show and tell last year," Mrs. Slaughter pipes.

"We can get you set up," Ted offers. "The important feature is cross cut. You don't want a strip shredder. Thieves can put those babies back together in no time."

"Really?"

"Yup," Ted says, "Hey, can I ask you, how many kids in this room speak Spanish?" It's a careening digression for which I'm im-

mensely grateful. Never mind that I've prepared considered answers to all the questions we faced at Emma's conference in the fall. I have even compiled a detailed list of things that Emma has told us about school. But now I'm willing to sacrifice the sharing of any of it for a speedy conclusion. Slow to process, I'm still working on 'SLP.' That one wasn't in Nicole's list of acronyms. Of course, if I'd finished college, I'd be able to match the acronym to the correct specialist in a nanosecond. This thought comes from nowhere. Stunned and bullied by it, I reach down for the back of a blue tiny chair at a table apart from the rest of the gang and sink low into it.

"None. No one speaks Spanish. Why?" Slaughter blinks at Ted.

"The labels. English / Spanish."

"It's the exposure." Slaughter leans in here. Ted is the lucky recipient of a secret.

"You know, the other teachers don't do it. But I think it's beneficial to expose the kids to a different language. It makes them curious. Shows them there's something else out there beyond their own little world. Besides, I'm a huge fan of ethnicy things. Other languages. Anything tribal. Bamboo. I love skin with some dark tones to it. And I don't mean tanned. In fact, I volunteered to take both the ESL kids in my class." She pushes up her sleeve to reveal a silver cuff adorned with hieroglyphs. "And this is from Laos."

"You've been to Laos?"

"No. I got it on Ebay."

"So the Spanish is just for show." He crosses his arms in disapproval.

"Exposure," corrects Slaughter.

"Thi," says Mrs. Willis, making a joke that everyone ignores.

"It's like the multiplication table." Slaughter points to the wall behind the bank of mailboxes bearing each child's name. Over them hangs a multiplication chart. The numbers are an unnaturally bright royal blue. "The other teachers on my team don't have that in their rooms either. But I think, when multiplication and division come 'round to greet them for real in second grade they'll think: *Wait a minute. This looks familiar. I know this!* And inside, they'll thank me."

March 21st

On the days that I can accompany her to school now, Emma walks a half a block ahead of me. I am superfluous: the tenth bridesmaid following the bride. She rounds the corner and disappears from sight. I think it is in those moments, when she's turned the corner and I haven't, that she grows up and I learn to let go of her a little. Maybe this is also when her little nuggets of baby teeth loosen their grip a bit, preparing to relinquish their miniature dominion over her mouth.

We have one freaky day where the temperature climbs near seventy. Temple and I gather the kids together and on the way home they pull ahead on the sidewalk.

"It's so warmb," Maxi squeals swinging on her mother's arm.

"W-A-R-M. Warm," Temple spells while watching a sparrow land on an empty cement planter in someone's yard. But it used to be C-O-L-D," she spells distractedly.

"Whee," squeals Maxi, lifting her feet off the ground.

Temple hauls her daughter up by the hand and looks her in the face. "Maxi. The word."

"Oh, cold!" Maxi shouts and she throws her head backwards as Temple lowers her to the ground. The rest of the way home Maxi and Emma fight over who should bring home Snowball over break.

Starting two weeks before, solicitations for the guinea pig's vacation home have come home in the backpack. The last one was written as if from the pig itself. "Please help me find someone to love me over break." Beneath the sentence was a crude drawing of what was supposed to be a forlorn guinea pig. Only the artist had given him thick eyebrows. The end result was a vicious rendering whose real-life counterpart would be the last thing you'd want glaring at you from the cage on the floor next to your kitchen table. But then, I was a half hour late for the douche spot callback because Emma had to find a light blue skirt in her closet. Emma doesn't own a light blue skirt and after twenty-two agonizing, tempus-fugit minutes of her tantrum, I lost my temper. Before me, I saw the opportunity to land a national douche spot vanish. Whipping the skirt hangers off her closet rod I'd shouted, "Pink, Flowered, Another pink, magenta, purple. That's it, damn it. That's all we've got. Pick one." And I'd hurled them all on the bed and left the room.

That afternoon, still guilty from the morning, I caved. I met Emma at school. Without meeting Slaughter's eyes I told her that we'd take the pig. Then I looked squarely at Emma and added, "Under one condition: his cage stays in the basement."

An hour later we're positioning the cage on one side of the workbench opposite the vice. Of course the thing stank. Would you clean the cage if you knew you were handing him off in a week? Ted was miffed I didn't consult. "It's getting a pet, Jen. This is a family decision."

"It's babysitting a pet, Ted. I didn't commit to adopting a litter of Great Danes. Besides I thought you two were buds. That you'd like him here."

"I liked him there."

Basement door closed, just in case, Emma cuddles Snowball on the bottom step while Ted and I clean the cage. "You're so cute. *So, so cute.*"

He is cute. With warm imploring eyes (no brows) and an explora-
tory nuzzle. Emma baby talks to Snowball. And the guinea pig makes
his squeaky wheel sound back at her. And he makes his squeaky wheel
sound every day while Emma spends an hour forcing celery greens and
cucumber wedges through his wire cage. And he makes his squeaky
wheel sound while I scoop whites from the drier. And then, on the
seventh day he rests. Falling into a deep sleep. A furry ball of sleep.
A sleep seemingly absent of breath or consciousness. A sleep that en-
dures while I run a screwdriver along his metal cage to rouse him.

"Emma? What's with Snowball?" Huffing from the climb from
the basement, I stand at the door to her room. She had popped the
heads back on the Barbie and Ken only in reverse. She was playing a
trans-gendered game. Ken with his enviable ta tas and slender waist
was inviting Barbie with her inexplicably missing manhood for a
playdate after school.

"What?" she asks, banging the dolls' faces together.

"Did something happen to Snowball?"

"Why? What's wrong?"

In seconds she's next to the cage on the workbench. There she
works a finger between the wires of the cage. Cajoling the still animal
she pleads, "Wake up. Time to wake up. Please." And I watch in
excruciating witness as my child's heart breaks. And some large hairy
hands reach in, and take my own heart in clumsy fingers, and wrench
it in two, like a loaf of crusty French bread.

"Honey. Don't open that."

Emma tugs at the cage door. "We have to getted him better."

"Honey. You can't touch him. He's . . ."

"Why?"

I can't answer. I don't know why. "There are germs, I think."

"But I just holded him at lunch. I gave him my carrots and I
kissed him and squee . . . hugged him. Why can't I hug him now?"

We leave him in the cage. Emma finds a blanket that belonged
to one of her dolls and we cover him, leaving Snowball's nose exposed

in case we're wrong. A pall of mourning slips over our house. Emma and I sink into a silent afternoon of PBS programming. I watch with her, like when she's sick. Occasionally a tear slips from the corner of her eye or her breath catches. And I think that I would do anything, anything in the world to prevent one more tear from sliding down her baby face.

The last time she cried was when I asked her about the domino story. Her thumb found her mouth and she stared at her lap. Then she looked up at me sorrowfully. "I wanted to say about them." As if the wanting was enough. And for me in that moment, it was. It was enough. When it's my kid you bet I'll reward intention. Besides I'd already made an appointment for Emma with the one-footed SLP, if only to disprove her need for him before the school district holds registration for next fall. Turns out lots of kids have issues. They couldn't get me in until June.

When Ted comes home I intercept him at the door and tell him about the pig.

"You think she killed him?"

"No. I'm not saying that. I think maybe she hugged him too much or too tight."

He leans over the couch and kisses Emma hard and long on top of her head. The next time I see him he's at the back door with a plastic Target bag in his hand. A round lump weighs it down.

"What are you doing?" I hiss, hauling him back into the kitchen.

"I'm taking him out to the trash."

"You can't just throw him out. There has to be like a ceremony. A Stride Right shoe box painted with a rainbow and a little family funeral with a reading of an Emily Dickinson poem."

"Jen, it's been raining for days. Even if we wanted to, that couldn't happen until the ground dries out. And where would we keep Snowball until then?"

Emma plays with the volume on the remote. Suddenly we hear, "Boo Bah teaches kinesthetic awareness and enhances gross motor skills." Neither of us tells her to turn it down. We both turn to the TV as if the dancing colorful blobs on the screen hold our answer.

"I got it," Ted says. "I'll be back."

Twenty-five minutes later he's transferring the new Snowball from the PetCo cardboard carrier to a fresh lining of cedar mulch in the basement cage. He's tickled with his solution although the new version of Snowball is like a bionic version of the expired Snowball. He's a good third bigger with fierce black eyes and a swatch of brown fur under his chin like a goatee.

"He looks kind of like a mad Frenchman." And, ironically, very much like the guinea pig on the solicitation with the eyebrows.

"'Allo," Ted says in really wretched French. "Je suis Monsieur Snowball Duex." The pig snuffles with a noise like Maxi makes in the winter.

"He doesn't squeak. He makes a totally different noise than the first. It's like a different language."

"Duh. Je parle francais."

Emma is thrilled. She buys the swap: hook, line and sinker. "I told you he was sleeping!" Her lashes are still wet with tears and she appears not to notice the beard. There's no way we'll be so lucky at
192   school. The next night is sleepless wondering how to put it to Mrs. Slaughter and the rest of the class.

In the end it's Ted who has to take Emma to school the first day back from break. I'm downtown early for an audition and I'm beyond relieved. That is until the afternoon when Ted turns all obtuse and cryptic around the subject of the drop off.

"Good. It was fine. The kids were sure glad to see Snowball. I've never been so popular. Sixteen kids all sticking their fingers through the cage before I could even get it in the classroom."

"What about Slaughter?"

Ted shrugs. "She said Snowball looked healthy."

"You didn't tell her?"

"How could I tell her? There were kids everywhere. It was crazy. One of them was holding his dick with one hand and tugging at me with the other begging for a playdate."

"Yeah. His name is Duncan. Shoot. I knew it. They'll all suspect."

"I don't think so. As soon as this huge girl slipped and skinned her knee all they cared about was the trickle of blood that got on her sock. I set Snowball down inside the classroom and left. Hey, is that woman kind of a flirt?"

"Who?"

"The teacher."

"Slaughter? No."

"Hmm. I swear she winked at me."

"Shit, Ted. We absolutely have to tell her. How can we raise a child in a household that values honesty above all else if we aren't clear with the teacher?"

"What about Emma? We just colluded on this switcheroo because we couldn't bear to see her distraught. You know if she grows up to be a serial killer it's on us, Jen."

"Where's that coming from?"

"I'm just saying, it's how it starts. With animals."

After school Temple arrives at our front door accompanied by Maxi, Emma and Duncan who broad jumps past me into our living room. Ted neglected to tell me the part about actually inviting Duncan today after school. Now the boy drops his backpack, sheds his coat on top and says, "Do you have a juice box and twizzlews? Or how 'bout fwuit gushews. Do you haved any fwuit gushews?" I hand him a Scooby Doo fruit snack as my cell phone rings. It's Blane. They are holding me for the part of the friend in the douche spot. It's the best of both worlds. They want to cast me in the commercial but not as the doucher, the part I read for. I am to be the friend of the doucher. I struggle to remember if she even says anything. And because of the certain money from the shoot, I dig out a bottle of Merlot from under our sink for us to have with dinner.

Duncan turns in a circle here and announces, "I like youw house. It smews like Snowball." An hour later, after eating half my private home-stash of M&M's Duncan throws up on Emma's Groovy Girls Car. Emma weeps. Duncan locks himself in the bathroom and we spend the last hour of the playdate watching Shrek and waiting for Dashenka to come pick him up.

April 23rd

With unusual exuberance Emma hauls me into school to see the duckling eggs in Miss Barbey's classroom. Against the wall, just inside the door, four hatching eggs quiver under the yellow light of an incubator. Next to it a corner of the classroom is cordoned off with chicken wire, and a bed of straw inside awaits the hatchlings. Low dishes with water and food pellets the color of milk chocolate occupy one corner. The scene is home spun and ingenious, aglow with the golden light of the incubator. Of the eggs, three are cracked. In the furthest along, a tiny beak pokes through a jagged hole he's made in the shell. Emma crouches, the whole of her is no taller than the wire coop.

"Let me out!" squeals a sassy girl into her gloves with no fingers. The gathered audience laughs. Then half the crowd follows her from the room. Baby animals of all stripes adorn the bulletin board next to the door of Miss Barbey's room that, other than the cage, has a whole different aura than Slaughter's room next door. A lamp with a red scarf tied artfully over the shade warmly illuminates the rocker in the reading area. And somewhere there's a Glade Plug-In at work because, despite the animals, the room smells like lavender. It's a day spa compared to Slaughter's room. And while I feel like a trespasser here, I also feel a tiny flicker of teacher envy. What sort of year would Emma have had with this teacher, in this room? Bet she'd talk eagerly to her. Here I'm pushed aside by a huge boy wearing a Cubs jacket and a ratty backpack with a split zipper. Inside I can see a whole electronics warehouse: a Nintendo DS, a cell phone and an iPod Nano. He whoops as the hatching egg before us suddenly cracks. From the number of upper-grade kids who stop by to shove in for a look before the tardy bell, the annual duck-hatch has clearly made Miss Barbey a star.

Emma has had enough. She bolts from the room with me in tow, and weaves with me through the hall towards her own classroom. I don't mind, because I'm dressed today as a businesswoman who likes the fresh produce at Meijer's. I've got on natural makeup and a cobbled together beige pants suit. In the hallway, drawings of tulips, bees and butterflies adorn the bulletin boards. The new season has brought Ted success as well. He's signed two clients, both of whom own franchises with multiple locations across northern Illinois. The business has lightened him in the way that Temple's math calls do.

On Thursday I have a 6:00 A.M. call to shoot the douche spot, so Ted walks Emma to school. My agent has confirmed that I do, in fact, have no lines. "Just a reaction shot," Blane announces. "You'll be in and out."

"In and out?"

'Yeah, babe." He misses the joke.

"It's a douche spot, Blane." That I have to explain it kills the humor. Besides actors are never 'in and out,' given that they have to pay you for the eight-hour day, and they always feel entitled to keep you for at least half of that, even if you must only pout deeply in one shot because vaginal itching has got you down. That's it. That's what I have to do; sit on a stool, jut out my lower lip and nod while all the viewers at home imagine my prickly privates.

"Hmmm." The makeup girl examines my face, turning my head to the light. I can smell tobacco on her fingers. A tattoo of intertwined hearts encircles her right bicep. "They don't want me to pretty you up at all," she says. "What's the line you have to react to?" Is she serious? "Vaginalitchinggotyoudown?" She knows the line. She's just sadistic. I see her tight smile when she turns back to her voluminous makeup kit. She has created an up-do with her own hair using only a pair of chopsticks. I find myself studying the creation while she picks through her tackle-box of tubs and tubes.

The director goes over what he wants from me quickly, while simultaneously conferring with the lighting man over the look he's trying to achieve. The douching woman, who turns out to be the same red-haired Sean Connery impressionist from the Adventist Hospital shoot, gets the "Vaginal itching got you down?" line. At least she's not talking directly to me. She delivers her bit straight to the camera as well. They spend extra time on her makeup as if her whole person; her tight, shiny curls and voluminous eye-lashes have resulted from the purchase of a Spring Morning Douching Kit. When she sees me from her turn in the makeup chair she says as Sean Connery, "First we meet over fibroids and now the itching. Anything else you'd like tell me about before we roll?" The line sets off collapsing laughter among two of the crew as they peel off long sections of black tape and use the strips to secure together huge plugs at the end of a tangle of industrial cords.

Emma's school lets out at 2:50 and though it does, indeed, take less than an hour to film my nodding pout, they don't release me until 2:30. Figure in traffic, and the earliest I can get home is 3:30. Ted answers his cell on the first ring.

"Hey. You have to get Em. I'm just pulling onto the expressway."

"How'd it go?"

"Leave it at humbling. I don't want to talk about it."

"Okay. . . ."

"Okay, you'll get her, right?"

"Aren't you going to ask how it went for me?"

"How walking her to school today went?"

"Yup."

He's smug and prideful. I resent him instantly for it.

"So . . . we're at school early because I thought you said it started at 8:45."

"Nine. She starts at nine. Ted, I told you like three . . ."

"Okay. That's not the point. The point is, we get there and we're the only ones. Emma forgot her coat so we're freezing on the playground and who flies out of the school but that other Kindergarten teacher."

"Miss Barbey?"

"Yeah. And she's freaking out. Apparently some fourth grader stepped on the side of this cage she has in her classroom yesterday, and she used duct tape to fix the thing. Only she wrapped the tape around the outside, sticky-side in."

"Yeah?"

"Yeah. So overnight all these furry baby ducks got stuck to the tape."

"The ducks got stuck to the duct tape?" It's amusing. That's it I think, but still he talks.

"Exactly. So Miss Barbey comes into school this morning to find six, stuck, dying ducklings. She was freaking out about the kids coming in and seeing them. She wouldn't even let Emma into her classroom. So this Barbey woman spent like fifteen minutes with Emma out in the hall while I separated the ducklings from the tape. Which, by the way, was not easy. That tape is supremely sticky. That's the whole point, so the stuff will stick on a seam in a duct-run from the furnace – no matter whether it's heat or AC you've. . . "

"Good."

"So I freed the ducks and rebuilt the cage for her. Only I used a double layer of tape, sticky side in on *both* sides."

"Wow. Saved the day, huh? Excellent. So you'll walk her home? And Maxi too? You've gotta get both kids today."

"No problem. But that's not the best part. The best part is that when I finished with the cage I go to leave, and Mrs. Slay . . ."

"Slaughter."

"Mrs. Slaughter is in the hallway. She stops and shushes me cause here's Emma at that table in the hallway with her back to us. It was hard to hear, but she was reading a book about buying a pet dog with Miss Barbey."

"Well, that was nice of her to read to Em. She would have done so much better with Barbey as her Kindergarten teacher, I think."

"No, listen, Jen. *Emma* was reading Barbey the book. Miss Barbey was listening."

In the course of it, so many milestones are missed because the mother has a trial, or a management conference, or because she's busy cleaning the upstairs toilet or sneaking a cigarette behind the garage. But no matter the reason, what the missing produces in the mother is the same wound as a saber plunged and withdrawn would leave. A wound that gets tweaked, when, some years hence, she overhears a coffee shop conversation between two women about the date little so and so first rolled, walked, or learned to read. And I am so unfairly miffed at her: at Emma the accomplished. As if her timing was deliberate. Night after night it was the two of us in her bed surrounded by books. Crawling through syllables at a pace so slow and plodding, the sound, without amplification, could be a newfangled method of torture. Couldn't she have waited? Or trotted out a glimpse of her talent while I sat on the edge of her bed the night before listening to her improvise story number twelve? The only snippet of the scenario that salvages my humor is that Ted was witness. He got the fruits of the labor. That's okay. It's more than okay. Between the duckling rescue and the reading show, he'll be in certain good humor when I get home.

By the time I burst through the door, with a celebratory box of assorted Munchkins, I've talked myself off the maternal ledge and am eager to join in a little family celebration. Only I find Ted nonplussed and Emma at Maxi's. He scrutinizes the donuts as if the box harbored several kilos of hashish. Begrudgingly, I explain the occasion; the reading for Miss Barbey that he witnessed. He listens, and then turns back to the donuts.

"Yeah, so? It's good. But it was also eventual, don't you think? Everyone learns to read. I mean it's not like she did a page of trig or something." And he plucks out a donut. A round glazed sugary ball, and pops it into his mouth.

April 27th

I fish for recognition of Emma's progress from other quarters by walking her into the classroom later in the week. I'm emboldened and feeling a little like I've arrived a day late for the dinner party clutching my lukewarm gift-bottle of Two Buck Chuck. Seeing the caterpillars in Slaughter's room are my ruse and my efforts don't go unrewarded.

"The other day Emma read a few little words out loud, to me and Miss Barbey." Mrs. Slaughter's eyes meet mine. She has on a fantastic pair of silver hoops within hoops. Around her neck is a blue gauzy scarf woven with silver metallic thread. And before us is a cage containing three, slanting, leafy branches. Stuck to them are several verdant tubular insects the size of my pinky. Now, as I recall, Ted said it was a story. She read a whole story out loud. I think there's quite a distinction between a few words and a story.

"A story, you mean."

Mrs. Slaughter chuckles and gives me her weary, tolerant smile. Then she extends her glasses on their beaded chain, shelves them on her nose and looks at me over them.

"She'll get there. Don't you worry." And she turns to stare into the cage.

Henry materializes between us, pulling his eyes down to show us only the whites. Then he turns to face Mrs. Slaughter. "I'm not going home after school because my mom is going to get a thing removed. They're giving her something that makes you count backwards. She loves that part. It's not serious but it's brown. Brownish red. I'm going to Nana's. She has nut cake and hard candy in a bowl in her cabinet. Only it's scotch butters not chocolate. I take them when she's not looking. And my mom will only have a Band-Aid on her shoulder when she comes home. That's all. And two stitches. She's gonna show me. Only I cannot touch it for a year."

I'm not *worried*. If it was a story then give the girl credit for reading a story. But I can't quibble because: a) I wasn't there that morning, and b) Henry is still speaking. So we move on, the difference between *words* and *a story* hanging between us, unsettled.

Slaughter looks at me now, over babbling Henry, to share a confidence. "You know Miss Barbey has ducks in her room. She insists on it every year. She goes through the whole process of that ridiculous pen. It's a bit over the moon if you ask me, when there is so much more to be learned from this life cycle. A larva as it becomes a pupa."

We gaze into the cage together. Slaughter sighs. "Yes, they're ship shape this year. Despite being busy like a bee, I remembered to line the cage with the six layers of newspaper. One year, you know, I forgot to do that, and when they started to emerge they all fell. Many to their deaths. The ones who made it were, shall we say . . . challenged. They hopped around with bent wings: flappers that really couldn't fly. It was really very sad. And you know what was even stranger? I had such an odd class then. Only one reader by May. And over the course of the year," here she counts on her fingers, "one, two, three students broke their arms." She's very close to me now; I can see her eyelashes and the hypnotizing circling of her hoops-within-hoops-earrings. Something has slipped away quietly during our exchange this morning. I feel it instantly, the shift. I no longer care if I please her. I check the time on the CLOCK / RELOJ just over her head as if to note the exact moment I was liberated from the need for her approval. She doesn't notice.

During our interlude by the cage, the pandemonium in the classroom has escalated around us. The twins have gotten new tennis shoes and they're showing a group of three other boys how fast they can run. Not to be outdone, all the boys must now show how fast their shoes are. They whip back and forth from the BOOKCASE / EL ESTANTE PARA LIBROS to the CALENDER / CALANDARIO. On the other side of the classroom Aubrey weeps loudly with her head tilted back on her neck and her eyes squeezed shut because she's not going for a playdate with Katie and Maxi is.

"SHHHHH." Mrs. Slaughter flickers the room lights and then claps out a rhythm with her hands and creepily the running boys freeze. Aubrey rights her head and they all turn to face her. As one, the expressions drain from their faces. Then without missing a beat the classroom of Pavlovian percussionists clap the same rhythm back at their teacher.

"People let's line up!" Slaughter barks. "Line up! Who is my line leader today?"

I stop in the hall to call Ted so that he can clarify for me the exact details of the Emma-reading-the-story-morning. While pushing in numbers, I completely miss the first, "Mrs. Lansing?"

Mr. Klein is uncomfortably close when I spin to him. "It's taken a long time to catch up with you," he seethes. "I've observed Emma in class you know." Instantly the image of him squatting in a classroom corner under the list of kids who takes the bus home, takes full shape in my head. I can envision his left hand curling over his pen as he scrawls on a clipboard balanced on his knees. Next to him is a Starbucks cup. Periodically his wonky eyes rake over my little girl as she struggles to write the word wall words in lower case letters, and his comb-over quivers with diagnostic delight.

"You . . . what?" I stammer. "No, I didn't know that. This was never discussed." My words come fast and furious as if a little combustible can that contained them was shaken and set into place by

Mrs. Slaughter: all ready to be exploded open in this moment by the weasely man grinning before me.

"You listen to me," I say, gaining traction. "I've thought about everything you suggested. And I completely disagree. Screw the team, I will not allow her to be held back."

He parks his briefcase on the floor and opens his mouth to speak.

"And as for you," I say, cutting him off. "My answer is, no. No. . . Theodore. No puppets." My hands are flying about now. I've been primed for this outburst for two months and there's no turning back now. Passion and persuasion combine in a symphony of oration here. And I am blazing, because it is my daughter, my child. And I am nothing, *nothing*, if not her advocate. "No Theodore. No introducing other kids one at a time. No extra testing. I want none of it. My daughter is fine. She is *fine*. She is *five*. FIVE!" All the fingers on my right hand are splayed in front of his eyeballs in case, in addition to wandering, they don't see so well. And still he smiles at me with that peevish grin that just spurs me on.

"She's five and she's reading! She reads already. Isn't that crazy? Emma is shy. SHY. That is all." In the climactic scene of the original *Charlie and the Chocolate Factory*, Gene Wilder, as Willy Wonka, unleashes on Charlie and his uncle. At the end of his rampage, he dismisses them both with a bitter, spat, "Good Day, Sir." It chills me every time I watch it. That phrase in its brutal finality says it all, and that line is on the tip of my tongue here. To complete the scene, to form the concluding button on the end. I ache to deliver it, turn on my heel and take my leave.

But my momentum crests and begins to plummet as the little grin still plays at the corners of Klein's mouth. He takes in my rumpled Baylor Bears tee shirt and my fleece pants. And when he should be retreating, he seems to settle in, as if my outburst has proven something. As if he's won. When he hasn't won. I have won, damn-it! And in order to win, I have uncharacteristically left my substance, the very matter that comprises my being, somewhere else.

I feel in the waning of emotion here, completely insubstantial. Like all my important, load-bearing elements have gone soft. It is as if I am paper, a May Lunch Menu standing miraculously upright on nothing but the fine edge, waiting for the certain gust that will blow me over.

When Klein speaks, his voice is low and quiet. "Why Mrs. Lansing there's no need to get so . . . agitated. I was just going to say that I've observed Emma in class, and I think . . . you're right."

His eyes dart to the left. If he were a frog, his tongue would follow and reel in a fly. "She's five. She's shy."

What? Is he agreeing with me? Here he fumbles in a rear pocket and produces a business card. It is bent, holding the curve of his ass. He holds it out to me between two straight fingers. "But should *you* have any – needs. Here's my card. Oh, and one more thing." He bends and sets his Starbucks on the floor. Then he removes a money clip from his pants pocket and takes out a dollar. Before extending it to me he looks around to make sure no one's watching. Then his face collapses and he sucks in his lips in an expression of profound pity.

And this is how I find out that my Homeless Coalition PSA is airing on cable.

Also Margaret sees it during *The Ace of Cakes*. She calls to me at dusk from the far corner of her side yard. Well aware of the chemical perils of lawn fertilizer, she's applying hers in a disguise that is both protective and terrifying. A WWII era mask covers her face. Her legs are completely encased in thick rubber fishing boots that disappear mid-thigh under a dark navy slicker. Yellow latex gloves designed for dishwashing cover her hands. At first she says only, "Hey." If I didn't recognize that as her trademark greeting, I'd be flying back into my house rather than bustling on to the PTA meeting that started ten minutes ago. She looks like a beetle. An oversized version of the yard pest she seeks to prevent by the application of whatever grey and yellow toxin is heaped high in the galvanized bucket at her feet.

"I saw you last night on TV." She shifts the mask up to rest on top of her head. It looks now like the beetle is swallowing her whole.

She's got a wary humor about her. "Very clever, Jen. I don't have a dollar on me, but I'd say you must be raking it in from that appeal, hmm? Wished I'd thought of that. Although, it's a kind of a lie isn't it? You aren't *really* homeless right?"

I try to explain that the spot benefits the Homeless Coalition and not me, personally, but she won't be budged from her beliefs. The more I sputter, the keener her admiration becomes. She's either been drinking or the protective gear has failed and the herbicidal toxins have made her woozy and incapable of succinct discourse. In response to my polite subject-changing questions about the yard stuff she's applying, she launches into a tirade about the weedy contaminates that infiltrate her bluegrass. After ten more minutes I excuse myself, explaining about the PTA meeting I'm headed to. Now though, it's too late. I can't walk in. They'll already be on to their discussion of plans for the lobby fountain dedication this summer.

"You *wanted* to go tonight?" Margaret looks surprised.

"I did."

"You know they're nominating the chair-people for next year's committees tonight. You go you're as good as committed."

"I know."

"Why do you think I'm doin' the yard instead. Besides it's gonna rain tonight. Gotta get that weed killer on there good before it comes." And with that she's done with me. Her mask comes down and she leans over and grabs a fist full of grit from her bucket. Then she chucks it at the struggling grass, not two feet from where I stand.

May 15th

With only a few weeks left in school, word passes around the playground one warm afternoon that some of the Kindergarten moms are getting together at a local bar for a little mom's night out. Pippa invites me. We're standing next to the "No Dogs Allowed" sign, and with smiling apology, she interrupts my conversation with Dashenka. Mercifully, because I'd been struggling to explain, in terms she can understand, the precise difference between crocuses and daffodils.

When I get to the bar at 7:00, several moms are already imbibing. A line of them holds court at the long bar. Crosby Stills and Nash sing *Carry On* over the sound of silverware meeting plates from the adjacent restaurant. Duncan's mom, her trademark blazer nowhere to be seen, is at the far end of the bar. She's undone a couple of buttons on her shiny blouse, with an eighties bow for a collar, and nearly falls from her stool when she spins it towards me in greeting.

"Hi, Duncan's mom. How are you?"

"Hi, Emma's mom." Her voice is more sing-song than usual. Her first words come at a high pitch that falls as the thought progresses as if they will conclude with a burp that never comes. As she identifies me correctly, she pushes at my chest with a manicured finger. Then she spins towards the bartender and when she's got his attention, draws imaginary circles around the bar, her empty shot glass and me.

I order a Sam Adams and jump right in. "So what do you hear about the first grade teachers?" Because I've thought of them. I don't know who they are, beyond the last names I've heard in conversations on the playground. Couldn't even point them out in a line-up. But I've thought of them. Even gone so far as to imagine what sort would be best for Emma. And I've wondered, often, whether I should lobby Principal Otis on the point. These questions surface when I'm lying in bed, on the off-nights when I'm not reliving the confrontation with Mr. Klein. Since that day the whole subject of repeating Kindergarten has evaporated. Vanished. I wander through the hallways at school now baggage-less and emboldened. Eluding nobody. But then, in the dark I think, what if they were right. What if she's really not ready to go on? What if she flounders silently at her desk through the next year, too shy to ask for help? Unable, even, to thrust up her hand and ask what page they're on or when the persuasive essay is due? And for a split second, like the Road Runner's cartooned-gulp-moment; the one in mid-air, right before he plummets into the canyon, I allow myself to think maybe she'd do better in the long run if we did keep her back a year.

Crosby or Stills or Nash sings, "To sing the blues you've got to live the dues . . ."

Duncan's mom brings me back by lurching suddenly towards my chest. "Duncan will have Mr. Ashika for first," she says. "Because Ms. Kliest is married and thirty-four. You see where I'm going? With the man, you don't have to worry about them getting pregnant and leaving your child mid-year." One arm flings out over my head to prove her point. Her speech is noticeably slurred. I wonder how long she's been here.

"You already know his teacher?" A fist of jealousy shoots up through my sternum.

"I do." Unable to resist a smug smile she continues, "I'm not supposed to, but Otis showed me the list and there he was. The very first name." She leans into me. "It's all strategy my friend. You gotta be on top of it." Here she studies her fingers and their clumsy attempt at snapping. The bartender delivers our beers as well as a shot of Jack Daniels. Duncan's mom downs the shot in one impressive gulp.

"What do you mean, *strategy*?" The word sounds cruel and unfair. Something to avoid, not aspire to.

After suppressing a burp she lists towards me again. Her intoxication has bloomed in the moments since I arrived. "I'm gonna say, right now," she says. "Here's an e.g. for you; Duncan. Duncan has a bad hockey birthday. He's l'il. He's l'il." Her eyes cross, seeking the word. "He's young. Last year I got him some private stick handling lessons and the best coach in the Mites." Here she raises her voice and her glass and glances around seeking an admiring audience. "Now, at six, he could play Travel." To this notion I have no objection, but she presses on anyway. "Seriously, he could," she slurs. "Mark my wors."

The sort of robust parental influence she's describing galls me on the one hand. But on the other, I'm certain that the next question will be about what Emma's doing this summer. And I'm suddenly mindful that Emma starts her exclusive session of Discovery Summer Camp in two weeks and also of the seven phone calls it took to get her in. I am just like the mother before me, I realize. No different. Strip away her cinching belt and my frayed at the heels denim and we are underneath, one: lobbyists on behalf of our offspring. Here I'm spared any more steps down the rugged road of self-examination because Duncan's mom seems perilously close to setting her cheek upon my breast. "By the way, my name is Louise," she announces to my collarbone. Then leaning backwards with a firm grip on the bar, she takes me in fully.

"Hi Louise. I'm Jennifer."

"Jennifer, can I nominate you for something next year? She leans into me again with the question, Her fuzzy eyes fixed to my face. And she sings quietly, "It's a position with the PTA."

"And you want to nominate me?"

"Yes!" Her face goes blank then slack. And she squints at me, "Sorry, what was your name again?"

"Jennifer."

"Right." She raps on her head with her palm. "I need to hear it three times before I get it. We really need someone really nice like you to cold call the new parents and ask for donations to the Fine Arts programs." She pets my arm. "What with the district cuts the budget for the spring play, and sheet music royalties and such, is really in the shit hole."

I feel like I've just been recruited to play Tree Number Three in the school play.

"No," I sigh, as from the speakers John Denver's voice croons, "You fill up my senses like a night in the forest. . . "

I successfully hook Louise's eyes for a second. "I don't think so." I tell her, "I mean I'll do something. Just not, that."

Mothers in groups of twos and threes have pressed into the bar. Inside the door, Rico's mom is laughing with Henry's mom. I slide off my stool and excuse myself but before I can take a step, Duncan's mom, Louise, catches me by the wrist. In a parody of thinking she taps her forehead roughly with one finger. "I've got the perfect thing." She leans in so close I can smell her makeup along with the pungent exhalation of Jack Daniels. "You could co-chair the wrapping-paper-sale-fundraiser in the fall. We really need a mother who knows the school for that; the teachers, the schedules, how to get things home in the backpacks."

Here something fluttery happens deep inside my rib cage. And it isn't the beer. "You mean," I say, "I am a *Mother Who Knows*?"

She leans her head back and hoots at the copper ceiling, "Yes! That's a cute way to put it. Yes, exactly, a *Mother Who Knows*. I love that."

She shoves me here. It is a move that's meant to be endearing and good-natured – but her buzz fuels it and it nearly topples me. "You are!"

"Whoa there." It's Henry's mom. She has my back, literally. "Are you okay?" As she speaks I get it: the voice: it's Wheezy from Dragon Tales. It's everything I can do not to tell her she sounds just like Wheezy. But suddenly the bar is loud with greeting. Raucous with the entry of a huge group of Kindergarten moms who've pressed in en masse. I'm shocked to see Temple behind the shimmying mom from the fountain brigade. Tonight the mom wears a halter shirt that plunges down between her bosoms like she's on a date.

"Told you I'd show," Temple breathes out of the side of her mouth after threading her way through the standing crowd towards me.

"Goddamned travel soccer tryouts ran late."

"Maxi's doing travel soccer?"

"Nah, not till next year. Just Karla. It's good, it's just, God, I can't stand the other moms. So freakin' competitive. Tonight was tryouts. That's all. The season hasn't even started yet and these two mothers get into this bitchy brawl about which of their daughters is a better forward." She has to shout to be heard. The music, the amalgam of voices has swelled along with the numbers. "They don't have their own lives those moms. That's the problem. They live through their babies, you know what I mean?"

Henry's mom is standing silently beside us. "Are the moms like that in pee-wee football?" I ask her.

"What?" She hasn't been listening. Shouting, I repeat the question and she takes a long gulp of her wine and stares into the glass.

"I don't know. Henry refuses to go." She shrugs with apology. "He likes rhythmic gymnastics." A splotchy blush rises in her neck and she looks as if she might cry. She's in need of reassurance, that's clear.

"Isn't that the one with a ribbon?" Temple asks.

"Yes." Henry's mom's face crinkles into a weary smile. "Also a hoop. Or sometimes a stick. Please don't repeat this."

"I think that's fantastic." I lean my head back and shake the compliment out from my hair like Pippa, the outgoing PTA president would.

"Me too, darlin'." Temple squeezes her arm.

"Really?" Henry's mom winces.

"Oh yes. Absolutely."

She looks at me. "Can we go to dinner sometime this summer with our husbands?"

"Yes. Sure. I'd love that. We'd love that."

Her squinty grin returns and her fingers play with a circular silver necklace with a stick figure etched into the center above the word *faith*. "I'd love for you to repeat what you said, about the gymnastics being okay, to my husband. As it is now, I tell him we're off to a Pee-Wee conditioning class at the Y when I take him over to the studio. I'm so tired of lying."

Suddenly, from a high table next to the bar, we hear little Becca's mom. It's the same keening wail that drew me to her on the first day of school.

"I don't know." Her howl slices right through the chatter and din. Even patrons on dates, who aren't with our group, interrupt their conversations to stare at the woman draped over the high bar table bawling unabashedly. Becca's mom lifts her head and wails, "She just doesn't get it. I mean here we are, at the end of the year and every night with the rhyming families and the sounding-out and the word wall words." She's complaining to no one and everyone at once. "I mean some words aren't even words, they're just letters. 'I,' what's hard about that one? It's a single letter! 'I,' 'I,' 'I,'" She thumps on her chest with each declaration then runs out of steam with a jagged inhale. "I don't think she'll ever read." It is her final, dying wail. She sinks back onto her chair and suddenly it's like a mother's radar for a child floundering in the deep end has been activated. Temple is there, waving a fist full of cocktail napkins in her face, as the rest of us surround her and jump in for the rescue.

Henry's mom pipes eagerly, "My kid still can't tell the difference between a circle and a square."

Another mom says, "My daughter has been in ballet for three years, and she still can't skip." From the bar here, Duncan's mom bellows, "Hell, my son is six, and he still can't wipe himself." She spins around once on her stool, sticks her drink in the air and hoots, "Then again, neither can his father."

Then the most surprising thing happens. Duncan's mom comes to attention on her stool. She smiles radiantly and I follow her eyes to find Margaret standing off by herself beside the old jukebox. The thing pulses with neon color in time to Journey's *Don't Stop Believin'*. Margaret's hoodie is pulled up over her head, and she expressionlessly scans the room. Here Duncan's mom stands on the rung of her stool and waves like crazy. Her smile is so wide I can see the grey of the caps on her teeth at her gum line. Margaret acknowledges her with an upward jerk of her head and starts her migration towards the bar. To my amazement, mothers turn and great her warmly as she passes.

Temple sees my open jaw and whispers in my ear. "Margaret's always got a joint if you're interested."

Out of the blue then someone shouts, "Hey, everyone! Let's toast to first grade!"

"First grade!" A unison cheer from the gathered.

There's a smattering of applause as if somewhere there's a winner about to step forward. I'm ebullient with the rush of friendship I feel in the room as well as the welling warmth from the Sam Adams I just downed.

"First grade." I thrust my bottle into the air and then take a last, robust swallow of beer. Only then do the ominous words sink in, to squelch my burgeoning buzz. First grade. I swallow so much beer in one gulp my throat hurts.

The next morning I stop by Temple's on my way downtown for a Sears Back-to-School-Sale audition. Yes, it's May. I should have said no because I have to wear a bathing suit and it's not pretty. At least I get to wear sweats on top for now.

"It's fine. 'Real' is *so* what they want," Blane said on the phone. "And that is *so* you!" I have no script in advance so I can only hope it's a tight shot on my face with lots of copy. What I lack in svelte

I can make up for in delivery. Besides, Miss Barbey runs a morning Get Ahead Reading program twice a week over the summer. I want Emma in, and it's not cheap.

Temple's house smells like baking cookies. Right away I take in the ambrosia of cooking dough and resolve to stay until they come out of the oven. I'm sitting on Karla's bed. Her room is like a sunken pool. There is no visible meeting of the rug and the wall because on all four sides the junction is lined with a continuous pile of papers, notebooks, paperbacks, stuffed animals and the American Girls, Kaya, Josephina and Molly. Party favor bags spill out their lip-gloss, sticker, pencil contents. I wonder silently if this what Emma's room will look like in seven years. Temple pulls a pair of jeans from the mounds. She looks inside and rolls her eyes.

"So she wouldn't let me in the bathroom with her but I knew right away she got it from the way she stormed through the front door and screamed, 'Leave me alone!' before I opened my mouth. Also her hoodie was tied around her waist. Kinda tell tale."

Here she sniffs the pit of a tee shirt. "Mary, Mother of Jesus," she says, wilting. She tosses the shirt out into the hallway. "And she's mad at me for making her a girl. That's what she says through the bathroom door. And I want to scream, 'What about your father, darlin'? For once couldn't you be mad at him? He had something to do with it, too.' They had sex-ed last year. She should know that. Anyway, I try to talk calmly through the door. I tell her, 'You have to take off the wrapper and put it in the middle hole.'" She freezes with alarm then speaks to me. "It is the middle right?"

I have to think for a second before I agree. "Yeah. Middle."

"'You mean the place you told me not to touch?' she screams back at me."

"'Right. It's okay now!' I say. 'Just put it in there, darlin'. Sometimes it helps to lift up your leg. Stick a foot up on the potty,' I tell her." Temple's on her knees now, raking up open books, balled up camisoles and dirty athletic socks from under the bed.

"'Just put it in?' she screams back at me. I can hear her hysteria but she won't open the door. And when she repeats my instructions they sound wrong. 'No, sweetie,' I tell her, 'Shoving is better. Just shove it on up there 'til it disappears.'"

Temple leans against the bed clutching her armful of dirty clothes from the floor. She seems near tears. My brain works furiously over how to make Emma skip puberty entirely.

"Did she get it in?"

"No, she opened the door a little and her face appeared in the crack all red and streaked with tears. And she spits out, 'First you tell me not to touch. Then you tell me it's private and I can only touch it very gently when I'm by myself, and now you want me to shove this huge thing in there? Make up your mind, Mom.' Then the naked tampon sailed past my head like a flying mouse and she slammed the door."

"Wow. What are you going to do?"

"I have no damned idea. I can tell you what she's *not* gonna do. She's just not gonna to do swimming for awhile that's for sure." And then her face falls open in alarm. "Shit!" The clothes forgotten, she flies down her stairs into the kitchen. From her oven she pulls a baking sheet filled with the florescent hues of ocean coral rendered in miniature.

"There," she says proudly, pulling off oven mitts that are shaped like carp.

"Oh. Not cookies. I thought we'd eat cookies."

"Lord, no. Diorama on aquatic life in the Caribbean. You got your fan coral, star coral. These tentacles will sting, but they also collect food. Didn't do finger coral – too hard." Here she points to a green terraced glob. "That's your lettuce coral."

"What the heck is all this for?"

"Final project for Earth Science. It's not due until Friday, but I thought I'd get a jump on it. Karla'll do the spiny lobster and porcupine fish when she gets home." I move in closer.

"Hey. You even think about eating one of these babies I'll cut off your arm. Took me all night to do 'em."

The coral bits are incredible: intricate, lacy miniatures in florescent hues of orange and green. Many are mottled and if you look closely, all have teeny eyes the size of cracker crumbs. They leave me speechless.

"What?" Temple's studying my face. There's a steely aggressiveness in her expression that makes me want to run. "What?" she demands again.

"Nothing. They're fantastic, but . . ."

"Come on, Jen. What?"

"It's just that. I don't get it. I can't figure you out. It's like you don't care about school, but then you do this . . . masterwork of coral. And you find teaching opportunities in every moment with Maxi."

"Who says I don't care? I do care. I mean I try not to. When Karla settles down to her homework. I open some Cabernet, grab my Real Simple and tell myself it doesn't matter. But then I just can't help myself. Next thing I know I'm reachin' over her shoulder, pencil in hand, to change 'there' to 'their' on her page. You'll see. Especially with the oldest. It's like the cord between us is still there, I swear. Just try to back off. Try to not prowl through their middle school backpack when all you get from them about school is, 'It was fine.' And they say 'fine' like you've been interrogating them all mornin'. *Fine*. Lord, I detest that word." She's agitated. The southern accent coats her speech and she rubs at her cheek with her whole hand.

"God. Me too. *Fine*. What does it even mean?" I say.

Here an uncomfortable, radio silence settles between us. Temple's eyes land on a Plexiglas frame on her fridge containing a picture of Karla at five or six. In it, her mouth is open in a laughing grin. Temple sees me watching her. "I mean look at that baby girl, with her bangs and her missin' front tooth. It was easy then. You know what I mean?"

"*Easy* isn't the word I'd choose."

"It is, darlin'. It's so easy now. You just wait. When they hit fifth, sixth grade you try to let them sink or swim but then everyone else's kid is out there setting pool records. They don't just *do* the project. They film each step, edit it in iMovie and make a DVD of their *process*. Then they burn copies for the whole class and put it on You Tube just in case yours won't play on your Dell. And you see the look on your kid's face when they come home feelin' like their project doesn't measure up and you try to tell them the other parents did most of the work for their kids but they don't see that. And you're talking really fast cause they'll only listen to you for fifteen seconds before they shrug and shove their goddamned ear buds back into their ears."

While she rants, she yanks open a junk drawer and retrieves from it a tiny video camera. "So you bake coral. And you edit their papers. And you pop a Xanax the day they take have to take all their placement tests for next year. All of 'em in one freakin' day!" She gestures with the camera. "And you lean on the teacher, and you hire a rapping sixty-five fuckin' dollar an hour math tutor."

I shake my head.

"So you see the shrink and pay the fee and hire the tutor because they're your babies. And you just want them to be successful." Here her voice catches and, covering her mouth, she hands the camera to me.

"Just shoot the coral," she says, waving her hand over the cookie sheet. With a loud sniff, she bends down and removes an errant piece of fuchsia clay.

In the viewfinder I frame the coral bits. "Lean down, Temple. It's cutting off your face," I say.

She is aghast. Popping up, she retreats to the safety of her inadequate countertop. She leans against it wiping under her eyes.

"Lord no. I don't want to be *in* it," she says, her eyes wide, as if she'd done something wrong.

June 9th

The bulletin boards outside Mrs. Slaughter's classroom are empty of artwork and assignments. All that's left in the primary colored expanses are collections of twin holes from a year's worth of staples. The time has slipped through my fingers somehow, irretrievable as water. And yet I long to gather it up again. Cup it in my palms. Preserve it in all its fullness and dimension, not simply the school photo and the teeming contents of the basement boxes. Over the PA the Principal's voice fills the school after a squawk from the mike, "Hola children and parents. This is Doctor Otis." The Principal had used the occasion of Emma's final team meeting to announce that she had completed her doctoral studies and would like to be addressed now as *Doctor* Otis. It was the highlight of an otherwise mercifully, perfunctory exchange. The whole of it took seven minutes during which papers were signed and straightened. And the file before her that bore Emma's name, closed.

An electronic squawk fills the hall here, and the announcement continues. "A reminder that pick-up is at 10:50 today. Please don't forget to empty those lockers completely boys and girls. Happy summer everyone!"

At the classroom door I wax nostalgic over the memory of Emma's vice grip on my hand from the beginning of the year. I watch as she skips into the room and hugs her friend, Rico. Something inside me

218

constricts as I realize she hasn't touched me at all yet today. She doesn't even say goodbye anymore. No turn. No choking hug. No shy, close to her belly, wave. Instead she charges towards Duncan, who races from her towards two cardboard containers packed with classroom books. He leaps atop one as Mrs. Slaughter bellows, "Young man, off the boxes. Do you hear me?" The bell rings, and sets off a slamming of lockers in the hall.

Temple bustles up behind me hauling her daughter by the wrist. "Hey, Jen. Crap, Maxi, you are late. Get in there, darlin'."

Slaughter materializes before us, her back to the classroom door, and her hand on the knob. "Thank you for joining us, Maxi," she says. The teacher is decked out today in a long crinkle skirt and red Crocs studded with large silvery rhinestones. Without looking up she says, "Hello, moms. Excuse me. I'm just going to close this door today." It swings in its arc and clicks shut before us.

"Damn," I say to Temple. "I'd kind of wanted to stay in there." My voice catches at the end and a teary brew of emotion wells up within me. Her jaw drops and her lip curls. "Not me, darlin'."

"I've been meaning to ask you. Did you ever get the coral project back?"

"Oh, that thing?" She brushes it off with a flip of her hand. "Turned out fine. We got an 'A.' Leaves us in good standing for next year. And did I tell you?" She grips my arm and squeals, "We're going for the granite counters. It's between Uba Tuba and St. Celica. I'm off to the Home Depot. Wish me luck!"

Al, the janitor, passes me with his push broom. His face lights up when he sees me in the hall. "How're you doing today?" he asks.

"Good, Al."

He studies my face for a moment and continues on. Then, by Miss Barbey's room, he stops, and reaches for his back pocket.

"Hey." Margaret steps between us. She wears a long black trench coat and chunky black sneakers. A plastic CVS bag dangles from her wrist and here she opens it so I can see its contents.

"I got extra. You want to hand them out in Emma's class?" she drones.

In the bag are 12 oz. packages of generic jellybeans, gummy worms and Swedish Fish. Al waits sheepishly behind her; his broom pole resting under his arm and a dollar folded in his hand. It's easier to reach around Margaret and take it, than to launch into the whole explanation of what is real on TV and what is not. It briefly crosses my mind that next year, when the Spring Morning commercial airs, my vaginal itching will be the playground topic. Instead of dollars, mothers will slip medicated douche kits and herbal remedies to me at the Fall Festival. Here I peer deep into Margaret's bag.

"No thanks," I say to Margaret. "You do know there's a wellness policy thing against candy in school right?" She closes her bag and stands there. Her head lists to the right and something like a twinkle lights her dull eyes.

"Yeah, but it's the last day. What are they gonna do?" she drones. "Besides, what do you think inspired my little crusade?"

"The wellness policy. Of course, I get it."

"You know my twins will be in seventh grade next year." A heavy sigh travels up through her shoulders.

"I know. That's gotta be strange."

"Ummm Hmmm." Her eyes swing up to me. "Hey, there's a seminar at the middle school on cutting Wednesday night. Wanna drive together?" She hooks the grocery bag over her wrist and shoves her hands into the deep pockets of her black trench to wait out my response.

"No. I don't think so. But you go and have fun!"

"Okay." She sighs deeply. "You can take some for yourself, you know." She opens her bag again and holds it out. "Go ahead."

I wonder, glancing up at her sly expression, what she knows, but think the better of a confession here because underneath the generic gummies are grape Laffy Taffies and I haven't had those since I raided Emma's Halloween pumpkin.

My hand is deep in the bag when I hear, "What have we here?"

Doctor Otis materializes beside us. Her nose is fast inside the bag and before I can get to my treat she swoops the thing away. "Ah, ah, ah. Mrs. Glastheme. We've spoken about this before, have we not?" And she leaves it at that, with a turn on her heel and a sashay back down the hall towards her office, the bag clutched to her tummy.

When I turn back to Margaret her mouth hangs open in a grin watching Dr. Otis retreat. Tiny, yellowed teeth peek out from inside her mouth. "That lady cracks me up," she says. "Otis doesn't like the gummy stuff," Margaret explains. "Otis only likes dark chocolate; Special Bars. Doves. Those little Ghirardelli Squares. Gravely likes the gummies. And Cheetos. She took the bag for her."

"You get Otis dark chocolate?"

"Yeah. Of course. It's the price of doing business. Compensation for looking the other way, if you know what I mean." After a pause she turns and follows Al's clean path down the hallway. Then, unceremoniously, she brings a fist full of candy wrappers from her pocket and drops them behind her onto the floor. I am alone now, surrounded by the soprano mingling of students' voices that wafts from the open doors of other classrooms. The rectangular window in Mrs. Slaughter's closed door beckons. I rise on tiptoe to see through it.

The Kindergartners are all gathered on the story rug for the last time. That is, everyone but Duncan is cross-legged on the rug. Duncan is running in small circles at the back of the classroom, his hand jammed down his shorts. Ignoring him, perched on her high stool at the front, Mrs. Slaughter is bent forward, elbows on her knees, addressing the class. She says something I can't hear and then Rico pops up in front of her. Slaughter straightens, says a few officious words to him, shakes his hand once and presents him with a rolled up little piece of paper. He salutes. Several boys hold their ankles and roll backwards in laughter. Something tightens in my throat when I realize that the roll of paper is a diploma. They're graduating. I watch as two more boys collect theirs and eye each other on the way back to their spot on the rug, telescoping through the rolls. And then it's Emma who stands up and shuffles towards the front, past the word wall and its tormenting list of high frequency words. 'Ball, be, bus, but.'

In front of the class Emma's arms are crossed on her chest and she stares at the rug. Mrs. Slaughter dips her head to catch Emma's eye. Then she lays a hand gently on my girl's arm, extends a little diploma roll, and says something. Emma has her little chin on her chest. Her head rises and falls in the smallest of nods. Mrs. Slaughter dips her head again, sets Emma's diploma in her hands, and rubs my girl's shoulder. And then Emma, hugging the diploma to her chest, looks up and pipes, "Thank you." Mrs. Slaughter's whole face opens and she brings her hands together in surprise. Then she gathers Emma to her. Emma hugs tight to her teacher; the gauzy fabric of Slaughter's top bunched in each little fist. Emma's eyes are closed, but her whole face is lit with a smile. Affection for Mrs. Slaughter blooms in me, and with it the scene beyond the window blurs.

At home there's a message on the voice mail from Temple announcing a last minute graduation party for Maxi. She goes on and on about serving simple cocktails and Sam's Club hors d'oeuvres. The invitation comes in her complaining tone like someone behind her is forcing her to make this call at gun point. She ends by saying, "Really hope you can come. And lord, don't worry too much about the gift darlin', please. Just any ole thing'll do: somethin' from the back of a closet or a re-gift. Really."

An hour later Nicole and I take the kids to the vegetarian café for a little graduation lunch. The kids stare at each other over black bean burritos and miso soup, while Nicole tells me about the fantastic new school she's found for Adam for next year.

"I've got an appointment Tuesday to suck my way in," she says.

"He's not in yet?"

"No, he's in. I mean suck the Principal." She catches herself with a laugh. "Not literally." Then after thinking for a moment into her soup she furrows her brow and says, "Well, sort of literally. I mean I'll offer myself up? Maybe write a Solar-Panel Grant Proposal for them like I did at his last school? You know, something like that. Do some good. That way even if the teacher's shit, the Principal will side with me when I complain about her." She shrugs, smiles and ruffles Adam's hair. He recoils like an adolescent.

"You mean some physical addition to the school."

"Exactly. That way they have to think of you every time they look at it. Credit where credit is due."

"Like a fountain for the lobby or something?"

Her spine straightens against the booth. "A lobby fountain?'" she repeats slowly.

"Yeah. You could do a mosaic lobby fountain. Get the kids to make the tiles in art along with an artist-in-residence program."

"A mosaic lobby fountain." She turns the words over slowly on her tongue. "Where'd you hear about that?"

"We're doing one. It's almost done. There's a community dedication next week. You should come."

"I absolutely love it. Running water." She snaps her fingers.

"And it reuses the same water over and over. Ever flowing." I'm not certain about this, but it seems feasible. I'll have to call the SIC committee woman when I get home.

"It's restful."

"Water reduces stress."

"Exactly."

"And it's the *same water*. It's so green! I love it! I'm gonna do it!" Looking at me, she reels in her excitement here. "That is if you don't mind."

Afterward lunch we're walking back to our cars when we pass a Baskin Robbins. "Nicole, Let's . . ."

"Oooo, Jennifer. That's dairy." She shudders and pulls down her mouth.

"Just this once?"

Nicole purses. Then her nose stud twitches. She sighs and enthuses,

"Adam, look! They built an ice-cream store here." She presses her palms against the glass door in fabricated wonder. "This must be new. Come on kids!"

When the kids have their cones, we find a bench outside and sit. People in short sleeves pass us on the sidewalk. There's a hint of lilac in the breeze. And I can't watch Adam eating his ice-cream cone because his tender tickly licking verges on the sexual. This seems to prove some point to Nicole who watches him with an ironic smile. That is when she's not demanding her own bites. Each time she's able to coax the cone from her son, she devastates it by thoroughly packing her mouth with wafer and ice cream. The load requires the use of her fingers to catch and push in the errant bits and drips.

Emma licks circularly around her cone. "Hey, Mommy you know what?"

"What, Em?"

"I am going to be a grader next year. Really, in a whole grade. For real."

"I know, sweetie. How do you feel about that?"

Emma licks her cone. Then flattens her tongue into the top. "Look a potty!" she announces, thrusting her cone under my nose. Then she settles, frowns a little and says, "Good. But a little scared."

I study her for a second. And then can't help but add, "Me too."

In the backpack today:

A folded over and stapled piece of unwieldy poster board containing fourteen half-finished paintings and pastel drawings and six, wrinkled, blank sheets of colored construction paper

A handful of loose, broken crayons

A Skittles wrapper

A wet, blue tissue

A fistful of pencils with broken points and worn erasers

A Summer Fun Reading List with three pages of suggested summer reading.

Her pink ruler

Her lunch box containing an empty cherry flavored Capri Sun bag and an unopened single serve applesauce and plastic spoon

A stapled 42-page packet entitled *Summer Fun With Coins and Clocks*

A snack-sized Ziploc with two prunes inside

A school supply list for first grade

An empty, open Elmer's glue bottle

Registration procedures for the fall

Thank yous from the PTA for such a great year and

The final report card

I rip open the envelope. Inside all the marks are "Meets grade level standards." Even the one about contributing to class discussions.

At the bottom there's a typed note.

It reads:

"Dear Ms. And/Or Mr. <u>Lansing,</u>

I've enjoyed having Emma in class this year. I'm sure she'll make a wonderful first grader. No worries.

REGARDS/ SINCERAMENTE

M. Slaughter

P.S. None of the first grade classrooms has a pet. So you're safe there."

The End

(photo Brian McConkey)

Tracy Egan is the playwright and original performer of the stage play, *Who's Driving the Bus? My Year as a Kindergarten Mom*. She has also written and performed numerous essays for Chicago Public Radio's award winning *Eight Forty-Eight* program. She lives in Evanston, Illinois with her husband and two daughters.

LaVergne, TN USA
29 November 2010
206603LV00004B/36/P